DOWN THE WELL

JOSEPH BLACKHURST

ISBN Ebook: 979-8-9884843-0-1
ISBN Paperback: 979-8-9884843-1-8

ATTENTION

The following is a printed reproduction of a handwritten diary originally scrawled on thirty-three canvases of various sizes (the "Canvases").

The Canvases were found buried among the rubble and corpses of an unknown town in Appalachian Kentucky. The horrific scene was discovered by a pair of hunters in December 2017. No earlier record of the buried town exists and its location is classified. Further, although the scientific community has designated the event the "Carrington Tragedy," no proof has substantiated that the town was in fact named Carrington. No survivors were found. Up until now, the investigation has been kept entirely confidential to prevent panic and conspiracy theories from permeating the general population.

The Canvases came across my desk as the subject of a property dispute. I represented the hunters against the federal government which claimed eminent domain over the Canvases as evidence in the ongoing genocide investigation. As part of the settlement agreement, further details of which I cannot disclose, my clients retain ownership of the Canvases in exchange for a limited license to print and reproduce the words written on the Canvases for public distribution.

The purpose of this license is to help locate the author of the diary, Richard Maltessouri[1]. No other record of him exists and none of the living individuals

---

1 The author's assumed name since that is what he calls himself.

mentioned in the Canvases have any memory of such a person. All leads dead-end.

Past attempts to transcribe the Canvases in full have failed. Photography cannot capture the ink due to its unique characteristics and the problem is exacerbated by the writer's frantic handwriting. The first attempt at a complete transcription (the "Wade Transcription") failed. Only twenty or so Canvases were transcribed before the attempt ended in tragedy.

Fortunately, I am entirely colorblind and therefore immune to the adverse effects of the ink. For this reason, the rest of the members of the Investigation Oversight Committee (the "Committee") voted eight to one[2] in favor of delegating the task of transcription to me.[3]

The Committee also voted to send me and another attorney to Lexington, Kentucky, to depose witnesses as my transcription of the diary identifies them. My partner volunteered and was approved by unanimous vote due to her unique connection with the matter. Sahar Ayubbi and I leave for our "expedition" tonight.

I am enamored by the predicament—how could a man who doesn't exist leave behind a diary? I've read the Wade Transcription hundreds of times and, admittedly, I feel empathy for Mr. Maltessouri. Despite his atrocious narcissism and problematic opinions, I can't help but feel sorry for him.

Of course, this is assuming he was ever real in the first place. I concede the possibility that this is a wild goose chase. That the diary on the Canvases might be a piece of immersive art by a Banksy or what have you, or some sick practical joke that achieved the goal of being

---

2 Dr. Terrance A. Milsap opposing.

3 All footnotes are my own interjections to provide pertinent context and information.

taken seriously. Your jaw would drop if you knew the amount of public and private resources that have been spent searching for Mr. Maltessouri.

Nonetheless, despite every rational explanation, the Committee cannot yet discredit the possibility that Mr. Maltessouri's account of the events that caused the tragedy might be true. After all, it isn't every day that a couple of hunters stumble across hundreds of corpses in the middle of nowhere.

/s/ Joseph D. Blackhurst
Attorney
October 1, 2022

Please submit any and all information
you have concerning the author of the diary

RICHARD MALTESSOURI

to federal or local law enforcement.

CANVAS ONE

I wish the marionettes would stop trying to break through the windows. Incredible. I'm not entirely convinced I'm still alive. I seared my thumb pouring the jar. Tried to be careful. Hands shaking. Get rid of it. Get rid of it. Write write write writingwritingwriting.

[Spirals][4]

Around and around. Around and around. I can't believe I did that but he deserved it. I hope it hurt. I hope he slowly dies. Have I gone mad? I don't think I've gone mad. I don't think you should trust a self-alleged madman's opinion of whether or not he's gone mad. That is, assuming I'm still alive. Writing writing writing. Maybe I got shot in the motel or died in that car accident. I don't think she stabbed me with the pickaxe, but maybe she did. Ghosts could be real at this point. Might as well believe that too. Ghosts who don't know they're ghosts. I gotta be a ghost. Yep, that's it.

Outside, the blizzard is pitch black from the coal, I think. Or because of whatever evil all this is. The black ashen flakes blot out the light except for the white eyes of the marionettes watching me. I'll be snowed in soon. There's no end to it. Looks to be about a foot. In New York, I once walked in a blizzard and an old man walked toward me. Sam was old like him and Sam got me killed. Bastard. But Sam couldn't walk. The old man in New York was bent over, inching along pathetic

---

4 Certain compelling visual details of the diary are of course lost in this printed transcription. Namely, how tiny and crammed together the words are. The sheer amount of scribbles on Canvas One is unnerving. Violent, sharp depressions take up half the surface area. The pen pierced through in several places. In the scribbles, you can make out certain shapes. Arrows, stars, a poorly sketched merry-go-round. These may be irrelevant—I find myself partial to doodling while on the phone, for example. Still, I note these details in the event you, the reader, understand something I don't and perhaps these details may in fact be psychoanalytic clues to where Mr. Maltessouri might be found.

and decrepit. The high snow on the sidewalk narrowed to the width of a shovel blade and I crossed it without stopping, making the old man wait his turn. Why won't the baby stop crying and let me write?

[Scribbles]

Sam got me killed for his wife. Figures. Women ruin men every day. I slaved (unnoticed) to lay more and more brick down the lonesome boot-strapped path of success toward the spotlight of their recognition and, head down, I was brought to darkness instead. Women operate on whims, not reason.[5] My mother worst of all. She doesn't even deserve to be called that. Why am I writing about her? She must still be alive since I'm dead and she's not here. But maybe ghosts don't work like that. Sam made me his puppet. But first he killed those children. Then he killed me. Writing writing. Great, now I'm crying and my stomach is so cut up it hurts.

[Scribbles]

Too much power for a stupid old man. Write writing writing some more. I don't get what's in the well. Is it really just bugs? It bugs me. Ha ha hah haaha. If I'm dead, maybe I can ask god what's going on. How do you get god to show up when you're dead? Maybe that's not the way god works. Or maybe this is purgatory.

It's kinda funny watching the marionettes get covered in snow. I hope they freeze in the cold like bugs.

---

5 Apologies to any readers who take offense with Mr. Maltessouri's words. These are his alone and are views not shared by myself or the publisher. No part of the Canvases will be edited or omitted during my transcription to preserve a complete record of the evidence in order for the public to assist with the search.

Might restore confidence in my own faculties to figure this thing out with the entire statement of facts. Rule derivation rule application. Rule derivation rule application. Columbia really did teach me how to think like a lawyer. Sam said this tint[6] had rules he couldn't figure out. Yeah, well, Sam was retarded.[7] So I'll review the record de novo.[8] March forth my army of tiny logic ants! Euph, too soon.

What the well does with the dead is awesome (in the true meaning of the word, not the trite meaning my generation's overuse has depreciated it to like so many termites). Actually, awful is a better word for it. In both its horrific and reverential meanings. The well eats the living. I don't know why the well wants us but I know the well in fact wants us and helping the well is, itself, the well of endless reward. Yes I know the use of "in fact" is poor writing. *See* Strunk and White *The Elements of Style* page whatever 4th edition year whatever.

There. Happy, Scott? Everyone every. . .one.

[Puncture]

Oh har har har. Red pen that all you want, but I like the ring of that sentence. It's sassy rhythm. (I hate parentheticals but they eat up a couple extra drops of tint.)

Gotta figure all this out. Women ruin men. I bet Sam killed his wife like he killed me. Amara, I think he called her. I gotta hand it to him. The portrait he painted of her is good. I look at it next to me in true awe. Hahahaha. Oops woke the baby back up, speak of the devil. Wow that's ironic. Or déjà vu or something way crazier. The baby doesn't like it when I try to hold it. Better to just let it work itself out. What's that sound?

---

6 The ink the Canvases are written in.

7 *See* supra n. 5.

8 The appellate standard of review in which no deference is given to the lower court's determinations of law or fact.

The portraits Sam painted are pretty. I guess I'll give him that. I hope he didn't die on impact. I want him to freeze slowly. Yes, freeze really slowly. With broken leg pain. Wait, he wouldn't feel that. He must still be alive since I'm dead and he's not here just like my mother isn't. Or maybe the problem is I'm still alive and they aren't. Seriously, what's that sound? Gonna check.

Great. The marionettes are battering the doors now. I wish they would just hold their horses and stop.

One is holding the horse. I need to lay down. I mean lie down. I need to understand. I wish I knew what Sam knew.

[Spirals]

EXPEDITION NOTES
OCTOBER 2, 2022 | 12:10 A.M.

It's nonsense, I know. I transcribed Canvas One—and now write these notes—shortly after midnight at our terminal where our flight has been delayed for six hours. Sahar objected to me taking the Canvas out of the carrying case. She insists it's dangerous to both the Canvases and bystanders. I insist it's important I use every spare minute to make progress on the transcription to inform our witness selection and fact-gathering decisions during our expedition. It takes both our keys to unlock the case. We compromised by having me sit in the corner, on the floor, away from prying eyes.

Not much can be said about Canvas One to aid the reader. It makes as much sense to me as it does to you. So many unanswered questions—the marionettes, the motel, the car accident, the bugs, the baby. Ramblings of a lunatic, it seems. He may be as dead as he suggests for all we know.

Sahar went for a walk. She says it's a headache but she didn't look at the Tint. I know how she gets when she's upset. The airline wouldn't let her bring Borlú as a carry-on and so they put him in a kennel in the cargo hold. The bag check manager apologized for Sahar's impression that her emotional support animal paperwork was enough. Apparently, there's still a strict size limitation, and a 6-month-old German shepherd clearly exceeds it. How anyone could turn an angel like Borlú away is less clear.

I'm sure it doesn't help Sahar's anxiety knowing the Canvases soon mention her.

CANVAS TWO

The night Sam saw the tint for the first time went like this:

A bunkhouse in a mining camp in the 1950s. Sam drawing some woman with a piece of coal—patterns of crosshatch shadow. I assume his mother.

"Make the titties bigger. Lord'n knows them's the best part," some other miner said. Sam's mouth tightened at the words. Sam hated loud noises and the miner was so drunk he was shouting. Sam chipped the coal to a finer point with his blackened fingernail. Drunk miner burbled his words between swigs of shine and drooled sooty dew down his whiskered chin. "Her hips lookin' good. Draw me one next. Not a lotta ladies down the tunnels." The drunk drooled on Sam's sketch and Sam got upset.

"You got her wet," Sam said.

"I tend to do dat," drunk miner said. (I hate writing plangent ball-in-a-cup pang uneducated 1950s Southern dialect. Stop it. (And stop these parentheticals.)) Baby is asleep at last, thank god.

A third miner playing rummy got off his bunkbed and stomped around laughing at drunk miner's joke about making a drawing of a lady wet. "You a Kentucky boy?" rummy miner asked. "Why you in Carrington?" Drunk miner's eyebrows raised. His eyelids like half-closed seraglio curtains above cheeks red from burst blood vessels. "You're a strange one, kid. You got a family or something in Carrington?"

"Momma had a baby last week," Sam said. Drunk miner draped his arms around Sam's shoulders and Sam's coal rocketed off. "You broke it. Get off. You smell." Sam shoved drunk miner and drunk miner fell on his ass and got mad.

"Go out there with your own kind," drunk miner said. "They're mad you're in here with us."

"Who is?" Sam asked.

"Damn, you slow," drunk miner said. "Those white boys out there."

"The coal turned me the color black too," Sam said.

Drunk miner laughed hard. "Can't say I didn't say something."

[Puncture]

Watching all this Sam memory shit in my brain is like daydreaming but awful. Seeing these things swim in front of my face with the marionettes behind them. Marionettes all icy and sliced up and bleeding with broken arms and stuff. Great. Now I'm hyperventilating. But I have to look forward. The tint's too bright to look down.

[Scribbles]

Later, a bunch of white men much older than Sam were picking on him around a campfire. Pine trees contorting in the firelight. Moonshine. Sam had never really drank before. Felt sick. Sam already had enough trouble making sentences. Always had. Especially around grown men. They made him uneasy. Their deep voices made the words bleed together. To him, their voices were like coarse textures. Like the coarse log he sat on that nettled and hurt his skin and distracted him and the trees looked like the coat rack his mother would hang all those coats on but she died. But still the trees made him laugh. His mother would comfort him when he was bullied for laughing at nothing in particular but, like I said, she died. A mean miner asked who Sam was always writing letters to. Sam said he likes to draw because he doesn't know how to write or read.

"How you not know how to write, kid?" mean miner said causing more laughter. Mean miner pressed his hand down on his knee and flexed tendons in his forearm like harp strings. "You run away from home?"

"Yes," Sam said. "Violet."

Drunk miner stumbled out of the bunkhouse and tripped and fell face first into the mud out cold. White men laughing. Sam ran over and turned him on his back and drunk miner drew air like a garbage disposal.

Baby woke up and interrupted the images but now she's done crying.

I want to continue seeing Sam's first memory of the tint.

Mean miner removed the flat cap from his sunburned head and beat form into the leather with his fist. "So you run away from things," he said. More laughing.

Sam stood up. "I'm not scared," he said.

"Kid, if you ain't a coward, go find Davis."

"Who's Davis?" Sam asked.

Mean miner squat forward and prodded the fire with a shovel and sparks flitted and died.

Why are there so many medical textbooks in here if Sam couldn't read?

"Davis never ate," mean miner said. "He was all ribs and cords like those Jews after the war. Real strong though. No one talked to him. Couldn't. Devil Davis had no tongue. Just sorta hissed back deep in his throat."

Sam swallowed the metallic salt moonshine aftertaste.

Mean miner continued his story. It went like this:

Years and years ago, mean miner was sleeping in the old mine and got woke by screaming and the kid lying next to him had his skull cleaved open at the eyes through the brain. Kid's tongue flapping like seizure, still crying. The back of mean miner's hair matted in the kid's blood. Kid's hairline sideways on a shovel edge like a platter balanced on its edge. Davis wrenched the shovel loose and the scream stopped. Davis turned to mean miner next so he rolled and Davis got his shoulder.

Sam felt sick. Mean miner opened his eyes wide to the campfire embers as if seeing visions in the flame. He continued:

Shoulder bleeding, he tackled Davis down and ran for the ladder shaft past dim lanterns and dead men once friends gagged in the throats with stones. Torn off limbs. Gutted out genitals. Writing on the mine walls in the blood. Mean miner climbed to moonlight hearing the clang of shovel on rock and bone and Davis' hiss down beneath him. He got help but the marshals couldn't find Davis. He never came up from the mine. They searched every inch of the tunnels and lifted twenty loads of body parts before the pulley gave out. The foreman said it was better to just dynamite it all and leave Davis to starve down there with the dead men after they get too rotten for him to eat. Mean miner held a shaking grip around his knees, eyes toward the void. He turned to Sam. "Kid, I got an idea to show you ain't a coward."

[Rigid scribbles]

Sam stared down the deep mineshaft dug in a plateau a mile's walk up forested switchbacks. Circumjacent pitch pines cowered around the mesial baldcypress standing tallest like some proselytizing suzerain. Sweet, sweet locutions. I mean words. I'm so pretentious. Rowan was right.

The light from Sam's headlamp dissipated in the damp below. The decrepit ladder stung Sam with a sliver on the way down. Gossamer wrapped his shoulders and tickled his ears. A bead of sweat dripped, or something living skittered, through his hair and down his collar. His foot struck sudden ground and he followed the crossbeam arches as benchmarks deeper into the light from his headlamp.

Seriously, why does Sam have so many books if he's retarded? The splashes of paint along the spines of the books on the bookshelves' bottom rows is nice. Nice, normal paint. The colors are all so kind and normal. The splashes are at such odds with one another—jutting and twisting this way and that way. So many years of paint splashes. Splashes like a conductor of an orchestra flipping his wand thing. Or like orca whales flopping down for crowds at SeaWorld, only the water is paint colors that are normal and don't glow or change or nauseate like the tint. Sheens of bloody ice on the marionettes' faces.

Sam's ankle rolled on a rail edge. Dirt from the ground

caked beneath his fingernails. The headlamp flickered off. He twisted the bulb and the light came back. Chandeliers of roots. There was a high-pitched sound. A sensation. Shrieking yet silent. The thrum, the racket, the scream, the cacophony you hear and feel that isn't quite there but oppressive all the same. Like a floater on the surface of your eye.

The sound, and the odor of earthworms and coal mixed into burps of heartburn moonshine gave Sam a headache. He reached a dead end. A wall of stones where the marshals must have trapped Davis. Sam saw a glimmer of color behind the stones. Abnormal color. Back a ways beneath the fallen rocks. The tunnel wall leaked rainbow liquid. Sam wriggled into a tiny space between the dirt wall and the piled stones.

I can smell the corpses in the basement getting worse like bleach and hot cheese.

Rocks pinned Sam's arm to his hip as his other arm pulled him deeper into the narrow space. He sucked his stomach in and crawled on. The colors were beautiful and out of reach. The colors changed in the flickering lamplight. Jade then to amber then to lapis lazuli then to citrine. Then sunstone then larimar then kyanite then ametrine. Then topaz then nephrite then aventurine then tourmaline. And then he saw Violet.

[Sketch of an old woman's face]

And then it moved. Sam's own shadow appeared at once contorted on the wall beside him and skittered above him like a tarantula. Adrenaline injected behind his eyes.

He turned over, screaming, and between his boots he saw mean miner grabbing his ankle. His headlamp cast the shadow. "You scream like a girl, kid."

"Let go."

They walked back to the mineshaft and climbed toward the sepia light of morning spilling in. Sam's hazy head throbbed from the shrieking thrum inside his skull. His eyelids weighed heavy. The thrum continued to pulse. The savage morning brightness made him dizzy and he puked grits and moonshine. Jagged ladder rung after jagged rung. Obnoxious, scintillating overcast sky. His muscles spasmed and his foot slipped. Thirty feet down Sam's legs hit first. Yellow bone poking through the skin.

[Sketch of a merry-go-round]

Weeks later he was in a colorless insipid hospital ward. Banal, wispy drapes. Monotonous white beds bleeding seamlessly to the bleached white floor. Ferguson Memorial Hospital. Pops of poinsettias to parcels of places p word p word p word can't think of a p word for hospital. Pops of pastel poinsettias placed prominently, parallel to patients' pillows. No people visited Sam.

Sam ignored the doctor's words. The nurse was too pretty.

"Ms. Bray is not a nurse, Mr. Alley," the doctor said. "She is finishing medical school at the university and is studying beneath me."

Ms. Bray's eyes were buried in a clipboard. She yanked the beige blanket from Sam's atrophied legs. His cheeks blushed. She held her fountain pen in her mouth. The fountain pen I now write with. I hope she disinfected it. I burned my fingers filling it. She prodded his frail knees with cold calipers, swapped instruments, noted something with the pen, swapped instruments again. She leaned close, her hair like a bouquet. "Any trouble controlling your bowels, Mr. Alley?" she asked.

"No," Sam said, red in the face.

"Thank you, Ms. Bray, that's enough." The doctor unfurled the blanket back over Sam's legs. "Mr. Alley, your paralysis is permanent. Hard labor is out. How's your math?"

"Can't," Sam said.

"I can teach you," Ms. Bray said.

"No," the doctor said. "That won't be necessary. The assistance Mr. Alley needs is quite beneath your qualifications,

Amara."[9]

[Sketch of a tree]

Sam spent months of rehabilitation at the hospital. An eddy roiled beneath the thin ice covering the hospital courtyard pond. Amara was the first person who was patient with his slow speech. It took his full focus to put together sentences except when talking to her. They sat together on an iron lattice bench under an oak tree.

Holy shit I just remembered.

I wish for Hundred Suns to let Mel[10] go if they didn't kill her.

"Look up there," Sam said. "Down my finger."

"Good morning, little finchie," Amara said. The finch flitted off. "How do you suppose he knows his way back to the nest?" she asked.

Sam scrunched his face, hard in thought. "She has a compass like an explorer. Inside her brain," he said so serious. He made her laugh.

He sketched her a lot at breakfast. Whenever she'd sneeze he'd cover his ears and close his eyes to the coarse-textured sound.

"Are you keeping your soul inside?" she would always say. Over sixty years of marriage Sam came to love her sounds. Even her sneezes.

---

9 No record has been found indicating an Amara Bray or Amara Alley graduated from either the University of Louisville School of Medicine or the University of Kentucky College of Medicine. Or any medical school.

10 Melanie Cybulski, born in October 1995 in Mound City, MO. Resident of Orange County, CA. *See* Los Angeles County Missing Persons Search, oag.ca.gov.

EXPEDITION NOTES
OCTOBER 2, 2022 | 2:33 A.M.

We finally boarded. Sahar is beside me trying to sleep. She was furious that I took Canvas Two out on the plane but she couldn't make a scene.

I suppose I should bring you up to speed on the framework of the Carrington Tragedy investigation team. The team is made up of approximately ninety individuals with various expertise. The team is further divided into four subgroups: Units C, B, A, and the Oversight Committee.

Unit C is the largest subgroup, accounting for over half of the team. Unit C consists of forensic scientists, archeologists, and excavation contractors and their crews. Unit C excavated the mass grave. It took all of 2018 for Unit C to unearth and preserve the destroyed town—Canvases and corpses alike. The layout of the town matches the hypothetical town of Carrington as described in Mr. Maltessouri's diary.

Unit B is comprised of relatively new PhDs who carry out the grunt work research, chase down leads, and otherwise perform tasks assigned to them by Unit A. The past two years, Unit B has primarily focused on tracking down Mr. Maltessouri.

Unit A is the primary thinktank of the Carrington Tragedy investigation team and is comprised of nineteen doctors and professors at the forefront of their various areas of expertise. Unit A performs analyses of the data gathered by units B and C, formulates and tests hypotheses, and oversees Unit B. Unit A contains experts on everything relevant from geology to psychology to genocides and mass atrocities, etc.

The last group is the Oversight Committee. The Committee steers the investigation itself, coordinates with various federal and state bodies, and seeks funding, to name a few of its duties. The Committee is made up of nine individuals including Sahar and myself.

At this time, the Committee has adopted the explanation of the tragedy put forth by Dr. Terrence A. Milsap, the Committee's head of science. The theory is that an insular valley town was destroyed in total by a flash flood and later someone buried the Canvases at the site for unknown reasons. That's the entire theory.

Sahar woke up. She made me laugh.

"I hope Borlú isn't scared. Find the creep yet?"

"Richie? Getting close," I said.

"Sure. It's almost like he isn't real. What time is your dep?"

"Nine."

"Sucks for you." She peeked at my laptop. "Are you writing about Milsap?"

"The team in general."

"Don't forget to mention his Napoleon complex."

CANVAS THREE

I fell into the tint again. It's like being inside a womb. Like tossing and turning inside an eggshell padded with awful patterned wallpaper, rolling around. I must have fallen off my chair. The wood floor is so cold and calm. I could stay laying there forever. I mean lying there forever. I think the baby's crying cracked the eggshell and pulled me out of it. All she does is cry, I swear.

I want some baby food.

I guess that works too.

Objection! Relevance! F.R.E. 401.[11]

Amara bought the manor on Eldridge Lane in the nineties. I despise descriptive passages about architecture (blah blah wainscoting) or physical appearance (blah blah milky skin, broad flat nose). Molasses-laden quicksand slogs of technical, hyper-specific, authorial constraints with all the muse of a user guide. Reminds me of Sister Chloe. If you were out of bed after eight you had to polish the banisters and the orphanage was three stories high. Sam and Amara's house is big and pretty with a big pretty veranda and the study is lined with big pretty bookshelves filled with so many of her big boring medical textbooks. Sam still couldn't read. The textbooks are on topics like, I don't know, myalgia. Oh and the study has a nook of windows like a greenhouse and they're drafty as hell. I'm freezing under them now.

Amara beckoned Sam with a flapping gardening glove through these windows. She wore denim overalls. She loved to wear denim overalls. Sam went outside and the humidity dampened him as he wheeled down the veranda ramp.

"Come see what I found," she said.

She pushed him to a path through the thicket of woods at

---

11 The Federal Rules of Evidence test for relevant evidence. It states: "[e]vidence is relevant if: (a) it has a tendency to make a fact more or less probable than it would be without the evidence; and (b) the fact is of consequence in determining the action." Baby food is more likely irrelevant.

the back of the yard. "Let's paint the entire house white," she said. "I think it'd be cleaner. Wouldn't that be lovely, Sam? We'd even paint the floors." Sam laughed and she laughed but I didn't laugh because her joke wasn't even funny and then the path opened to a clearing.

Now see the well.

[Large sketch of the well]

A round stone basin. A mossy A-frame roof. A red iron crank. A rope. And beside it stood a birch tree. Amara ran across the grass and leaned over the edge. Sam sat resolute at the edge of the clearing. She reeled the rusty crank and he grit his teeth from the interstitial screeches of iron. The worst texture he'd ever heard. He flapped his hands to shake it away. She leaned out over the darkness and her foot rose in an arabesque.

"It's got a little bucket," she said. She ran back to Sam. "Could you paint it for the bathroom?"

"I need to finish my face first," he said. "For your Alzheimer's." That's sad. Bummer Sam.

She became so sad. "What would happen if you're on your own?" she said.

He took her hand. It was his favorite texture. "One of my picture books has a rainbow," he said. "You called it the spectrum. We're all like that. Red, orange, yellow, green, blue, indigo. We can see those colors, but there's more colors. So we don't go away ever. We just turn into colors we can't see."

She smiled through the tears. "You forgot violet." That made him sad.

They held hands a little while longer before turning home and he felt relief as the screeching thrum slithered back down the well to wait, itself, just a little while longer.

[Scribbles]

Her mind tore away. She punched him once in his sleep so he slept in a cot down in the study after that. She'd wander off and the police would bring her home. She'd call it hide and seek and that made Sam laugh, but nervously.

He was in the kitchen the night it happened. Amara's cat cheeked up against the wheel of his chair as he wheeled to the foot of the stairs. He got startled by his own painted face staring back through the study doors. He hated that self-portrait and how long it had taken. He called to her up the stairs. "Want coffee?"

"I want to paint the house white," she said.

"Well, I'm gonna make coffee if you want a cup."

"That would be lovely. Just leave it on the white stairs."

Sam fell asleep swirling paint and pinching the awful texture of the paintbrush bristles against the metal ferule. A drop splashed into his mouth and he woke up coughing. His self-portrait bled real blood from the forehead down the slanted canvas and pooled between his feet. The drops began to drizzle. Above him were the floorboards beneath Amara's bed. He threw his body onto the staircase and the mug of cold coffee spilled and soaked his clothes. The balusters cut creases in the spaces beneath his fingers. I had to polish the orphanage balusters at least thirty-six times. Sam's ribs sawed across each stair as he pulled baluster after baluster. Her bedroom door was ajar. Her mattress was against the wall. The open window and the flapping curtains. The blood-covered knife. The dead cat, hacked to pieces, bleeding through the floor. It wasn't hide and seek because the police never found her. Sam never saw her again. Well, that's actually sorta not true.

That cat later saved my life but died again.

EXPEDITION NOTES
OCTOBER 2, 2022 | 3:29 A.M.

Sahar wasn't always an anxious person, at least not to the degree she is now. When she first joined the Committee, I would have described her as resolute. Bullheaded even.

She was first contacted in the very early stages of the investigation. It was inevitable she'd end up at the top of the list of individuals to subpoena. Her role in Mr. Maltessouri's diary is significant. His adoration, turned resentment, for her is significant.

Understandably, Sahar asked to join the investigation to stop what she believed to be slander. She was nominated to the Committee in less than a month. No one burned the midnight oil quite like her. She was hell-bent on determining who made up what she claims is a false story about her being somehow connected to an alleged massacre. I'm disappointed she now buys into Milsap's flash flood theory.

I don't blame her for giving up. Her anxiety grew with the evidence. The only other Committee member who burned the midnight oil was me. It became our routine to go out to greasy, hole-in-the-wall burrito joints as late as two or three a.m. The two of us in our rumpled suits debating theories about a mass grave between drunk college students and burnouts. Me posing questions like how Maltessouri was able to see Sam Alley's memories; Sahar telling me about persons from her past who might have stalked her to the point of fabricating such a tale. I miss those nights.

Sahar no longer goes out at night. The sun once set outside the windows during a Committee meeting and she had a debilitating panic attack. I found her in the ladies restroom in a heap. I sat with her on the tile.

I talked to her to comfort her. She said nothing and I talked about nothing important. In those moments, it's just good to hear someone talk.

"What if he's still out there?" she finally said.

"We'll find him," I said.

"We don't even know who he is. Every guy who looks at me, I think—he's who wrote the Canvases, he's the one watching me—and then I picture him grabbing me. Holding a knife or knocking me unconscious. Taking me to his—"

"It's safe here. It's just us and a bunch of bathroom stalls."

She laughed and wiped her eyes. "I'm still getting a guard dog." And so she got Borlú. But Borlú couldn't hurt a fly.

CANVAS FOUR

I wish to see my memories of the last month. I've come to discover two patterns in my life. First, nearly every setback I've faced was a woman's fault (or Sam's). Stood up at prom. Caught in a lie by feminine intuition. Abandoned at the age of four, etc., etc. Second, my personal resilience and steely work ethic, alone, have corrected everyone[12] of those setbacks. Top of my class at Columbia (who's too good for who now you prissy sissified prom queen). I hate parentheticals. Cut it out. (Okay. Sorry.) That being said, of all these setbacks, my Salamanca NYC interview was deleterious beyond the rest combined and served as the cataclysm that set me down the viatic digressional detour ending with me hunched over a damn canvas meandering through puzzle piece vignettes of two sides of the same story until every last drop is gone. The jar is still full and dumping it doesn't work. It's like snot, basically.

[Swirling scribbles]

The interviews were in the dorms. The door opened and another 3L[13] stepped out and said good luck and the interviewer said gimme a second to get myself in order and she winked and closed the door and a minute or two passed. She made a plywood-door-muffled phone call and then the flimsy door reopened.

There's like thirty marionettes crammed in the hallway outside. Bones sticking out of their skin.

"Thanks so much for being patient. After you do twenty interviews in a row, the interviewees start to bleed together without the occasional break. Please come in and take a seat."

I stepped inside. The mattress leaned against the wall and a small card table with two chairs had taken its place over the dust outlines and the carpet indents and crummy

---

12 [sic]

13 Colloquial term for a law student in their third year.

discolorations. The mini fridge buzzing in the corner.

"Do you like Dick? Rick?"

"Richie," I said. Such a childish hypocorism.

"Well, Richie, when we interview the top of the class it's usually just a formality," she said. "The firm maintains our number one status by swooping up the top of the class like yourself at the most competitive salary."

I can tell the baby hates me but I hate it back. It isn't even human I'm sure it's bugs like the rest of the marionettes.

The partner asked me why I don't want to go to a California firm where I'm from. I told her I'm not from anywhere, I had so many foster families. Then she joked I looked too pale to be from California. Then I told her she doesn't look like how I pictured a partner.

"Well, there are key intangibles beyond looks," she said. And then I said something else sexist and I didn't get the job.

EXPEDITION NOTES
OCTOBER 2, 2022 | 3:50 A.M.

I should come clean. In a footnote, I wrote that no part of the Canvases would be edited or omitted during transcription to preserve a complete record of the evidence. However, certain inconsequential edits will be made at the decision of the Committee. These edits will be innocuous. For example, "Salamanca NYC" is not the law firm Mr. Maltessouri interviewed with. In fact, it isn't a law firm at all, I made it up. Mr. Maltessouri interviewed with one of the most prestigious firms in the country. The Committee thinks it best to not drag a Vault Top 100 law firm into the transcription to avoid potential libel litigation by persons whose jobs are to be the best litigators. I assure you no such edits are at all material to the substance of Mr. Maltessouri's diary.

One of the first assignments assigned to Unit B (after sorting through birth records) was to scour the student records of every primary school in California during the relevant period. After the discovery of several Richard *Mon*tessouris, and the subsequent clearing investigations of each of them (and the subsequent subsequent absurd debate of whether Mr. Maltessouri had misspelled his own name in the Canvases (a dubious hypothesis put forward by Dr. Milsap)), Unit B expanded their search into every other state. The expanded search was also fruitless.

A search for Richard Maltessouri in foster care programs also turned up nothing.

CANVAS FIVE

I met Mel shortly after that interview. Light of my life, fire of my loins. Mel, the tip of the tongue taking a nap along the length of the palate.[14]

September first, the night before my first day at the hole in the wall law firm that did hire me. I sat in my unfurnished Lexington apartment packed full of unpacked boxes. My laptop balanced atop a lopsided, crushed box. Video chat.

"Happy birthday, goddess," I said.

"Baby, I'm so old," Mel said.

"Twenty-two isn't old."

Her shoulders slackened beneath her pronounced pout and her piercings teased through her two-sizes-too-tight cami. "When does my present come?" she said.

"I shipped it express."

"What is it?"

"A surprise."

"Gimme a hint."

"The most expensive thing on your list."

"Can't wait." She took a hit of her vape. "How you liking Kentucky, babe?"

"Only three days and I'm already a racist."

"Wait, really?"

"It was a joke."

"Oh. Nice. Well, I'm going out in a sec."

"It's a little late to be going out, isn't it?"

"It's early in L.A."

"It's midnight there."

"Like I said, it's early in L.A. If you wanna play, I'll stay."

"I can't, it's my first day. Will I see you tomorrow?"

"Obviously."

"What time?"

"I'll start at ten again." She was texting. My eyes were

---

14 I prefer *Pale Fire*.

drawn to the most recent prurient comment by one of the degenerate slugs.

"You're so pulchritudinous," I said.

"The fuck?"

"Pretty. It means pretty."

"Ah. Okay. How sweet. See ya, babe." She logged off.

Can't get five minutes without baby crying.

I spent that night sleeplessly analyzing Mel's demeanor. Were things off? She seemed annoyed. Birthday blues? Was she mad at me? Was she mad at the slugs? Was she even mad at all? Was it something I said? I should text her. No I shouldn't. Maybe I should. Cold sweat ruminations like these had become my nightly routine since we met. When she acted distant, worry and subconscious self-consumption would swarm me (I once chewed my cuticle to a pulp and it still hasn't fully grown back—flayed and bloody like Kellan's cheeks). I said cut it out with the parentheticals. (SORRY.) But when Mel acted affectionate, those luscious flowered vines of true love at long last arrived, twisting around me like my tossed and turned duvet. Either way, I lost a lot of sleep because of Mel. And the merry-go-round. How could all those people watch a child go around and around for over an hour? Eventually, the attendant took me to the security booth.

I want to continue to recall and describe the events of this past month in crystal clear clarity.

The next morning, I got dressed worrying about Mel and walked to work worrying about Mel. I walked blocks of historical brick strangled by contemporary university steel with brass lettering like "Henry R. Clum Visitor Center," surely "The Clum," colloquially. And the "Carol Hiance School of Applied Appliance Science," Carol actually being an old wealthy man.[15] Trust fund buildings. Every store, restaurant, and bar were painted blue and white to prey on school spirit. I passed a smorgasbord of nasty "late nite" hangover troughs. I passed the mirrored windows of a campus bookstore. The sort of glass you normally use to inspect your hair and stretch your double chin, but that morning I was looking down at my dress shoes, worrying about Mel.

"Felicityyy. Want some waterrr???" A ditzy falsetto voice assaulted my eardrums as I passed a group of meretricious copy-pasted sorority girls in pink pageant sashes stumbling like flamingos out of a Greek house. Few know that felicity was once one of the finest words in the English language, holding the sacred charge of conveying one of the purest of all meanings. But as these things go, the inexorable tide of woolly headed women in the hangover of childbirth cheapened the word to a name. "Felicity," now defined as a sorority girl in a cheap velour skirt she can't pull off. And I use "pull off" to mean both wear in an aesthetically pleasing way and take off. Felicity puked on the sidewalk next to my dress shoes.

[Puncture hole]

I was above every one[16] in that town. My collarbone keeps clicking. Sort of electrical shocks around my ear when I lift my arm. The bruise reaches all the way down to my navel. I'm an idiot. I want my body to heal. Incredible.

I reached a ludicrous fountain I'd later become intimately familiar with of stampeding iron horses puking water from their chipped mouths like so many Felicitys. On the fault-line where the campus met the measly skyscraper downtown, at

---

15 Likely a joke reference to the University of Kentucky Gatton College of Business and Economics, named after Carol Martin Gatton—who is male.
16 [sic]

the corner of Pizza Place Lane and Yet Another Liquor Store Boulevard, I came upon my new office. The windows of the federal courthouse had those spiky pigeon repellents you picture piercing a climber's bloody palms. Across the street from those windows was the building of my new employer who didn't have the budget for window spikes and so the window sills were covered in pigeon shit.

There was a one-man-in-suspenders certified public accountant firm on the first floor and the gold mirrored elevator emitted a strident whine for oil as it lifted me up the shaft. The inspection plate confirmed elevator maintenance was a cut expense like the window spikes. I should sue them for that elevator. The firm was on the top floor; a decadent power trip of gazing down upon the peasants from the third floor of a geriatric prohibition building towering dozens, I say dozens, of feet into the sky. On the door, the frosted glass "Litton" and the frosted glass "Steenken" had chipped away while the modern sandblasted "Mendez" sat beside the withered "L.L.P."

[Doodle of an elevator]

The humidity was more than the window units could handle. The thin gray carpet had a smattering of pink. The walls were lined with that pointless abstract office art that begs the question of—was this free?

"You must be Richieeee!" A wretched, cheetah-print-wearing woman came around the reception desk whining the last vowel of my name the entire way while flapping her hands like Sam.

"Hello," I said, holding out my hand to shake hands just in time to stop her from hugging me. She shook it like a can of whipped cream.

"I'm Emma, your admin assistant! Oh wait, maybe I'm the girl's. I forget. Better check with Scott. Ohmygosh I love your tie." She said all this while holding my hand with her awful warmth long after the handshake had ended.

"Thanks. It's Ferragamo."

"Ooo is that Italian for silk? Such a smarty pants. Sounds fancy. I just love fancy. I was broke for six months after Macy's opened at Man o' War. I'm a shopaholic, guilty as charged! Have you been?"

"I'm sorry?"

"Man o' War! It's uh-may-zing. The best shops and restaurants. The mall, not the horse, obvi. Actually there is a statute of the horse in the food court. You can see both! You don't wanna shop at Donovan's though. They only hire those kids that just sit on their phone. It's like, hellooooo, come up for air! Gosh, Scott told me to tell you something but now I forget."

Emma gave me a tour of the office and a migraine. "The break room is where we all just really cut loose and get silly. We're all really fun like that. You'll be lucky if you don't gain ten pounds. Want a piece of cake? Scott turned forty last week." She raised the plastic lid on a stale sheet cake yellowing around the edges.

"I'm good," I said.

[Puncture]

My office had four walls, an empty shelf, and a window with no window spikes. I kept it that way until my last day.

"Got any questions?" Emma asked.

"I'll find you if I think of any," I said. "Your desk is down the hall and out of sight right?"

"Oh my gosh, such a quick learner! I'll send Scott when he's done getting the new girl set up. Sahar! That's her name! I remember now, because it made me think of the Sahara Desert which made me think of Toto because they have that one song. Shoot, what's that song? Sahar got here at like the crack of dawn, bless her heart. She's a real catch, you know. A real smarty pants just like you. You two are lucky being so smart at your age. I wasn't smart until my thirties. So spill the beans, are you single?"

"I'm seeing someone," I said.

"Oh my gosh, who? Do I know her? What's she look like?"

"I should get started on all this new hire paperwork," I said.

"Jeez Louise. Dangle the tea then pull it away, why don't ya. Okay, buh-bye!" She finally left. My Emma migraine now had a touch of Sahar-the-Type-A-coworker-I-had-no-idea-about-got-here-earlier-than-me-and-made-me-look-bad fury. If anything, it makes me the punctilious one. And better at reading comprehension. "Monday at nine" means Monday at nine. Not that I really cared. The plan was to lateral out of Litton Steenken and Mendez as fast as possible. But still, people should follow directions.

Been writing all day. Every pop or crack in the house sends adrenaline through my body. Couldn't sleep if I tried. Writing writing writing.

EXPEDITION NOTES

OCTOBER 2, 2022 | 4:42 A.M.

Enter Sahar. She hates Canvas Five. Good thing she's asleep in her seat. I spent the summer before my second year of law school working for a mid-size law firm in a small city in Michigan. Maltessouri's description of such an experience is apt to say the least.

Canvas Five receives a great deal of focus from the Committee precisely because of its connection to real persons and places. Melanie "Mel" Cybulski lives in Los Angeles and does indeed have the millennial demeanor Maltessouri describes. She was a principal witness for much of 2018 until her involvement in a separate federal criminal investigation took precedence.

Emma Freeman, Maltessouri's administrative assistant, is an actual employee at Litton, Steenken & Mendez. She is the first deposition scheduled on Sahar and my expedition. It starts at 9:30 a.m. tomorrow. I can't wait to meet her and witness the Emma experience in person.

I should really get some sleep. Never drink coffee after midnight. Another Canvas or two and I should get tired. Couldn't sleep if I tried. Writing writing writing.

CANVAS SIX

"Welcome aboard captain!" Scott Mendez was the khaki pants and tennis shoes of the legal profession with a belt that would bite you if the fangs hadn't been removed. "How's the digs treating you?" He surveyed my unembellished office as though in true awe of its melancholy emptiness.

"No complaints," I said.

"Great. But seriously, if anything isn't up to snuff let me know. Your experience and development here are paramount."

"I'm excited to get started."

"To be honest..." Scott checked over his shoulder and leaned in close, assaulting me with his truck stop coffee breath. "To be honest, things were getting pretty stale around here with some of the old dogs. We need fresh blood. You and Sahar starting the same day is like Christmas morning. Oops, sorry. You Jewish?"

"I spent some time in a Catholic orphanage, but I'm not Catholic."

"Gotcha. Wanted to be accommodating either way, you coming from New York and all." He punched my shoulder with a force that conveyed a high school football history ending in marriage to his cheerleader sweetheart.

In hindsight, Scott was well-meaning.

Scott took a seat in one of the visitor chairs in my office and rocked his weight in a quality control test. "These chairs suck," he said. "You like sports?"

"No," I said.

"I got the game ball from Super Bowl thirty-seven in my office. The pirate bowl. Mint condition. Well, mint condition in terms of after the game. You gotta check it out. There's a little blood on it. Little brown spot next to the laces."

"The whole ball is brown."

"Different brown. So I started Sahar off on drafting some interrogatories. Easy stuff. UK's a great school but I gotta check she's up to snuff. I'm comfortable starting you on the hard stuff. You ever think about how being number one from

Columbia makes you literally one of the top five new lawyers of all law schools combined?"

"I never thought of it like that," I said. I had nearly every day.

"You're too humble. You're like winning the draft lottery." He slapped me on the lower back in a politically correct snap decision to quell his latent high school football spanking habit.

[Sketch of a football]

Could probably get the marionettes to rob a bank or kill a political figure or something, but I'm not evil.

Later in the day, I was staring at my wall or something.

"Brought you some yummy coffee," Emma said. I sipped the oddly salty contents of the Taz mug and winced a feigned smile. "It's instant I bring from home," she said. "The stuff in the break room is way too weak," she said. It was, but at least it wasn't salty.

"Mmm," I said.

"Finally someone with good taste. Scott teases me and says it tastes like there's salt in it. Ever think of growing a beard?"

"No."

"Oh," she said. "Maybe once it cools off. Speaking of men, if you ever drive in, you gotta listen to Mark and Mantis!"

"What?"

"The morning show![17] They got all those billboards off 75! Mantis is my man."

"So, he's funny?"

"No he's actually my man, for real. He's one of those real man men who just draws you in like a magnet. We met in the audience of Springer. He was so brave. We'd be married if it weren't a system for oppressing women. He taught me that, you

---

17 The radio show 'Man Tits in the Morning' was cancelled following a slew of sexual assault allegations against both hosts.

know. Oh right, I gotta take y'all's picture for your business cards. That's why I came to get you. The break room light is best. Sahar's there waiting."

[Sketch loosely resembling Sahar]

Sahar's fangs smiled from lips of Ruby Woo.[18]

"Sahar, hon', can you step out of the frame?" I forgot Emma was in the room with us. She had been fiddling with the settings on a digital camera with one of those wrist straps to protect it from falling overboard during whatever kitsch Niagara Falls vacation it was tasked with documenting. Any phone would take better pictures, but the firm wanted to keep the poor quality headshots consistent across the website.

Sahar prodded a wrinkle in my suit and prinked my already perfect necktie.

"You two look cute together," Emma said, shooting me a covert wink. "When's the big day?"

Sahar tugs her necklace when she gets nervous. A small silver cross hangs in the shadowed valley of her breasts like a symbol of paradox. Its presence grated my nerves. I'm not against religion any more than astrology. Let us latch ourselves to a word or phrase in the horoscope of a Sunday morning sermon or the natal chart of the good book written god-knows-how-long-ago by that god-knows-who unreliable source. My god, how that magical word or phrase hooks our soul by a loose relevance to some worrisome shadow over our personal lives and before we know it, behold, coincidence vindicated as cryptic, heavenly divinity. Lawyers especially should be more skeptical of their beliefs. Sahar was otherwise perfect, I thought at the time.

"Wasn't it a beautiful ceremony?" Sahar said, linking her

---

18 One of MAC Cosmetics' most popular vintage lipstick colors. Sahar insists she's never worn it. I've never seen her in makeup.

arm in mine high above my elbow.

"Ohmygod ohmygod ohmygod," Emma said. "You may now kiss the bride."

"Close your eyes," Sahar said. My heart rose to the top of my chest. The sour marzipan taste made me gag and I spat cake crumbs. Sahar steadied herself against the kitchen counter, laughing. Her hand clutched the smashed piece of sheet cake.

"I got it on video," Emma said.

"You owe me a new suit," I said. I used the dishcloth to wipe my face and dab a purple fondant flower from my necktie.

"Let's say I owe you a drink," Sahar said. "I'm going to the Copper Roof tonight. Meet me there? A band is playing. I think they're great, but I'm biased. I'll give you my number."

[Spirals]

The area around the Copper Roof was mostly fast food and I couldn't risk bloating so I planned to get a salad at the nearby upscale grocery and arrive just before our date. Everything went swimmingly until my arrival at the upscale grocery where to my dismay the only so-called healthy salad they had was a concoction of Kalamata olives, oil, and cheese. That isn't healthy. Worse yet I was trapped in line behind a horrible old woman as she palavered with the deli clerk over what sort of cheeses makes the best charcuterie in the age when smartphones exist to answer all questions.

I often find myself gummed up in time and space waiting behind insufferably lackadaisical old people. The predicament itself an overt, blackjack-over-the-head metaphor about the generational passing of the torch to an increasingly impatient posterity. The greatest then the silent then the boomer then the X then me then the infernal Felicity. Generations beget generations the way a bookbinder rounds the glued spine of a hardcover's chapters over one another with a claw hammer. The chapters of human life—vicissitudes of calm to agitated back to calm. The undying heartbeat of man mimicking the deft tension of a literary classic. But as any high school student will tell you, the classics are very long and very boring. This particular boring old lady made me late. The worst old person I've met is Sam. Sam ruined my life. I left the deli line and got a so-called healthy prepackaged turkey wrap instead.

[A series of dots]

I needed caffeine so I stopped by what would become my new hangout—Cafe Coffeel. The clay-tiled floor was obnoxious on the eyes and knees but created a refreshing freeze that hit you in the face the moment the door sucked away from its frame. Night owl med students sat in sinking leather booths studying topics like, I don't know, myalgia. Sparse chalkboard menus contrasted against the god awful $300-per-square-foot community art pieces harassing from the walls like buskers.

I waited to be helped for at least two minutes at the counter beside the plexiglass muffins and blotchy bananas. Bananas black as death. Who even eats those? Between the beaded backroom curtains I saw the crossed legs of a fat barista hunched over a tattered book. I made the amplified sniffle our species utilizes to make one's presence known in such situations. Bathroom stalls, etc. She emerged and strolled toward me slowly as her eyes continued to sweep the words on the page. She tossed the book on the counter with nihilistic indifference and it landed on crushed pages like a bird with broken wings.

"Sorry, dude," she said. "I was washing dishes."

"I'll have a medium black coffee."

"Medium roast or medium size?" Her voice was the vocal equivalent of the feeling of pencil metal scraping as the eraser nub smears black smudges.

"What's your medium?" I asked. She pointed to a stack of cups. "Large then," I said.

"Medium or dark roast?"

"I already said medium."

"Room for cream?"

"I already said that too. This is getting repetitious. Black." I skipped past the tip option tapped no receipt, and swiveled the "register" back. The macabre eighties music complaining over the radio and the greasy hair beneath the barista's beanie pretty much filled out the rest of her personality.

"Have a night, dude," she said. My generation has a terrible habit of dudeing one another without considering the other's status or education. Sam made me fall in love with that horrible barista. Disgusting. The taste of her, still in my mouth, makes me gag. Sam must have finished our portrait while I was on my way to the airport. He ruined my life.

To my surprise, the coffee was the best I've ever had. You'd have to be crazy to not love that coffee. The door sucked again and I stumbled back out into the humid South.

EXPEDITION NOTES
OCTOBER 2, 2022 | 5:09 A.M.

I got Canvas Seven all ready to transcribe on my tray table. When I came back from washing my hands, the Canvas was back in the carrying case.

"The steward said it's bothering other passengers," Sahar said.

"They're asleep," I said.

"Said it's a safety hazard, too."

Later the steward came back to offer me a mask and blanket. "You finished drawing, I see," he said. Sahar had fallen back asleep.

CANVAS SEVEN

If human beings are just another instance of matter rocketing through space along the chaotic indefinite reckoning charted forth by the propulsion of the Big Bang, then a sports bar packed full of drunk college students is surely a gaseous state.

I arrived at the Copper Roof late and did a thorough sweep of the obstreperous college crowd and confirmed that, although Sahar is the early bird in matters of work, she is the snail in matters of play. I texted her and sat at the bar sandwiched between the backs of two polo shirt alphas projecting their drunkenness. I could see these jocks' future—destined to become NFL sportscaster lookalikes seated in tailored suits with fastened buttons straining over midlife fat drowning the abdominal muscles of their prime. But that night was still their prime and I looked like a child beside them. Somewhere, a girl bleated, "That's ironic." A word of considerable precision charged to convey a most rare relationship now beat into submission to serve as a placeholder for "that's interesting." To ye youths who've come to eviscerate our fragile mother tongue I say stand before me armed with thy frail YouTube education and be thyself eviscerated! Come and see if you can swerve me![19] Of course, I said none of this out loud as I generally have no desire of getting my jaw wired shut by NFL sportscaster lookalikes. Sahar left my text on "read." Only the manipulative turn read receipts on.

[Sketch of a merry-go-round horse]

A blue and white painted merry-go-round horse was suspended by wires above the bar. I needed air. I stepped

---

19 The use of "swerve me" would appear to be youth slang, however, given his status and education, Maltessouri is more likely quoting Captain Ahab in Herman Melville's *Moby Dick*. Ahab repeatedly uses the phrase throughout the novel. E.g. "Swerve me? The path to my fixed purpose is laid with iron rails, whereon my soul is grooved to run."

outside where, as physics dictates, a crowd of smokers had spilled out onto the patio area like smoking intestines through a bayonet wound in winter. I'm freezing.

I wish this room was seventy-five degrees.

I sat on the bench of one of the picnic tables. Sahar finally showed up a half hour late. "Sorry," she said. "We were pregaming. I meant nine at the earliest. You remember college party protocol."

An impeccably dressed guy with a cleft chin was standing behind her and closer than I would have preferred.

"We haven't met," I said.

"Sorry. I'm tipsy," Sahar said. "This is my friend, Aaron. Aaron, this is my coworker, Richie."

"Sahar was telling me about you," he said.

We played pool and Sahar reached the rosy point of drunk.

"Richard, where did you study?" Aaron asked.

"Columbia Law. Harvard English undergrad."[20]

"Call me impressed."

Sahar interrupted. "Aaron was second in our class. I was first."

"I was first of my class too," I said.

"Seems I've met my match," Aaron said. "Solids or stripes Richard? You can have whatever you want." The meaning flew over my head.

The women in the crowd flocked magnetically like a murmuration of locusts towards the stage. The front man rose above his female congregation like a puissant priest adorned head to toe in two shades of denim with an unbuttoned Henley framing a four-year oiled beard. He tuned a mandolin by ear.

"Look at that pussy," I said.

Aaron dropped the billiard chalk and for a moment the sound of the crowd seemed to have died in a vacuum.

"Pussies are actually really strong muscles," Sahar said, turning from pixie to succubus. "But, I wouldn't expect you

---

20 Further support of my hypothesis regarding Maltessouri's use of "swerve me." Unit B found no record of him at either institution.

to know anything about that."

"This is my stop," Aaron said. He left us to go chat with an equally well-dressed man standing at the bar.

"I wasn't being sexist," I said.

"Oh really?" Sahar said.

"Yes, really. Do I really need to explain to you the origin of the word pussy?" I said. "Pusillanimous. Look it up. It's not my fault society wrongly associates a timeless, eloquent insult for wimpy men with female objectification."

"Wow. Thanks for putting me straight," she said.

"I suppose you'd rather just stand there and get crushed by whatever idiotic snowball is rolling downhill," I said. "If the educated of society like you and I don't put our foot down then who will?"

"You're right," she said. "You're my hero. Protect our words, hero. They're so important. You're so important! Every one[21] else is wrong. My instinctual emotional reaction to pussy is my own problem. I really need to work on that. You're right, hero. You're so right."

"Someone has to be," I replied.[22]

Her glossy eyes relaxed their focus and washed over me with pity. "You know, I was trying to set you up and you blew it. Aaron's a bigger feminist than I am."

My heart sank. "Wait. You think I'm gay?"

---

21 [sic]

22 Sahar has researched this point further and wanted it noted that records exist proving "pussy" was used as far back as the 15th century to mean a girl or woman exhibiting characteristics of a cat. *See e.g.* T. Wright *Songs & Ballads Reign Philip & Mary* (1860) lxxiv. 209 ("Adew, my pretty pussy, Yow pynche me very nere.") Further, there are uses of the word as coarse slang referring to the female genitals dating as far back as 1699. Further still, Sahar is correct that, even if "pussilanimous" were the origin of the word, everyone in the 21st century associates it as a derogatory word for female genitalia and therefore it's offensive because society deems it so. I asked her why she's so determined to win an argument she claims never happened with a person she believes doesn't exist. She said it's the lawyer in her.

The front man interrupted. "Y'all gather round now. I'm feeling the love tonight. We've been on the road an awful long time but there ain't no better place for chicken pickin' on God's green earth than our sweet Kentucky home." The audience applauded at a ratio of three women to every man. "Now this here's a brand new song. True love only comes once a lifetime and when it does, boy howdy, you better grab it by the reigns and never let go. This one goes out to my fiancée. Baby girl, I'd be adrift at sea without you. This one's called 'Sahar Star.' You're my north star, babe." The women in the crowd, and my soul, groaned a despondent murmur as the wretched twang of strings filled the room.

I wish for Sahar to get dumped by her fiancé.

[A hangman game he lost to himself. The word has to be "lynx"]

Later that night, I sat on a one cardboard box chair at my two cardboard box desk and waited for the website to connect.

"Hello, goddess," I said.

"Thought you forgot about me," Mel said.

"I thought about you all day. I hate it here."

"Aw. Come to L.A., babe."

"I'd have to take the bar again."

"Aren't I worth it? Don't you wanna be with me?" She smacked her chewing gum.

"What if I actually did move?"

"Then my bed wouldn't be so cold and lonely."

"What about the stuffed animals?" Her bed was infested with plush animals and a litany of teddy bears in tiny outfits.

"They're just friends. Don't be jealous."

"They aren't the ones that bother me."

"Not this again."

"Why won't you quit?"

"Are you gonna pay my bills?"

"Hold on." I fished my wallet out of my rumpled coat in

the corner. The slugs fall for the trick of buying only what they need which leads to a feedback loop of overpaying. I always bought the maximum 10,000 Coinz for $200. It's a 40 percent better deal. It's just smarter.

Mel took off her dress. "Do you like it, babe?"

"You got my present," I said. "It fits you perfect."

"Will you help me unwrap it?"

I paid 50 Coinz and went into a private camgirl chatroom with goddessMELgoddess and, like Pavlov's dog, she licked her lips to the soundbite cha-ching of Coinz.

EXPEDITION NOTES
OCTOBER 2, 2022 | 9:58 P.M.

It was a rough morning. Our plane landed shortly after eight and by the time we made it through baggage claim and got our rental car it was past the time the deposition was scheduled. I felt hungover I was so tired. Got a second wind right now though.

Needless to say, we had no time to drop our luggage off at the hotel. On the drive over we called Litton Steenken to ask if Emma would be amicable to rescheduling the deposition for later in the week. She informed us she couldn't because she was leaving for Cancun tomorrow. To make matters worse, Scott Mendez—whose deposition was scheduled for tomorrow—gave us the ultimatum that he had changed his mind and would not cooperate unless he was deposed today as well. A case had conveniently "blown up."

We were driving down Versailles Road toward downtown. "So I'll take Scott and you take Emma," Sahar said.

"You're conflicted out."

"What?"

"You can't depose someone you know. I can do both if we halve each witness' time."

"You can't cover everything in three hours," she said. We were already entering downtown.

"Okay. But I'm taking Scott."

Selected portions of the deposition of Scott Mendez below:

BY MR. BLACKHURST:

Q Did the firm hire any associate attorneys in the fall of 2017?

A Yes.

Q Who?

A Sahar Ayubbi.

Q Was it typical for the firm to have only one junior associate at a time?

A The last time you conspiracy theorists called, I gave you our payroll records. I don't know how many more ways I can keep saying the same thing.

Q Mr. Mendez, I need you to answer the question. Did your firm usually only have one junior associate?

A No. Not usually.

. . .

Q Are you familiar with the matter Rothacker v. Souers?

A Yes. But it's very fuzzy.

Q What is your understanding of the substance of that case?

A My understanding? It was my case. Object to form.

Q That objection seems baseless, but let me ask it a different way. What were the circumstances of that case?

A That case? What case?

Q Rothacker v. Souers.

A I see. Gotcha. Your questions need to be more specific for me to be able to answer. Plaintiff filed a civil complaint against her ex-husband alleging he kidnapped their twin children. Defendant was my client--the father. Our motion to dismiss was granted in under a month.

Q Do you remember who drafted the answer to the complaint?

A Not off the top of my head. Memory is fickle like that.

Q Okay. Let me refresh your recollection. Mr. Mendez, can I ask you to please turn to Exhibit 074. Defendant's Answer in Rothacker v. Souers. Please turn to the signatory page. Page eighteen.

A You can. You can ask me. I will let you.

Q Okay. Please turn to page eighteen.

Q Okay. I'm there.

Q Please describe what you see.

A You want me to read it?

Q Yes. I want you to read page eighteen.

A Thank you for being more clear. I see my signature. I see it's dated October 31, 2017.

Q I was clear, but do you see the blank space above your signature?

A Okay.

Q Is that where a junior associate's signature would go?

A If a junior associate wrote it, maybe.

Q When a junior associate didn't write it, is it typical for there to be a blank space that large above the partner's signature?

A Formatting errors are typical, sure. That's seven hours. Rule 30(d)(1). Unless otherwise stipulated or ordered by the court, a deposition is limited to one day of seven hours. Do you remember the way out?

As you can see, Mr. Mendez's deposition was a waste of time. Sahar and I decided to order room service with the intention of turning in at nine to get an early start tomorrow. We were eating club sandwiches in my room.

"Get anything out of Emma?"

"I don't know," Sahar said. "She might have mentioned Maltessouri between asking me about my dating life and telling me about where she cut herself shaving this morning. You tune her out at a certain point."

"I'll check the transcript. There probably wasn't much to discuss on the dating front."

She jabbed me. "True. This sandwich is the most action I've had in years." She fed a piece of bacon to Borlú. "Good boy. You'd give your little life just to make me happy, wouldn't you? Wouldn't you?"

"Why did you quit?" I asked.

"Giving Borlú bacon?"

"No. Why did you leave Litton Steenken?"

"I left Kentucky to get away from questions like that."

"Too many house calls from Unit B?"

"Tons."

"How many?"

"Seventy-nine calls and fifteen in-person interviews."

"Jesus."

Sahar sat down on the floor to pet Borlú. "The poking and prodding by the investigation team wasn't the bad part. The stigma is what gets you."

"What stigma?"

"It's not a hot look to have FBI-looking creeps visiting you at work. Stopping by your apartment. Asking that you give blood once a week. Asking that you undergo a sleep study for six months. Not asking. Telling. I lost friends. My brother hasn't talked to me in a year."

I didn't say anything.

"It's like there's a line item in the federal budget for ruining my life."

We were quiet for a long time. "Let's meet in the lobby for breakfast," I said. "I'm tired."

"You have no idea."

CANVAS EIGHT

Seem to be making a dent in the jar.

I wish to see the day Sam found the tint.

He was looking at a stack of pancakes on a church pamphlet he couldn't read. He sipped chunks of instant potato and bulk carrot out of a Styrofoam bowl of flavorless soup kitchen water. Amara had a peculiar way of holding spoons that he subconsciously mimicked during their fifty years of marriage. Fingers far back on the handle. Handle held tight between index knuckle and thumb in that pompous gesture politicians use to make a point without pointing. Imitation is the sincerest form of flattery, and with it bad habits spread like mono. Sam copied her to fit in with society. But, like turpentine, the year he'd spent alone since Amara's disappearance began stripping him of her mannerisms. He ate his soup gripping the plastic spoon in his fist.

[Sketch of a soup can]

At the other end of the folding table, a kid was in an argument with his fingertips in the throes of madness strangers assume to be opioid induced when in reality he had almost suffocated during birth. Amara used to greet the kid kindly when she saw him around town. They had a lot in common but Sam couldn't figure out the words to make conversation. The kid was in his thirties but still a kid to Sam. As Carrington changed, the kid was one of the few familiar faces left and they held a tacit lunch date at the church where they ate together in the silence of society's ignorant pity. The kid screamed and lurched off his folding chair and out the door. Sam was relieved. He had a stressful enough day ahead of him without the kid's ramblings rattling his nerves.

[Smear]

A miner took the kid's seat. Sam watched the surface

tension of the miner's soft drink fizz and ripple as it wobbled with every forkful of food the miner shoveled down his gullet. Sam's own skin began to nettle him and the back of his neck began to itch so he scratched it with his coat collar by looking up and shaking his head. Visions of sticky black liquid coursing across the slippery plastic tablecloth and onto the bag of canvases leaning beside his wheelchair.

"No drinking, please," Sam said. The miner raised an eyebrow and moved his cup a few inches from Sam.

"Brought me a couple masterpieces, Sam?" Pastor Kellan caught him off guard and soup went down the wrong pipe. Sam coughed. "Goodness." She handed him a napkin.

"Got six," Sam said, wiping his chin holding the napkin in both hands like a squirrel.

Pastor Kellan clapped. "What a deal," she said. Sam winced. "Sorry the soup is dog shit." Pastor Kellan's shoulders shot to her ears and she focused on the cross hung by cables above the altar. Chapel by Sunday, soup kitchen by weekday. "Forgive me, Lord."

"He and me heard worse," Sam said.

She took a seat and crossed her knees. "Now don't keep a girl waiting, Picasso. Lemme see." Sam blushed and turned away. "Lord, it's always pulling teeth with you." She bent down and pulled the bag onto her lap. She brushed the crumbs from the table with the sleeve of her clergy shirt and one by one she affectionately laid out each painting.

[Sketch of a flower]

"These are beautiful, Sam."

"I start with bright green and then in front of it I put darker greens and little yellows and browns and then the bright colors." Sam pointed to places in the painted landscape of milkweed and false blue indigo. "See, they're dots not actually flowers at all."

"Is this Amara's garden?" Kellan asked.

Sam shut his eyes tight. "It's weeds now," he said.

"You really must let me put the youth group to fixing up your house. I'll find some psalms about work or charity or something. I'll make a lesson out of it. Bible's good for lesson planning just about anything. Just think how good it'd feel."

Sam rose his voice. "No. No. It's got old smells I like."

Kellan stacked the paintings and placed them back inside the tote. "All of us in this room are jealous of your gift, Sam." A yelp and a clatter came from the church kitchen. "Sounds like I'm needed," Kellan said. "Instant potatoes have three steps and I'm the only one who doesn't skip one. You're gonna knock the socks off Jurgens with these. I'm praying for you."

"Okay." Sam wiped his hands and sunk the napkin he'd torn to shreds into the bowl of cold soup.

I should eat something.

It would have been fine that the Corporeal Gallery didn't have a ramp if the entrance step weren't a foot high. Sam spoke into the Call-A-Ride driver's phone.

"Hello," the voice on the other side said.

"Jurgens. I need help with the stair. Bus driver's back always hurts from it." Sam loved the bus driver's coat and how yellow it was. The bright coat was such a sensory overload for Sam that he'd been too distracted to ask the man's name all year.

"Here to waste my time again?"

"Driver's got to go get someone else so I need help with the stair, please."

"So go with him." A long pause as Sam struggled to string together the words. He heard Jurgens mutter an expletive right before the phone hung up.

Jurgens' arm hair pinched in the chair wheel lifting Sam over the step. Sam wheeled through the entablature and into the showroom. The familiar mildew odor of the Corporeal pervaded Sam's lungs like a cloud of spores. Humidity is the cancer of oil paint but air conditioning was an expense Jurgens couldn't afford. He compromised with draw-down curtains of cheap canvas that bathed the showroom in an amber light that distorted the art like a heat mirage.

I wonder if the baby's cold.

I want a comfier crib.

[Solid block of Tint]

"Backroom," Jurgens said, pointing to the door behind the register. The art was the same as Sam's visit the month before. A charcoal face stared down in odium from its etched eternity on a block of yellow wood at Sam. The entire collection of sullen, wooden faces glowered like a gang of hyenas. Sam thought those paintings were very mean.

In the backroom, Jurgens sat down on a squeaking metal swivel chair as he taped a Styrofoam corner to a canvas bundled in brown paper. All were textures Sam hated.

"Did you sell it?" Sam said, gesturing to the painting on the desk.

"Yeah. eBay. Only thing keeping the lights on. It's nothing to celebrate. Whole thing's a wash after you factor mileage to the post office and back." Jurgens worked his thumbnail around the roll of masking tape. His toupee was crooked a few degrees.[23] "I was holding off on shipping to batch sales into the same trip. Gambling my seller's rating for filling up the truck. Buyers usually reach out before giving a bad review. But two weeks is two weeks and I got no other sales to batch it with."

"Going online is a bad thing," Sam said.

Jurgens laughed. "The hell are you talking about? Like

---

23 Like Milsap's.

chatrooms? The whole reason I'm going under is the internet is great for you. Artists can cut out middle men like me."

"You'll like these ones I brought this time. I did what you said on shadowing better like you said. They have more shadows on them this time."

"Christ." Jurgens let his spectacles dangle by the chain around his neck as he massaged his eyelids to purple and lime. "Come on, Sam. I'm old and you're twice my age. It's too late to be trying to make it."

"Okay, but you'll like these ones I brought this time because of the shadows."

"Sam, I don't even wanna look. Look, I'm sorry Amara's gone but the world keeps moving on and you gotta move on too. Someone needs to tell you that in plain English and I guess that someone's gotta be me. Everyone else keeps giving you hope when they shouldn't. Maybe take a computer class at the library. They'll help you make a resume. A lot of places hire guys like you. They got all these new hiring laws to help guys like you out. You're blowing Amara's trust on paint."

"We're playing hide and seek," Sam said. "She was just not where the police must have looked. The cat got her scared and she stabbed it from being scared. I'll find her, don't worry about that."

Jurgens lifted the shoddy wrap job from the office desk and leaned it against a file cabinet. "All I'm saying is computers are cheap and easy to use now. You could sell these yourself. Now hurry up and set them on the desk here and I'll take a look."

Jurgens flipped through Sam's paintings like records in a milkcrate.

"See the shadows?" Sam asked.

"Yep. I do."

"Worth two thousand, maybe. You think?"

"You really are crazy."

"How much do you think?"

"Two hundred."

"I don't think that's enough."

"No, Sam. You need to pay me two hundred as rent for the wall space and we'll see how they do and you can keep whatever you make."

"I don't have that much."

Jurgens took off his glasses. "See that hole up there?" he asked. Sam looked up at the molding ceiling tile. "You see that stack of bills?" Sam looked at the pile of envelopes. "These are my problems and they're as tough as yours, buddy. Your problems are for you to figure out and I'd be happy to point you along but I can't figure them out for you."

Jurgens helped Sam down the step and Sam's joints jolted from the roll down onto the sidewalk. The bag tore open from the impact and the painted garden laid face down on the concrete where Sam left it.

[Sketch of a daisy]

The only food Sam had was jars of preserves Amara made. Sam picked the green white fuzz from off the top and ignored the smell and ate it in small spoonfuls. He held the spoon in his fist. He sat in front of his easel. The black face faced him with smiling fangs. Its fur bristled around the blank spaces where its eyes needed to go. A happy cat until the day its blood stained the ceiling above him. Blood now oxidized to orange.

The stain is still there. Above where I write.

Painting the cat's eyes were the hard part. They were impossible to get right and made Sam pull his hair. They weren't the common yellow or hazel green but purple like Amara's jam while also shiny. Sam wasted tubes of red and blue mixing magentas. He usually liked the way the tubes looked like toothpaste but not that night. It was two in the morning. His head felt full of wet cotton balls. He pressed his thumb crushing the glade of stiff bristles against the sharp metal ferrule. He pressed and pressed and his forearm pinched an arthritic nerve he ignored and he pressed harder and pressed harder until the paintbrush snapped in two. Sam threw the palette across the study and it pasted itself for a moment to the spines of Amara's medical books before clattering to the floor with a splatter.

[Sketch of a cat head]

The bottom pantry shelf wasn't entirely empty. HEALTH HAZARDS: may be poisonous if inhaled or absorbed through skin. Vapors may cause dizziness or suffocation. Contact may irritate or burn skin and eyes. If ingested, call emergency medical care; if victim not breathing, give artificial respiration. Sam couldn't read the label but he knew the meaning of a skull and crossbones.

He poured ten ounces of turpentine into the jar of murky paintbrush water. He tipped the jar and the lukewarm liquid sat flush against his pursed lips. The odor of sulfide. The fluttering butterflies. Pastor Kellan would worry and check in after a week or two. She'd call the police. The surface tension tickled the hair on his upper lip. But what if she came to check on him herself, he thought for a moment, worried. The cloudy gray liquid. Like all first kisses, the act demanded courage. He relaxed his lips and drank. Horrid thorns stung his taste buds.

Then he heard it. He dropped the jar and it shattered against the footrest of his wheelchair. The turpentine went to work removing the blue from his jeans. He coughed and spat and rubbed his tongue raw against the inside of his smock. He suppressed his panicked breathing to silence. He sat in deathlike stillness. He felt the rapid pulse of struggling heartbeat in his eardrums. He focused his hearing toward the conservatory windows. The wind? The only sound was the faintest pitter patter of the turpentine dripping through the floor to kill the rats in the basement. Then the woman in the back yard screamed again.

EXPEDITION NOTES

OCTOBER 3, 2022 | 12:17 A.M.

The corpse of a female pastor was unearthed early in the excavation of ground zero. It's plausible the woman was Pastor Kellan. Forensic identification of the body was made impossible by its lack of red blood cell enzymes. This was true of every corpse exhumed. The individual DNA signatures all contained abnormalities that rendered traditional DNA matching infeasible. Further, dental analysis was impossible because the enamel of every corpse's teeth consisted of 99.34% organic substances as opposed to 98% inorganic substances and only 1% organic substances—the ordinary chemical composition of enamel. The body matching Pastor Kellan had suffered an antemortem fracture of the elbow, likely caused by the weight of the dirt and rubble.

As for the Corporeal Gallery, like all of Carrington, no record of the place exists. Unit B identified a Kentucky-based artist who creates charcoal drawings of faces on blocks of wood as Mr. Maltessouri describes, but this could just as likely mean that if the Canvases are a sick joke, the prankster included this detail to lend credibility to the ruse. That's what Milsap thinks. When I proposed to the rest of the Committee to have Unit C search ground zero for the Gallery's art to confirm the presence of the charcoal paintings, Milsap said: "[l]isten to the lawyer, we wouldn't want a copyright suit on our hands."

I'm not a superstitious person. I never was. I used to laugh at those who believed in ghosts and conspiracy theories. But now, I'm not sure how anyone could be sure of anything. Lawyers especially should be more skeptical of their beliefs. I am so alienated for leaving open even the slimmest possibility of a supernatural explanation. Milsap's flash flood/practical joke theory seems more of a joke to me than ghosts. You're telling me some joker dug thirty feet into a landslide packed with dead bodies to bury thirty-some Canvases as a joke? We're dealing with a town that doesn't exist on any map, in any book, or in any corner of the internet. How'd they even find it?

And then there's the Tint. Seeing is believing and beside me this very moment is a stack of Canvases covered in the stuff. I might not see colors but I see the words pulsing. I've seen plenty of regular ink to know it shouldn't pulse. The Tint is real—a compound no chemist or biologist has ever created or discovered, the composition of which cannot be determined. A compound that elicits the powerful sensory response Maltessouri describes. By ignoring the Tint's very existence, Milsap's theory is disrespectful to the memory of the Wade family.

Klay Wade was the original copyist of the Canvases. He underwent six months of controlled micro-exposure to build up his tolerance to the Tint. It's no surprise the Committee didn't consider using someone colorblind with Milsap as its chairman. Gradual deterioration of Klay's mind began to show in both the transcription and his life. Harmless grammar errors developed slowly into full sentences about events in his own life. Violent sentences. Erratic behavior. Paranoia. He was checked into a psych ward where he spent two weeks. Once his mania subsided, he was released. That night he murdered his wife and six-year-old daughter by suffocation with a garbage bag. He then lodged his head between the banisters at the top of the staircase landing and hurled his body down, severing his skull from his spine. The tragedy would have been avoided if Milsap hadn't vetoed me serving as copyist in the first place.

I hate that I can't transcribe anywhere else. The air in this room is so stale after midnight. Milsap's stupid "public safety" rule. Sahar doesn't care enough to enforce it considering she let me transcribe on the plane. But her anxiety is crippling at night, so I promised her I'd stop all fact-gathering after she turns in.

Still, I would love to walk the streets Maltessouri walked.

CANVAS NINE

The woman's screams caused Sam's hands to tremble as they fumbled under the kitchen sink between paint cans and expired household cleaners for the flashlight. He gripped the handle and shook its corroded innards like a Newton's cradle. The clunking batteries bothered the palm of his hand.

I desire to describe this moment perfectly. I need to understand.

Across the veranda, the beam of light assailed Amara's decayed garden and twisted it into a calamitous shadowed menagerie of claws and fangs. Limp beans and starved herbs hung like splayed entrails over gazebo prisons. Sam rolled from the ramp to the dirt and a disturbed floorboard groaned as it eased back up the rusted nail to return to its tranquil impalement. The hoarse wooden creak blended seamlessly with the woman's curdled cry.

"Someone help me," she screamed.

Sam's arms fought the resistance of the damp overgrown lawn gripping the tread of his wheels. He felt better knowing the scream was a grown woman's. He was first worried for the little twins who lived next door. Little arms like hollow wiffle ball bats. Arms pinned down. Arms snapped. No no no, Sam thought. Stop that, Sam, Sam thought. The scream grew closer as he reached the unkempt hedges at the back of the yard. Maybe a mountain lion. Sam rapidly shook his head. Thickets of bramble and thorn clamped their jaws around the reclaimed beaten path. Twisted foliage blotted out the moon. Sam steadied the flashlight between his knees as his hands pushed his wheels. She kept screaming.

I still hear it, faintly. Like high-pitched chirping bugs. A sharp noise, calling from the back of the yard.

Every rotation tore Sam's exposed skin. He tucked his chin and mouth into the neck of his jacket. A thorn caught his eyebrow and ripped a warm stream along the causeway frequented by tears. Her voice kept screaming. He stopped. He smeared his face with his sleeve. The voice kept screaming. A thorny branch rasped the top of his head. Blood drops dribbled ahead of him in the flashlight beam. He came upon the clearing and the voice stopped. Sam made three passes across the grass with the flashlight. He saw nothing except the perfect grass.

"Amara," he called out. "Where are you?" He sat still in the silence. His eyes dilated to take in the entire field of vision. There was a small movement. He shined the flashlight over the well. The rope swayed gently back and forth. The wind whistled past the cliffs like a faint scream. He finally took a breath. At once, the rope thrashed. Violent bashing of iron on stone echoed up the cliffs as the rope writhed.

"You're stuck," Sam called out. At once the rope calmed. He wheeled across the clearing. The muscles in his forearms burned white hot from the awful feeling of the freezing wind. He fixed his eyes on the rope. The clouds opened and the waning moon illuminated the stone basin. The A-frame roof cast crooked shadows that slithered across the grass and held Sam in the palm of its hand. He locked the wheels at the edge of the well.

[Smudge]

"Please help." The voice in the well was a breathless whisper.

"You hiding?" Sam said. He leaned forward and peered up with the flashlight into the well roof. A bird's nest rested in the hutch of the cross beam. The glossy yellow eyes of a baby bird squinted back. It peeped. "Finchie. You scared me," Sam said.

"Please." Her voice spoke from just below the lip of the well. The palm of Sam's hand crushed an ant against the stone surface as he heaved with all his remaining might. The feeling of the stone was the worst texture of all and he sat a moment on the well lip rubbing the texture off his palms. He steadied his center of gravity and peered down into the abyss. Darkness gazed back. The moonlight traced the presentiment of rope from the pitch below. The roof support creaked against his weight. His eyes adjusted to see the bucket resting below on its side. The bucket slithered in circles across the oily surface. Sam gripped the roof support and leaned closer. The beam above him rattled and the baby bird tumbled down trailed by feathers and twigs. The bird scraped the stone wall and landed in a broken heap below

[Large sketch of the well]

At once, Sam's pupils contracted with a sting as the flashlight reflected off the sudden silver liquid. It shifted to jade then to amber then to lapis lazuli then to citrine. Then sunstone then larimar then kyanite then ametrine. Then topaz then nephrite then aventurine then tourmaline. In a span of seconds the bottom inches of the well filled with the substance. Sam stared out over the clearing and tried to blink away the green and purple spots floating in his vision.

[Swirling blotch of Tint]

Keeps getting brighter. Keeps getting brighter. Keeps getting brighter. Keeps getting brighter.

He gritted his teeth as he cranked the rusted handle. He kinked his neck to keep his ear flush to his shoulder as the awful metal screech seemed to peel back the marrow in his bones like a craftsman's plane. One hand held steadfast against the opposing force as he reached with the other and grabbed the bucket.

As I write these words the emblazoning hues variegate and elude all physical description. Its colors are nearest to gemstones, unfortunately I've already stated the handful I know. I suspect the substance is alive but biology is a blind spot in my vast knowledge. The colors shift from one to the next in infinite multitude pulsing the glow of a lightning bug's thorax beaming a never-repeating pattern of ever-brightening hues. I have yet to see it repeat the same color twice and yet each color it shines remains forever embedded in the unfading composite. And this visual phenomenon is only a fraction of the sensory experience. The substance stains one's nervous system in pleasure. It rinses all sense of time in a warm bath of symphonies. It instills a cloying shock of sweet and savory that travels from the surface of the eye to the tips of the toes and then through time and back again in a hopscotch of tickling pins and needles. It giveth like God. It taketh like bacteria.

Sam named it the tint.

Sam poked it and it latched to his fingertip like napalm and seared off the skin. He scraped the tint off in the grass. It reformed on the ground into gelatinous droplets obstinate to waste itself in the dirt.

EXPEDITION NOTES

OCTOBER 3, 2022 | 2:12 A.M.

Before I transcribe the disturbing event that is about to occur, the Tint warrants a brief aside.

The Tint is as Maltessouri describes—a joyful assault on the senses. The members of Unit C who unearthed the Canvases, without exception, were reluctant to relinquish the treasures because of the pleasure and the sense of need and attachment it elicits. That is until they experienced the after-effects—severe migraines and seizures. Most of the individuals have since reported deep depression that they attribute to knowing they'll never experience the sensation again.

The Tint on the Canvases has somewhat faded over time, but it is still capable of inducing headaches and loss of the viewer's sense of time. Sahar rightfully avoids them at all costs. Milsap, with all his theories of how we should discount the Tint's magical qualities, has never laid eyes on it. Everything he knows is based on the partial (and unreliable) Wade transcription. It is an honor knowing I'll be the first to ever read the second half of the record.

To me, the Tint looks like the surface of a mirror. Black and white shapes in the words seem to shift and reflect motion from without. Except, the shapes the words reflect aren't what's placed in front of them. The reflections aren't of me. I've tried to make them out many times with a magnifying glass. It's like looking at a petri dish with a kaleidoscope.

Still, despite the Tint's devastating long-term effects on the viewer, I can't help but envy the sensory experience my colorblindness robs me of.

CANVAS TEN

Sam's passage back through the thorny path was made painless by the analgesic euphoria the tint coated his senses in. Sam rinsed the moldy purple confection from a jar of Amara's jam with the garden hose. Sam weathered the lacerating path through the thorny trail again and filled the jar with tint.

[Thick swirl of Tint]

It's nice how the jar is a sort of nightlight. Like those salt lamps idiots believe in. The glass is warm to the touch. Actually, it's more like how dry ice probably feels.

I wish for the skin on my fingertip to heal.

I lay down on the cot to sleep but the jar calls me back. I need to get rid of it, and yet it wants me to keep writing. Between that and the baby's crying I haven't slept for days. She is so damn selfish.

I want to see what Sam did next.

[Puncture]

Sunrise broke over the cliffs and speared through the fingerprinted glass of the conservatory windows to dance in the eyes of the painted cat. Eyes painted with tint. Sam gazed into those shifting jewels until exhaustion took him and he slept his most restful sleep since Amara disappeared. Sam was awoken neither by the pain of the infected cuts across his face, nor by the aching in his lacerated arms, but by the warmth and weight of the returned cat sleeping soundly in his lap.

EXPEDITION NOTES

OCTOBER 3, 2022 | 12:14 P.M.

This morning, Sahar and I got coffee at Coffeel. Finally! I've waited two years to visit it in person. Sometimes during Committee meetings (especially the long drawn-out, pointless ones led by Milsap) I'd flip through their social media photos, and in one or two instances, take a stroll around the neighborhood in Google Earth.

Coffeel lives up to the hype. The clay tile floor. The terrible art. The door tables! (More on that later.) Both baristas wore overalls with one strap off. Regardless of whether it's the uniform or just a coincidence, it adds to the immersive bohemian experience. I've sincerely never tasted better coffee in my life. Sahar said I was exaggerating and that the coffee is just fine, but I'm telling you there's a depth in flavor I've never tasted before.

We drank our coffee and played fetch with Borlú around the University of Kentucky campus. You can tell it's the week before all the leaves fall. Lots of Felicitys around. Sahar threw the stick and Borlú tore after it. He padded back to us carrying it in his mouth and melting the hearts of the students he passed. A perfect, cozy fall morning. Pleasant as can be until Sahar threw the stick again along with a wrench in our plans.

"I remember crossing this field after my civ pro exam crying thinking I'd failed," she said.

"I bet," I said. "Remember how painful the month waiting for grades to post is?"

"Month? UK took six weeks."

"Y'all take it easy round these parts."

"Nice Texas accent." Sahar threw the stick into a bush and Borlú dove in after it.

"Regardless of your grade, I'm sure Scott got you up to speed on the federal rules. He seems like a great mentor."

"Based on what? The dep?"

"You don't remember anything about having Scott as a boss?"

Borlú padded up and dropped the stick at her feet.

"What about Litton Steenken in general? Emma seems like a character. Do you remember horsing around with her at all? Any food fights?"

Borlú sat patiently for Sahar to throw the stick. She didn't. He huffed and laid his head on his paws. "I forgot to mention," she said, "I'm meeting a friend for lunch."

"What? Is it Aaron? He slipped my mind as a potential witness."

"Yeah, it's Aaron. Not that it matters. And before you ask, yes, we're getting lunch at the Copper Roof. He was my best friend here and I could really use him to vent."

"Totally. I'll be there to kick you under the table if you accidentally dive into anything confidential."

"I'm going by myself," she said.

"It's better to have a second chair in depositions and it's not like I'm busy."

Sahar threw her half-full cup of coffee in the nearby trash can. "I'm meeting up with a friend. That's all. Would it help you relax the rest of the trip if I let you depose me?"

"No," I said. "No. Sorry. You don't need that. I can always review the transcripts from your dozen other deps."

"Thanks. I'll call when I'm done. C'mon Borlú." Borlú was growling at the empty bench across from us. He wouldn't budge. "Jeez Borlú. Cut it out. C'mon." She yanked his leash and he finally followed.

So here I am cooped up in my room during what should have been a perfect day. Since when am I on her leash?

CANVAS ELEVEN

Mel was hungover so I was alone with my troubled thoughts. I was lying on the putrid, coarse carpet of my office with the door closed. I watched a ladybug make his way from the carpet we shared up onto the wall and across the pallor expanse of drywall. Mel is sexy but distant and vapid and too young and a camgirl and hungover.

[Smear]

There was a knock on the door. I had only enough time to crane my neck before Scott intruded.

"Hey, boss, you got a sec? Whoa, you alright?" Scott spoke with his usual air of retired jock bravado. Nothing asserts you're the boss like calling other people boss—the forty-year-old equivalent of dude.

I sat up. "Doing yoga, what's up?"

"Smart. More of a contact sports guy myself. Good to get the blood flowing. The office can be draining, I know. But it's like I always say. Greatness is grit through monotony." Scott offered me his hand and I pulled myself up by the edge of the desk.

"That depends," I said.

"Okay." Scott carried a collection of papers which he had rolled into a baton and thwacked against his palm like a prison guard. "What does it depend on?"

"On what the monotony is." I sat down at my desk chair before Scott could. He had a habit of sitting in the power seat regardless of who's office it was. "Say I work nine to five as a toll booth operator gritting my teeth through ten thousand hours of toll collection mastery. I guarantee the result would not be greatness."

"In the eyes of your toll booth boss, you'd be pretty great. Probably make toll booth boss yourself one day." He laughed at his own joke and hit my arm with the rolled-up piece of paper. I realized that by me sitting he had maintained a power position by simply standing. "Try to think of each work day as a page of a book you're reading," he said. "Bit by bit they add up and at the end of each day you dogear the page and look down the edge of the book and marvel at how far you've come. That's growth."

"But if the book is bad, then it's a benchmark of the time you've wasted," I said.

"Sure, but you gotta eat your spinach. Now as much as I love debating philosophy, I stopped by because I read your motion for the condo case and wanted to give you my notes in person."

"Something wrong?"

"Far from it. In fact, this the best work I've seen in a while." He unrolled the paper baton onto my cheap laminate desk. It was covered in red ink stitches. "Before you start sweating, most of these are formatting changes to match the filing rules. I love your point about the bylaws here but it could be even better if..." blah blah blah... I zoned out as Scott droned on. His suggestions were pedestrian and subjective.

But one was insulting: "Rich, do you know the difference between everyone and every one?"

"What?"

"Everyone and every...one." His emphasis on the last word blew coffee breath in my face.

"I don't follow."

"Everyone means every person. Every human being. If it isn't qualified by some limiting group or context then it means every human on earth. Versus every. . .one, which means each individual member of some specified group of something. Could be humans. Could be pickles."

"I know what words mean."

"Great. I figured you did. Just in a couple places here you've used them interchangeably. Incorrectly. Like this sentence here—every one else paid their association dues by July first." Scott underlined the sentence with his pen, carving yet another blood-red wound. "Every what paid their dues? Every tenant in the association? Every cockroach in the building? Every single person on earth?"

"I get it. I just didn't catch it."

"Don't be embarrassed. Take a breath, you're red. We all make minor mistakes and everyone has room to improve. Even the top of the class. I'm only hammering this home because I care about your development. Plus this is a court filing and tragedies are rooted in ambiguity. Strunk and White, fourth edition, page seventy-nine."

[Puncture]

"Great feedback," I said.

"Great." Scott tossed the defiled motion onto my keyboard and turned to leave. He tucked his hands down his snakeskin belt and straightened his shirt tails. "Remind me to bring a hammer so we can get your diploma hung up."

"Gotcha."

Scott tongued something stuck in his teeth. "Tell you what, how about me, you, and Sahar get lunch. My treat. I've never seen you talk. You've met, right? I can help break the ice."

If I am dead, this has to be hell. Trapped in a room arduously writing with a cramping hand ruminating about irritating conversations overlooked by a horde of hideous monsters. Eh, but if this is hell it's not as bad as it's made out to be. I'm pretty used to the faces and the baby is funny. I made her a little playpen out of her books. I really didn't need to. She just lays on her back like a flipped ladybug. She makes cute noises though. Still there's no way in hell this is heaven.

EXPEDITION NOTES

OCTOBER 3, 2022 | 1:50 P.M.

Maltessouri evidently didn't learn his lesson. There's instances in the record already where he's used "everyone / every one" incorrectly. For example: "[M]y personal resilience and steely work ethic, alone, have corrected everyone of those setbacks." Canvas Four, *supra*.

While on the topic of grammar, and not to state the obvious, but it is evident Maltessouri is slowly regaining his composure as his writing goes on. What began as terse stream of conscious ramblings has developed into (mostly) correct sentences. In a few more Canvases, he begins writing in columns of neat paragraphs. Through now, the paragraphing in the transcription has been entirely my own, but I like to think I've done the original justice.

The phenomenon suggests the Tint may actually be healing him from some kind of initial trauma. It may be that prolonged exposure is actually beneficial to the viewer if they can get past the initial mania and pleasure/ pain the Tint causes. The trauma Maltessouri originally wrote through may have been this initial phase of Tint exposure. On the other hand, he suggests he experienced external trauma in Canvas One. He writes: "[m]aybe I got shot in the motel or died in that car accident. I don't think she stabbed me with the pickaxe." It may follow that enough exposure will bestow a sort of transcendence to the viewer.

Sahar needs to hurry up. It's pushing 2 p.m. We're here to do a job, not catch up with old pregaming buddies.

CANVAS TWELVE

Sahar uh-huhed and oh-wowed like a parrot on Scott's shoulder at every stupid thing he said. We crossed the threshold of the historic brick and column section of the downtown into the outskirts of the seedier northside of rust and grass-stained siding. We reached a window with gold flake lettering: *Angelo's Ristorante*. The next window down: VASECTOMIES - TWO 4 ONE - THE SECOND BALL'S ON US! It was one of those kind of strip malls.

Scott checked his phone. "I gotta take this. Grab us a table by the window."

Sahar held open the door. "After you."

Strands of dusty plastic ivy hung down from the stucco walls. Checks impaled beside the cash register. The gum-snapping hostess sat us beneath a mural depicting a WWI trench battle dug into a large-breasted hillside.

Sahar scanned the sticky laminate menu. "Should I get the bucatini, the pulled pork, or the gyro?"

"I don't know what you like," I said.

The hostess glanced up from her phone to point Scott in the direction of our table. He held his gut in past the narrowly arranged tables. "Sorry to do this, kids, but I gotta get back. Cyrus Souers snapped his litigious fingers and cooked up another time-sensitive scheme to make his ex-wife's life worse than it already is. I swear, no matter how much I bill him it's never enough to get my lunch hour back. Try the mahi tacos, they're to die for." He handed Sahar his credit card and darted out.

[Sketch of a shattered window]

The tacos laid limp and soggy beside my empty water glass. The two of us ate in silence. Sahar was equally abstemious despite her Cobb salad appearing satisfactory.

I should try to eat. Hopefully I can keep it down now. What do I want? Wow I can have anything I want but I can't think of a single thing.

I want pudding I guess.

Ew vanilla.

I want you to give me chocolate pudding.

Sahar's phone illuminated from a text and she picked it up faster than I could read the name. I checked mine and was surprised to find Mel had messaged so early.

Babe, I need you really bad.

I replied: Busy. Tonight I'm yours.

Sahar set down her phone with a sigh. "So what's your plan after Litton Steenken?" she asked.

"Why do you care?" I said.

"Why would anyone from a top ten come to a nobody Kentucky firm? There's no way you're paying down your student debt."

"What's your problem?"

"Just saying it's nontraditional. I guess I like hearing about people's strategy."

"Oh so it's a competition?"

"I'm not sure why you're acting so threatened," she said.

"I'm not. Is the bathroom through the kitchen?" My chair leg rasped across the terracotta tile floor and a pair of old ladies peeped startled noises.

"Look," she whispered through clenched teeth. "I'm sorry for thinking you were gay. You're definitely just sexist."

"Is this you apologizing?"

"Pssh, why should I?"

"How fast do you think it'd take you to make partner?" I asked.

"I don't wanna make partner, I wanna work for the D.O.J.," she said.

"So you'll never make partner. You know, I did want to leave Litton Steenken, but now I think I might stick around. At least until you leave from all the pressure you can't handle."

Her phone lit up again and she glanced at it from the corner of her eye. She turned it face down.

"Fiancée?"

"Yeah."

"How's he?"

"Not an asshole, at least."

"How could a pussy be an asshole?"

[Sketch of a fork]

She threw her fork at me. It flew past my head and struck the window, the glass broke into a cobweb.

[Sketch of a cobweb]

Then a single shard broke loose and the whole thing came down and shattered across the floor. The hostess was nowhere in sight. Sahar took Scott's credit card off the table. "You pay for that," she said. She got up to leave as an old woman shambled in off the street through the broken window. Shredded leaves crowned her sunburned face.

"Is everything alright, mister? Ma'am? I don't want you to hurt each other. I saw her throw that at you. I saw her break the window."

"Mind your own business," Sahar said.

"I'm sorry. I'm only trying to get to my job down on Nicholasville Road and I need five dollars for the bus to get to my job."

"Sorry we don't have cash." Sahar breathed through clenched teeth, as though to filter the air from her tongue.

The woman spoke to the floor. "Please, ma'am. Sir, ma'am. I only need a five dollars."

"Where exactly do you work?" Sahar asked.

"Up on Nicholasville Road."

"That isn't a job. Do they let you take your shopping cart on the bus? Excuse us." Sahar stood up and the old woman clasped Sahar's hand in her own and shook it.

"Please, ma'am."

"Let go of me!" Sahar wrenched her hand away and wiped it top and bottom on the greasy table cloth.

The old woman mumbled to herself. "I was born without a mother or a father or a brother..."

"I'm Richie," I said. "What's your name?"

She wiped her eyes. "My foster mother was always yelling at me that it was Mary. Mary. Your name's Mary. It's a lie. Don't believe one word of it. My name is Violet. I've always been Violet."

"My mother left me too," I said.

"Did she die too?" Violet asked.

"No, just left. My foster parents were always nice but the children were awful."

"Yes," she said. "Always ganging up on us."

"Yes," I said while handing her a menu. "Order anything you like."

Even if Sam hadn't ran away from his baby sister they would have probably been separated by the system. That retarded murderer could barely take care of himself.

[Puncture]

The walk back was awkward. Sahar kept a step ahead to keep me in her blind spot. We went our separate ways to our separate offices. I threw the red ink-drenched motion in the trash. I read Mel and my texts:

Babe, I need you really bad.

Busy. Tonight I'm yours.

Not like that. Babe, I'm in serious trouble.

EXPEDITION NOTES
OCTOBER 3, 2022 | 7:55 P.M.

I'm going crazy. I need to go for a walk. Sahar and I had a fight. When we met up at the Copper Roof, Aaron was already gone. She was sitting at the bar. The place was exactly as Richie describes, although no merry-go-round horse above the bar. Sahar said there never was one but I asked the bartender and he said they took it down last year. Sahar said she was always pretty drunk when she was there. She was drunk this time too. "Why do you keep staring at me?" she asked.

"Because I think you're more interesting than the places we visit."

"That's a clunky pick-up line."

"Not like that. What I mean is it's more important to watch for anything that makes you remember Richie."

"You want a shot?" She waved the bartender down.

I leaned over and pet Borlú. "How long has he been sitting here? He seems sad."

"Pssh. Lay off. He's having a blast. He's the center of attention."

Sahar ordered two tequila shots. "We don't need salt and lime. Right, Joe? You don't need salt, right?"

I rolled my eyes at the bartender and he put one of the shot glasses back below the bar.

"I'll have his then," Sahar said. The bartender complied.

Sahar downed the first shot

"Is Angelo's far?" I asked.

She cringed from the taste. "What?"

"The restaurant where you and Richie…"

"It's far."

"Should we go tonight?"

"The food is vomit. There's a million better options."
"It isn't about the food."
She downed the second shot. "Then go."
"You keep drinking you'll break a window."
That really pissed her off.

CANVAS THIRTEEN

It became an irritating evening of distractions. I parked my laptop at a corner table of Coffeel for the purpose of researching federal and state usury laws. I spent an hour or so pounding espresso to stave off the effects of prolix websites and reading blocks of size five font. The amount Mel needed was a pointe above the limit for borrowers with credit as poor as mine. It still hurts thinking about the amount of money I dumped into Mel's cam shows. It must be in the thousands. I maxed out a department store credit card. Who even gets a department store credit card? Idiots who are bad with money is who. I'm an idiot. Or I was an idiot. I suppose one perk of being dead is I don't have to worry about debt anymore. Or what anyone thinks about me. The first distraction was the divots in the table beneath my pen. See, Coffeel doesn't have tables, it only has doors. Six panel doors, painted with flowers and peace signs and whatnot and suspended between two sawhorses and then thrust into a booth. I suspect the inventor of the door table pivoted around 3000 BC after discovering his invention was more useful as a privacy barrier between rooms rather than a desk that causes pens to pierce holes through paper.

[Puncture]

EXPEDITION NOTES
OCTOBER 3, 2022 | 8:40 P.M.

I snuck out. I guess I wasn't really "sneaking" so much as opening my hotel room door and walking through it. If Sahar decides to pass out, drunk, at 7 p.m., she can't expect me to stay in my room all night.

What better place to transcribe about Coffeel than Coffeel. To think, Richie's first cup was on a fall evening just like this. I asked the barista if he ever had a coworker named Rowan. He said he hadn't but that he'd heard something from the other baristas about the CIA or something coming in all the time to ask questions. He heard that's why the last owner sold the place. He asked me if "Mr. Maltese" was a serial killer or something. I corrected him.

It's puzzling to reconcile Richie's obvious intelligence with his addiction to cam shows. I do hope the remaining Canvases shed light on his past. I'd like to know what started him down that path in the first place. I suppose we all make mistakes. Some of us drink too much. Some of us are obsessive. We all have vices.

I'm even more interested in what Richie looks like. Obviously it would help finding him more than any other clue, but it would also color his decisions and personality immensely. It's naïve to deny that an attractive man falling in love with a camgirl draws a much different inference than if a homely man falls in love with one. The former is more pathetic than the latter.

I almost had a heart attack just now. I've been typing with my laptop on my knees while Canvas Thirteen rests on my door table. A little girl came over and pulled the Canvas right off the door and ran. I managed to catch her quickly and get it back. I scared her and she immediately ran outside where her parents must have been. Maybe she thought I was coloring or something. Maybe they're right. No more transcribing in public.

I'll do one more and head out. You'd have to be crazy to not love this coffee.

CANVAS FOURTEEN

Sam's desk is much nicer.[24] One of those solid wood executive desks under the conservatory windows. Why would Sam need a desk? It must have been Amara's. She must have had a good job to afford this house. Probably was a doctor for, I don't know, myalgia.

[Blotch]

The second distraction at Coffeel was my own foolish mistake of opening my bank statement in another tab. A stretching column of negative red transactions I had very little memory of. This occasioned the third distraction—a chewed fingernail sheared off at the cuticle—which of course I nettled with my thumb like a masochist. The fourth and fifth distractions were Mel and Sahar weighing heavy on my mind. Heavy like a brick on my stomach making me take shallow breaths. Heavy like those cheap sand-filled sculptures of plastic dolphins tourists buy at beachside gift shops. The prickly blue anxiety sand of Mel's financial troubles mixing with the red pissed-off sand of Sahar's rivalry swirling together in a plastic, kitschy dolphin starfish vessel weighing down on my laboring lungs pinning me to the floor.

[Puncture]

I'm being melodramatic. The sixth distraction was a different woman. Around the time my research taught me that loan providers operating out of Indian reservations were exempt from limits in both principal and interest, my interest was caught by the hottest girl I'd seen in a while studying at the door across from mine and so I took out my terribly smart looking copy of the federal rules and deliberately angled its

---

24 [than the door tables].

spine in her direction. I tried my best to look smart. I thumbed my stubble as I read. I jotted notes of gobbledygook as I tried to seem handsome and brilliant. Like that would come across. I'm cringing just thinking about it. It's okay, Richie. You're dead now. No one cares. The eighth and most intolerable distraction of all was a British man. (The seventh distraction was the emo music filling the cafe but that's par for the course at coffee shops.) Damn you parentheticals creeping back in. Out out out. You gossipy little parentheticals.

[Several punctures]

The Brit was dressed like an 18th century snuff box maker with loud socks. His Ichabod body craned like a buzzard perched over the counter where he sipped coffee through smiling baleen. "Know a good pub?" he said.

"Try Limestone," the barista said. "This is a coffee shop." She twisted a valve and the steam wand howled. I swear she got uglier every time I saw her.

"I could use a bloody drink," he said. She recoiled from his pestilent breath. The solipsistic prat rattled on. "Where do you pop 'round after you get off?"

"I never get off." She disappeared into the backroom. A long while passed and the sorry sod shot me a grin of falsely assumed camaraderie. She returned pushing a mop bucket by the mop handle.

"Need a hand?" the Brit asked.

"Nope. Perfectly capable here, dude." She wheeled around him toward the restrooms.

Ichabod slithered after her. "There's a film showing at the cinema—"

"Hiya Jimmy, how's the German coming?" She threw her weight beside me onto the booth and scanned the scribbles on my punctured legal pad. The Brit and I were stupefied.

I responded, "Oh, uh, I think you have me mistak—"

"Oh, you're doing great! See, it's not all that different from English being Germanic and all." Her thick elbow prodded my side beneath the door.

"Uh, jah," I said.

"Ich habe ein bischen arbeit, aber let's take a look at what you've got so far." She read my nonsense notes for six minutes before Ichabod rode out into the night.

"You saved my ass," she said.

"Who is he?"

"No clue. I swear he knows my schedule. The mid shift said he'll come in and ask about me and leave without ordering." She snorted and picked something from her nose and rubbed it into the black leather bench.

"You definitely impel him," I said as I closed my laptop and tucked it into my bag.

"Barf, dude. I'm surprised you don't recognize him. You come in twice as much as he does. At least you aren't creepy about it."

"Can I have my notes back? I'm in a hurry."

"Oh please. You were oogling that girl for an hour. Here's your doodles back." She peeked at my laptop. "So are you in debt or something? Mob coming to break your knees or something?"

"You stalking me or something?" I asked.

She rolled her eyes, removed her beanie, and beat her hair like a foyer rug. "Gotta keep a close eye on my students. Tutoring is tough when the student's a horny blow-off."

I flung my bag over my shoulder, wedging myself between the door-table, the booth, and the barista. "Can I get out? You're thronging me."

"Can you stop with the grandiloquence? It's the twenty-first century, Melville. You come in every day and you never tip and I'm pretty sure the only time you've acknowledged my existence is when you talk down to me about your order in fifty-dollar words. Do you know how to speak normal English?

Do you need a tutor?"

"I assure you," I said, "the worst lawyer on the planet is sharper than the brightest living barista."

She stood up. "I can be pretty perspicacious too, you know. Also, I'm not a barista. I'm doing research." She fished a business card from her hoodie pocket and flicked it in my face. "Rowan. Call me if you need English lessons." She got up and pushed the bucket of cold mop water to the bathroom and closed the door.

ROWAN RAYNE, MFA, PHD.
Assistant Professor,
English Literature and Linguistics
The University of Kentucky

Her photo beside the words. The card is here now on the desk. Her tragic mistake was giving it to me; my tragic mistake was putting it in my pocket instead of the trash.

[Scribbles]

My contracts class covered usury rates only very briefly—five minutes as a tangent during a cold call, at most—still, I knew I was treading barefoot up a glacier. I was hunched in the shadows behind the dumpster enclosure of my apartment building, my phone illuminating my dumbass face. Subconscious machinations must have commandeered my legs to deposit me in a most portentous environment to perform the act my ego knew was leagues beneath my status and education. Portentous just means ominous. Shit, maybe I am pretentious. Crouching behind a dumpster to take out a payday loan was like the full body equivalent of someone covering their bad teeth with their hand while laughing. Only instead of laughing, I was making the worst financial decision of my life.

[Puncture]

I think the baby is bored. She looks bored. I'd be bored.
We gotta empty the jar first. No one should have this power.
Even me. What would entertain her?

I wish for a bunch of stuffed animals.

That's good. That's enough. Stop. Stop.
I wish the stuffed animals would stop.
That got silly real quick.

She's loves the little elephant in a raincoat. Hell yeah.

[Sketch of an elephant head]

Hundred Suns was a payday lender loosely affiliated with
a casino on a Virginia Indian reservation, which meant they
were out of federal and state jurisdiction. Borrower protection
laws didn't apply. In fact, I'd come to find out no laws applied
to them. Truthfully, I still know little about them. As soon as
I leave Carrington, I intend to devote my career to exposing
them to justice. Oh wait, I'm an idiot.

I wish for Hundred Suns to pay for their crimes.

Much easier. I swiped past the fine print and interest rate
chart. My direct deposit would hit my account that Friday
and I'd pay the loan back then and live off ramen for the
following two weeks. No big deal. I entered my name, social
security, and account and routing numbers. I flicked the digital
wheel to $3,000. The website thanked me and the money was
transferred to my account an hour later.

Later, I sat at the flimsy cardboard boxes I used as a desk
as it strained beneath the weight of my laptop.

"You're my hero, babe," Mel said.

"Anything for you. I'm sending the money now."

"What would I do without you?"

"Your landlord is bending you over."

"Speaking of..." And so my private show began.

Wait. If I'm dead then how did baby die?

EXPEDITION NOTES
OCTOBER 4, 2022 | 1:20 A.M.

Unfortunately, I cannot provide further details regarding Ms. Rayne's professorship due to potential litigation by the University of Kentucky against the Committee involving claims of slander and intentional infliction of emotional distress as well as possible counterclaims against the University for spoliation of evidence.[25] Mediation is in progress. Litigation would be frivolous and solely to block the investigation from gathering any facts that might connect the University to a mass grave. While I'm on the topic, I've always felt "Carrington Massacre" would be a more appropriate designation than "Carrington Tragedy." But I suppose that would only increase the University's reluctance to be associated with the investigation surrounding Ms. Rayne. The point is Sahar and I are prohibited from interviewing anyone from the institution.

The barista is closing up. Time to head back and toss and turn.

Wait, where is the baby? No dead babies were dug up.

---

25 Scrubbing all files related to Ms. Rayne from online databases, syllabi etc.

CANVAS FIFTEEN

I wish to see all the things Sam killed.

The claws batted from below and scratched the bottom edge of the door. It meowed. It exhibited no unusual behavior the entire week Sam locked it in the pantry. He unlocked the door and the innocent cat padded out and cheeked up against the footrest of his chair. Purred. Sam studied it. The cat studied him back.

Sam drained a can of tuna and placed it on the floor. The can tapped as the cat lapped it along the edge of the wall. Sam studied it some more. Sam finally pet it. The soft contours of its shoulder blades. The pleasant warmth. There was no doubt in his mind it was Amara's cat.

"Eat up, friend. Big day." A yawn and a shiver overtook Sam. Through the sidelites he saw the white and red Call-A-Ride pull up to his driveway. He double-checked the tote was fastened to the back of his chair and triple-checked the canvas was secure within. Then he opened the door and almost had a heart attack.

[Sketch resembling Olivia Souers]

"Hi, Mr. Sam!" The tiny voice popped like a balloon. Sam caught his breath.

"Olivia. Knock please."

"Was 'bout to. Oh, kitty!" Olivia collapsed to her knees and began petting the cat.

"No." Sam grabbed it by the scruff and tossed it back inside. He wheeled out fighting the furry thing back and closed the door. "He is sick."

"Oh...Okee. Momma said ask see if it's okee we play out back on the ramp." Olivia's twin brother was beating the grass with a wiffle ball bat.

"What were Amara's rules about it?"

"Umm. No touching tools, no climbing, and no going in the woods."

"Okay, go play."

Sam stopped beside the hydraulic lift as the driver stepped down from the Call-A-Ride. He wore his neon yellow parka like a smiley face.

"Morning, Sam. You seem chipper today." The driver spoke between bites of an egg and cheese sandwich. "I see those scrapes are healing up. Glad you've gotten into gardening. We headed to Pawper's?"

Sam handed the driver his last dollar. "Gallery please first and then Pawper's please."

"Aye-aye, captain." The residential veins of the eastern side of Carrington, where Sam lived, flowed into the central artery of Main Street. It was the only road connecting the eastern neighborhoods to the heart of town to the west. The artery was clogged by a coal truck parked perpendicular across the road. A sun-shriveled miner signaled for the driver to stop.

"Better get comfortable," the driver said.

Sam watched the rain start and patter his window. The blockage was cleared. The driver folded his newspaper and shifted the bus into drive. "And they're off."

[Sketch of a leering face]

An automated voice answered the first three calls and informed Sam the voice mailbox was full. Jurgens picked up after the fourth call.

"God dammit."

"Hi, Jurgens. I need help over the step and the bus driver's back is—"

"God dammit."

The artwork hadn't changed, only accumulated more dust. The painted wooden faces stared at Sam from the showroom wall just like the marionettes stare at me now. I've really gotten used to it. Snow up to their hips. Can barely make out the tops of the kids' heads. Sam followed the tracks in the dust on the floor his chair left during his last visit. The backroom roll of brown paper was frosted in dust. Jurgens' overalls looked as sun-washed as the unsold artwork.

"I'm glad you dropped by. Better to have this conversation in person." Jurgens wiped the dirty swivel chair with the edge of his hand and sat down. "The Corporeal Gallery has come to the decision it will no longer sell the artwork of Sam Alley." Sam closed his eyes to separate the words. "The vote was unanimous, but don't take it personally. The Corporeal has come to the decision to stop selling all artwork."

"I'm not understanding."

"I closed on the gallery yesterday. That means I sold the building, Sam." A sudden sheet of rain drummed the roof and a steady drip of water collected in a five gallon bucket like coins in a fountain.

Sam slowly scratched his hair, hearing and feeling the pops like TV static beneath his fingernails. "What if I...How about...You could use my house. For free you just put my pictures in the internet for me."

"No, Sam. Between you and me, I feel excited for the first time in a long time."

"Would you come over and help me put my pictures in the internet sometimes?"

"No, Sam. I— What is that?" Jurgens' eyes locked on the sparkling corner of canvas peeking out from the tote. "What the hell is that?"

[Sketch of a mouse]

In the showroom, Jurgens darted from wall to wall waving the canvas like a protest sign. "Over there it looks orange but over here it looks silver, but I swear it's still green. Incredible. Is that oil? Seriously what did you use? What color even is this? Don't tell me. Don't tell me. You're using that paint gangbangers put on low-riders to make them purple and black at the same time. You're branching out in subject matter too.

Sort of futurism meets Andy Warhol meets...I don't know... LED signs? Blacklight posters? This is something else." Jurgens took a wooden face from the center of the wall and flung it over his shoulder. It broke against the opposite wall. He hung Sam's painting.

"So it is good then?" Sam asked. "How much do you think it's worth?"

"I was getting to that. Need to take a couple photos first. This is going on the site immediately." Jurgens pulled out his phone before falling into mesmerized awe of the tint. A minute passed.

"It's good then?" Sam asked.

Jurgens covered his heart and jumped a foot off the ground. "Christ, Sam, I forgot you were here. Wow, what just happened? The money. Of course. Money. Of course. Of course. One second." Jurgens backpedaled toward the backroom, his eyes stayed transfixed to the painting as if it were the barrel of a gun. Sam watched him turn the dial of a small safe in the backroom and rummage through its contents. He returned thumbing a stack of bills like a flip book. "Ten thousand seem about right?"

"I feel sick," Sam said.

Jurgens smacked him on the back. "Figured that'd make you smile. Pretty ironic too, don't you think?"

"What is ironic?"

"That's all of the down payment on the gallery. I don't see this as a gamble. I know this is worth twenty grand to the right bidder. I have to make some calls. Now go home, puke your guts out or whatever you need to do, and paint me more like this."

The hydraulic arm of the Call-A-Ride lifted Sam off the ground.

"I'll be damned, Sam. Haven't seen you smile in forever," the driver said. The clouds drew open and Sam squinted toward the gallery storefront window at the shimmering tint painting of a ten thousand dollar bill.

[Sketch of a ten thousand dollar bill]

At Pawper's, a woman pressed her hip into a heavy bag of kibble and held open the door. Sam's lungs filled with the woodchip, dander, and urine tang. A parakeet tweedled and bopped.

"What'cha need now, Sammie?" the owner asked.

"A litter box and whatever's cheap that cats can eat."

"Did we get a kitty?" Sam nodded. "A cat to keep you company is a wonderful idea," the owner said.

"Also need more mice," Sam said.

"You're overfeeding that snake. It's bad for him. I'll give you one."

"Three, please."

"One."

"I'll freeze two. It's not so easy for me to get over here."

"Well, I wouldn't want to see the inside of your fridge."

It was dark by the time Sam got home. The cat greeted the wheel of his chair with its cheek. The massive canvas was finally primed. He'd start with Amara's feet and work his way up.

Sam had a loose grasp on scientific methodology from the years of being Amara's sounding board. He'd done his best to isolate variables as he used the well. He learned that no tint came from dropping dead mice. He learned each living mouse brought less tint than the one before it. He'd killed seven mice that week. That night, the eighth mouse writhed by the tail where Sam pinched it. He dropped it in the well. No tint came. He slept beside the well beneath a wool blanket. At daybreak he checked again. Still no tint.

The Call-A-Ride didn't run on Sunday so Sam had to cross town on his own. Faint morning light cast prison bars from between the trees. Sparse branches speckled with steadfast leaves heralding the coming winter. Sam's arms burned. "I miss you a lot," he said.

An hour later he pushed open the door to Pawper's.

"Good lord, Sammie. I'll get you a glass of water."

Sam winced at his sunburned reflection in the store window and stretched his elbows. A clicking feeling like an imbedded BB rolling over bone.

"What's the emergency?"

"I'd like a dog," Sam said.

"Take your pick." She gestured toward the puppies in the store window.

"An older one I think, please."

She took him to the kennels in the backroom. "Say hi, Samson. Good lord, get it? Sam's son." The scabby retriever lifted an eyebrow where it lay like a discarded mop head. "He's at least fifteen. I understand if you aren't interested."

"He will work."

Baby has quite a grip. She got ahold of a dirty paintbrush and held it tight like a little squid. So cute. Oops, spoke too soon. She dropped her elephant and is now bawling.

[Sketch of an elephant in a raincoat]

The moon illuminated Samson's golden coat. Sam sat beside the screen door and put on his thick winter gloves and wrapped a scarf around his face. The dog's knees hobbled from the long walk. The dog picked at the ground hamburger on the porch boards. Sam scratched its coarse, matted fur. It nettled his fingers through the glove and he pulled it away. "Good boy."

Thorns rasped Sam's scarf as they pushed through the thicket. A branch snapped back and Samson whimpered. Sam brushed an ant from the red spotted fur above Samson's eye. They reached the clearing and it began to rain. Tiny craters formed from the raindrops falling into the dirt. They reached the well and Sam lifted Samson onto his lap and said a prayer. He pushed Samson over the edge. Sam couldn't cover his ears fast enough. He heard the awful snap and the yelp. He cried.

Sudden blinding light. The bucket floated across the tint. So much tint. He filled the jar and gazed through the glass and into the beauty. He came to at midday and the rain had stopped hours before and the mud beneath his wheels had already dried and caked and the well was empty again. He crossed the clearing toward the path. He heard the skittering and turned back to face the sound. The oily black mass marched toward him.

I wish to stop seeing Sam's memories. I have no desire to see what Sam killed next.

[Large sketch of the well]

EXPEDITION NOTES

OCTOBER 4, 2022 | 1:01 P.M.

I was awakened at noon by the front desk calling to tell me there were two men here to see me. Sure enough, it was Milsap and some patsy of his. They had taken a redeye. Milsap relished in reprimanding me for going out last night. See, there are two rules Sahar and I are bound to on this expedition.

The first rule is I can only transcribe in private for the protection of the Canvases and others. Sahar had been lax on enforcing this rule. She had given me her key to the carrying case days ago out of convenience. But now she will not give me her key unless I'm in my hotel room where I must remain for the duration of the transcription session lest I be removed from the Committee. Sahar called Milsap shortly after I left last night to inform him of my transgression.

The second rule is that under no circumstances are we permitted to visit Carrington ground zero. The excavation ended in the fall of 2018. In 2019, Unit C transitioned to restoration. The goal was to return ground zero to ordinary wilderness. The photographs confirm restoration was a success. Other than the rows of freshly planted saplings, what was once Carrington now has the appearance of an ordinary valley. All that remains is the latitude and longitude—known only by Unit C and the Committee.

The edict of no return was obviously Milsap's idea. He says we can't risk the general public following us and learning its location. "If it was a flash flood, who cares," I'd said. Then he said something like: "You're the one who thinks there's a dangerous magical well, lawyer."

What I do understand, as a lawyer, is that Carrington

is the best source of evidence. What was the oily black mass that spilled out from the well toward Sam? Ah, but wait, that was "a metaphor," Milsap concluded. Of course, of course. Metaphor of what? I don't know. He doesn't know. But of course that's the only possible explanation. I am such a dumb lawyer sometimes. Milsap, you wouldn't even know if we went to see Carrington for ourselves. But Sahar insists we don't go so I guess we won't. Wouldn't want her telling on me again. I don't think I've ever been betrayed by a friend. How did Richie describe the way Sahar made him feel?

Canvas Fourteen: "[T]he red pissed-off sand of Sahar's rivalry...weighing down on my laboring lungs pinning me to the floor."

Pissed-off indeed.

CANVAS SIXTEEN

Keep showing me the past week in perfect clarity.

"The bitch is a psycho. Syd, where's the pics?" Cyrus said. Sydney slid a stack of printed screenshots across the conference room table with her bedazzled nails. The screenshots were excessively marked up with red marker. Sahar closely examined every single one. I rolled my eyes. She knew as well as I did those weren't useful evidence in a kidnapping case. Show-off.

"See here," Cyrus said. "At nine a.m., someone switched their watches off. Then my unanswered texts to her." Cyrus rifled through the stack. "Okay, and now look here. Look at that. Fucking 5:28 p.m. GPS watches come back on. She keeps the GPS off during the time when it fucking matters. I already told her I'm calling the cops next time. I mean, you agree. Right, Scott? Look here it happens again, October third, same shit. September twenty-first, same shit. It's been this way all fucking summer."

"That's terrible," Sahar said. "I'm not going to leave the office until we find your kids, Mr. Souers." She spoke looking at me with a satisfied smile.

[Sketch of a watch]

"Cy, show Scott the text where Molly called me a cunt," Sydney said.

"He doesn't care about that." Cyrus paced the length of the conference room, smearing his sweaty face with the sleeve of his button-down clubbing shirt. His gold chain bracelet clinked against his gold watch. Sahar underlined portions of the screenshots and wrote notes in the margins.

"Scott, is this her first case?" Cyrus said. "She's making me nervous. Tell me this isn't her first case."

"It's not her first case," Scott said.

The blood left Sahar's face and I fought my laughter.

"Good. The judge said the GPS watches stay on the kids

at all times except to charge them at night. I can do it, so why can't she? She feeds me bullshit 'oh I forgot to charge them,' or, 'oh the kids turn them off when they get to school.' Oh yeah? Then how come none of this shit happens the week I have them?"

Sydney held a pack of cigarettes with her offhand as she rummaged through her handbag like a monkey grooming for bugs. "Cy, hunny, want a snack? It's almost two-thirty and the doctor said—"

"For all I know, the kids don't even go to school when she has them."

"You're preaching to the choir," Scott said as he stood up and struggled to button his suit jacket. It was the first time I'd seen him in a suit. He'd clearly put on a few pounds. "The judge ordered the GPS watches stay on the kids at all times out of the house, implicit in that order is that they need to be charged and turned on."

"She's drunk and on meth with that boyfriend of hers. I know they have the kids holed up in some shithole motel. This is all part of their crackhead plan to lock me up and take my money. The fake ransom note will come eventually, I know it. She's dangerous. She drops the kids off drunk every time it's my turn."

[Sketch of a one-story motel]

"When did you last see Olivia and Austin?" Scott said. Sahar offered Sydney a tissue box. Sydney's bedazzled talons tore through the thin paper.

"Of course this happened the month we filed for change of custody."

"Cyrus, I need you to answer the question. When was the last time you saw the kids?"

"I dropped them off at her house last Sunday," Sydney said.

"Must have been Sunday morning I saw them then," Cyrus said.

"You were in Vegas," she said.

"Wednesday then. It doesn't matter. Long enough to be my alibi."

"What did you tell the police?"

"To fuck off. I wasn't gonna talk to them until I talked to you."

"Okay. And don't talk when they come back either. They're gonna come back. If they come with an arrest warrant, cooperate, but still don't talk. Who served the complaint?"

"Some shrimp dick who followed the cops. I know a process server when I see one. Hit me in the face with it before I could close the door."

I tried to read Sahar's copy of the ex-wife's complaint upside down. The printer had conveniently ran out of ink after she printed herself a copy. Sahar is above nothing. Debating whether to wish her career gets ruined. It was suspicious Cyrus' ex-wife's lawyer was able to draft such an elaborate complaint in a day. Kidnapping, false imprisonment, intentional infliction of emotional distress, motion to amend custody order, it went on and on.

EXPEDITION NOTES

OCTOBER 4, 2022 | 9:16 P.M.

Sahar was in the hotel's indoor jacuzzi. Borlú was harassing a pool noodle. I'm certain you're not allowed to have dogs down there.

"Get your suit," Sahar said splashing me. The water soaked the leg of my slacks.

"I'm wearing it."

"Your bathing suit. Come on. It's Saturday."

"I've got a couple witnesses to add to the list."

"Are we gonna line up the baristas at that coffee shop and ask who's guilty of serving an invisible man? Did you notice any professors disguised as baristas doing undercover research? It's almost like people don't do that in real life."

"I already questioned one barista."

She sunk down so only her face was above the bubbling water. "Of course you did."

"I'm going for a walk. I need a phone charger. The Souers contracting office isn't too far. Cyrus Souers' business."

"Who?"

"The defendant in Richie's kidnapping case. From Canvas Sixteen."

"Right. Sure. I haven't read those in forever." Borlú padded over to us with the pool noodle in his jaws scraping the tile.

"Can I take Borlú with me?"

"Fine. I'll give you my key when you bring him back."

I put Borlú in his harness. "I've been thinking," I said as I clipped on the leash. "I need to depose you."

She sat up.

"Yeah, I think that'd be a good idea," I said. "We'll start at eight a.m."

CANVAS SEVENTEEN

Seeing Cyrus and Sydney off in the lobby was another ten minute ordeal.

"I can't tell the police to arrest your ex-wife. It doesn't work like that." Scott rubbed his eyelids.

"Aren't you my lawyer?"

"Cy, let's get some more lunch," Sydney said, digging her talons into his bicep.

"Saying I kidnapped my own kids. Can you believe that? The screenshots show how crazy she is. You make extra copies of those. I want the judge to get those."

"I'll take care of it, Mr. Souers," Sahar said. Cyrus stared right through her.

"I'll put both associates on it," Scott said.

"No. I want you on it. I pay you three hundred dollars an hour and you have this kid doing it?" Sahar got redder than I remember. I love it. This is like watching a movie in science class and taking notes.

"I sign off on everything. Richard and Sahar do the grunt work to save you money. We only charge one hundred for them."

"I don't care about the money. I care that the bitch goes to prison. Move lightning fast on this." Sydney trailed behind Cyrus as he stormed down the sidewalk.

[Blotch]

Scott unbuttoned his jacket and his gut spilled over his belt. "She's his best girlfriend yet. But he's right, we need to move fast. Those allegations are serious and Cyrus isn't the most sympathetic defendant. Plus the police are already in the mix."

"Do you think he actually kidnapped them?" Sahar said, moving to stand between Scott and I.

"No way. He's too hot-headed to pull a kidnapping off without leaving a trail of broken glass and witnesses. There's no way." Scott began to pace. "Here's the plan. Sahar, research the applicable standard and draft the answer. We should count on our motion to dismiss being denied so, Rich, you and I will start discovery."

She turned red again. "Shouldn't I do discovery?"

"You'll get there." Scott began to pace. "The ex-wife lives in a middle-of-nowhere mining town a couple hours south. The sort of place maps have as all green. A real bang your cousin sort of place. Which means everything is still in the nineties. Which means discovery is tricky as hell. Usually no electronic records in places like that."

"I can't wait to get started," I said looking at Sahar.

"That's the spirit. I called Coffey Niehoff this morning—mom's law firm—and Barrett Niehoff agreed to let us depose Mrs. Rothacker tomorrow afternoon. Barrett and I go way back. The sooner we depose her, the less time they have to think up lies." Scott squinted through the glass door. "Shit, Cyrus is coming back. I'll head him off so you two can get to work. Rich, we'll meet here at six a.m. It's a long drive." He took a deep breath and stepped out to meet Cyrus.

"I can't wait to get started," I said. Sahar punched the elevator button.

The sun's going down again. How many days has it been? I need to change baby.

The elevator doors closed like an accordion.

"I'm liking this job more every day," I said. "How about you?"

"Fuck off."

The elevator stopped, jostled, and dropped six inches. I braced myself by the handrail and Sahar fell into me. She shoved off and the elevator dropped another few inches and she fell to the floor.

"Stop moving!"

"You're moving!"

Above us, a tense gear groaned and clanked like a jack-in-the-box.

Every twist sent a reverberation through the elevator walls. Sahar laid on the morgue slab floor with her face drained gray. Clank...clank...clank. The elevator pre-dated the advent of the emergency call button. The clanking ceased and was replaced with the whine of rusty machinery. The floor seemed to sway. I prayed to my reflection in the gold walls.

"I think it stopped."

"Don't talk to me."

It took the fire department until nine p.m. to brace a jack between the elevator floor and the second-floor ceiling. The delay was partly caused by Scott's backseat driving telling the firefighters how to correctly use a jack. It only made matters worse seeing how much nicer the other offices in the building were. Sahar looked like a sooty pedestrian staggering out of a bomb's blast zone. The fire marshal's official diagnosis was "happens a lot with the old ones."

[Sketch of an elevator]

Spending nine or so hours in a five-by-five compartment swaying above your death is a terrible way to get to know a person you already hate. Sahar does this terribly annoying thing she probably doesn't realize. Every few minutes or so she draws a long, audible, feeble breath as if to burst into tears from anxiety and then sharply expels it like a shotgun blast.[26] Like the sound dogs make when they feel cooped up. Audible passive aggression with a suggestion that the other person should say something. Well I didn't say a thing. If she wants to say something then she should say it. God, and her smell, I'm remembering it now. As if the air in the elevator became mustier and obnoxiously sweet. But not a floral sweet or a pretty shampoo sweet but like a stale cinnamon bun

---

26 More like she does this every minute, at least.

sweet. Sweet tinged with the day-old smell of grease from a fast-food bag left in a car's passenger seat the night before. It was probably her awful sharp breath filling the compartment after every rattling exhale.

[Puncture]

I meandered the streets of downtown strung out on adrenaline. I must have bought one of those terrible triangle gas station sandwiches in my stupor. I chewed tuna salad perched on the edge of the fountain of puking horses. I had three missed calls from Mel. I called her back.

"Hey, babe. What's up? I've had a weird day."

"I need your help," Mel said.

"What's wrong now?" A police car crept by as the officers took stock of me. Satisfied that I was sufficiently pathetic, they picked up speed and cruised on.

"My roommate and I had a huge fight. She was screaming at me like it was me screwing her over."

"Why was she screaming?"

"Cuz she's been dating that guy I told you about for like three months tops and like it's been nice and all having the apartment to myself like every night but today she was cleaning out her closet so I ask what's up cuz I haven't seen her in like a week and she says she's moving in with the guy tomorrow and they seriously just met like yesterday."

"I guess be happy for them," I said.

"I can't afford two thousand a month by myself. What am I gonna do? I need your help."

"Can you find another roommate?"

"It took like six months to find this one. It's so easy to get a crazy person in L.A.. It's a nightmare. Really, it's dangerous."

I stared down at my tuna salad sandwich wrapper where a stupid cartoon fish named Finny winked up at me with a hook through its grinning lip. "I'm an idiot," I said. "I'm not your sugar daddy."

"What?"

"I bet you already have a boyfriend. What's his name?"

"What the fuck?"

"Have him pay for it." I hung up.

I've got baby up on my knee. She likes bouncing in my lap while I write. She's nibbling the raincoat elephant's trunk. It's past her bedtime.

I wish for us both to sleep great.

SELECTED PORTIONS OF
THE DEPOSITION OF SAHAR AYUBBI

OCTOBER 5, 2022 | 8:06 A.M.

BY MR. BLACKHURST:

Q Were you ever stuck in the elevator at Litton Steenken?

A No.

Q Sahar, come on.

A I'm sorry, was that a question?

Q Please turn to exhibit--Exhibit 24.

A What am I looking at?

Q Exhibit 24 is an emergency report from the Lexington Fire Department dated October twenty-five twenty-seventeen.

A Where'd you get this?

Q The fire station is open on Saturday.

A You said you were getting a phone charger.

Q I also bought a phone charger. Can you read aloud row seven? It's about midway down.

A I remember being stuck in the elevator. Okay?

Q Okay. Who else was in the elevator?

A No one. I was by myself. Believe me, I'd remember.

Q Really?

A I'm sorry, what's the question? You need to be clearer with your questions. Are you new to this?

Q Can you read row seven of Exhibit 24?

A Happily. It says--Four fifty-eight p.m., Response team dispatched. Female trapped in out-of-order elevator at two thirteen North

Limestone. Unknown cause of elevator failure.
Weight capacity tested at 2000 pounds. Cable
damage suggests limit closer to 200 to 300
pounds. Resolved eight forty p.m. Female
unharmed. Recommended inspection to determine
cause of weight capacity failure. Joe, are you
calling me fat?

Q I don't know. Do you weigh more than 200
or 300 pounds?

. . .

Q Why did you break up with your fiancé?

A You've got to be kidding.

Q I'll remind you you're under oath.

A Oath? Who are you? He dumped me.

Q Do you know why?

A Yes.

Q Why?

A Jesus. Because--when I-- Look, I felt
really sick that day.

Q Sick?

A Lightheaded and like sleepwalking. I
remember I was working late and got home at
like one in the morning. I remember I was
planning to pull an all-nighter but I came
home because my head was pounding.

Q Anything else?

A What did he say? He said something
like--it was really strange. What was it? He
said something like 'I'm breaking us up.' It was
some quick statement like that. So no I guess I
don't know why. Oh it was 'we're broken up now.'

Q Anything else?

A Not really. I remember crying and asking

why and sitting there while he picked up all his clothes and instruments and crap and he didn't say a word so I cried even worse and then he just left. It was like he was sleep-walking too. He didn't even put his clothes in a bag.

Q When was this?

A November second twenty-seventeen. Early November third technically.

Q You're sure?

A You don't forget breakups that weird. Why are you asking about this?

Q Checking a theory. How long after did you quit Litton Steenk--

A What theory?

Q Sahar. I ask the questions and you answer them. You know how this works. I ask you to do your best to not interrupt me and I'll do the same for you.

A I don't have to answer anything.

Q You do though.

A Or what? There's no fucking judge.

Q It's a deposition.

A With no consequences. Quit calling these depositions. There's no case until they find this made-up guy you think is a murderer. Well he doesn't exist. You're the only one who still thinks Maltessouri exists. Everyone else left that train. These are only interviews, not depositions. I only agreed to do this so you'd stop bugging me and staring at me like I'm some animal you're experimenting on.

Q Okay. I--

A Face it, Joe. This is a vacation.

Q If you can't perform your duties, I'll

let the Committee know.

   A   Tell on me.

[Ms. Ayubbi leaves]

   Q   Sahar, wait. You left your keys--We're
on break.

--Off the record at 10:49 a.m.--

CANVAS EIGHTEEN

I'm rested and thinking clearly.

I wish ~~the tunnels collap~~[27] I wish that, as soon as I leave, the tunnels collapse and all the marionettes get crushed to death.

I had the dream again. Funny, I don't think of my mother as my mother. She's just that woman at the fair.

I rode the merry-go-round around and around. I remember the horse best—intricate scrollwork and chipped paint. It's really my first memory. Every revolution brought me closer to her, then away from her. She was crying I think.

I remember picking at the chipped paint with my fingernail. I remember looking up and her not being there. I remember spending the night in the police station. Who abandons their kid like that?

---

27 Words crossed out by Richie.

EXPEDITION NOTES
OCTOBER 5, 2022 | 2:18 P.M.

Sahar had the TV in her room on at full volume and pretended not to hear me knock. I tried to give her key back so I don't feel bad for taking the Canvases to Coffeel.

There's something to Richie's wishes. Sam inadvertently brought back the cat when he painted its portrait with the Tint. He used the Tint to paint ten thousand dollars which he then received. It's possible that Richie's wishes are the written equivalent of Sam's paintings. This was the theory I was checking during the deposition.

On Canvas Seven, Richie writes:

"I wish for Sahar to get dumped by her fiancé."

And at the bottom of Canvas Fourteen:

"I wish for Hundred Suns to pay for their crimes."

The elevator emergency report was dated October 25, 2017, Sahar broke up with her fiancé on November 3, 2017, and the Canvases were discovered December 5, 2017. Therefore, Richie would had to have written the Canvases sometime between October 25th and December 5th. Specifically, he would have written Canvas Seven through Canvas Fourteen on November 3rd.

In addition to being the date Sahar and her fiancé broke up, November 3rd is also the date the F.B.I. raided Hundred Suns' headquarters in Richmond, Virginia.

The lender was a third-party money launderer doing business with a number of gangs and organized crime syndicates. In addition to its third-party services, the organization extorted dozens of white-collar professionals via usurious loans. Central to their tactics were identity theft and threats of violence.

In the middle of Canvas Two, Richie writes:

"I wish for Hundred Suns to let Mel go if they didn't kill her."

Melanie Cybulski, horribly beaten, sleepwalked into a Richmond police station on November 2nd, 2017. It was her who led the authorities to Hundred Suns' headquarters the next day.

CANVAS NINETEEN

Such an undesirable feeling to wake up after a fight to a single text from someone else:

Do you have a car?

I texted back yes and Scott called me a second after it sent. I buried my head in my pillow listening to him ramble on and on about how the condo case had blown up overnight.

"You're going it alone," he said.

"But I have no idea what I'm doing."

"That's not necessarily a bad thing. Nerves mean you're alert."

I asked a slew of questions in a raspy 5 a.m. voice. He batch answered them all with "you got this."

The oil in my car was months past due. The dashboard was a series of cautionary hieroglyphics. The engine seemed louder. The wheels transmitted a coarse sensation to my fingers as I turned out of my building's parking garage.

Emma waddled out in Bugs Bunny slippers when I pulled up to the firm. She stood in the street and handed me a binder of notes from Scott and a tape recorder.

"Do you live here?"

"Scott and I pulled an all-nighter. Says you're gonna do uhhh-mayyy-zing and to tell you not to push anything too far. Mom's gonna be in a bad mood." She handed me a flowery piece of stationary.

Coffey Niehoff, P.L.L.C. 16 Main Street, Carrington, KY.

"I wouldn't do that anyway."

"I know, sweetie, but he wanted me to tell you. Shoot I made you a thermos of instant coffee but left it in the kitchen. Be right back."

"That's okay. I better get going."

"Well, it's the thought that counts anyway. My goodness it's nippy today. Still dark out though. Bet you're glad you aren't walking." She rubbed her exposed arms peeking out of her Marvin the Martian pajama top.

"Gotta go, Emma." The automatic window raised. She drummed her nails against it in a cascade of acrylic clacks. I lowered it an inch. "I really gotta go."

"Mark and Mantis! Ninety-nine point nine! Starts at seven! You'll love it, they're real witty like you. If the signal goes out further south just scan and there's another channel with it. Buh-bye!" She waddled back and pushed a pull door she'd opened several times a day for ten years.

Who knows why Scott had me leave so early. The map said I'd arrive at ten. The deposition was scheduled for one. Annoyed, I drove to Coffeel.

An old woman dawdled ordering between her questions to the lemon-haired barista about his performance art degree. A predatory degree, if you ask me. I bit my canine teeth into the corner of my mouth to the white hot point of almost breaking skin. Wow, I'd had a canker sore since then but that's gone too. It's almost worth keeping the tint around for medical miracles. Except someone could just as easily make the sun explode.

"Look at you in your cute little suit," the old lady said. "Dashing. Bet you're in a hurry. And here I am in my own little world." She turned back to the barista. "What gluten free teas do you have?" I dropped my shoulders and my face rose to the ceiling and I expelled a puff of air. Wisps of aquarial light danced across the stucco ceiling like pine needles blowing in the snow. I turned around and Sam's painting pulled me in.

I hate visual art. Doesn't matter the medium—paintings, sculptures, terrible modern art like t-shirts nailed to walls—I hate it all. I hate the subjectivity of it. I hate the ambiguity. I hate the stupid, assumptive whims of the spectator filling that ambiguity with their own scattershot interpretations. I prefer the precision of words. Air tight with no room for error. Besides metaphor, I suppose. But metaphor is the art I do enjoy. Still, I recognize there's a time and place. Judges often misguidedly rely on metaphor in judicial opinions when they don't know precisely what they're trying to explain and it invariably leads to future confusion and ill-founded arguments. Causation—the great joining of tributaries into one ocean.

No man may say whence any drop of water is derived, but still they'll argue and try.[28] This coffeehouse painting was the first piece of visual art I've ever been blown away by. I gazed, mouth agape, at the canvas adorning self-portraits of Sam. One Sam walking and one Sam writing. The endless colors so commingled that all distinction between them ceased to exist. A feeling like syrupy amaretto.

Who knows how many people passed me in line.

"Ew, ew, ew. Oh, hey, Dick," Rowan swept the broom into a flip-lock dustpan around the ground I stood.

"Hello, professor. So did the University fire you? Shouldn't you update your business card?"

"Au contraire. I'm on sabbatical conducting research for my fourth book. It's on the importance of coffee shops to twenty-first century language and relationships. You might make a footnote.[29] Little bastards are taking over." She swept a mound of ants swarming a sticky spill at my feet.

"Yikes." I stepped off to the side.

"The owner should seal the door better. You'd think the cold would kill them, but here they are, gangbanging on the floor." She corralled the last of the ants into the pan and wiped her oily forehead with her hoodie sleeve. "Is that the only suit you own? Pretty sure you wore it when you were stalking girls the other night."

"No, I…" I felt lightheaded.

"If you came to bird watch today, you're doing a shit job at it. You've been staring at that pic like a weirdo for forty minutes."

I checked my watch. She was right. "Shit. I gotta go."

---

28 A reference to *Palsgraf v. Long Island Railroad Co.*, 248 N.Y. 339, 352 (1928). The seminal torts case creating the rule that negligent conduct resulting in injury will result in liability only if the actor could have reasonably foreseen that the conduct would injure the victim.

29 The works of Rowan Rayne include: *Precipice: the Erosion of Linguistic Barriers to Inclusion*, *Slanganese!!!*, and an erotica novel titled *Men of Honey*.

"It's chill. Literally every one[30] does it. I did it. It's actually sold already." She picked the price tag off the frame with her thumbnail.

"I..." I had a headache from the tint.

"You seem discombobulated, hot-shot lawyer man. I'm sure you've got big important justice to do so I'll skip the line for you. Medium, black, no room right?

"I...I'll actually take a large. I've got a long drive."

Rowan pumped me a cup from the airpot. "Our little secret, okay?"

"Thanks. I appreciate it."

"Wow. Were those actually manners?"

I sipped the lukewarm liquid and turned back to the tint. She grabbed me by the elbow.

"Door's that way."

"Right."

Leaving Lexington, I drove over the train tracks. I passed the fuming peanut butter factory. Tarp tents and cardboard beds. Personal storage buildings beneath personal injury billboards. Tall tufts of sidewalk grass. A torn sticker on a vacant storefront window warning me that EVERYTHING MUST GO!

I crossed New Circle Road. It's like crossing the border of food groups on a social strata food pyramid. From 6 to 11 servings of slums all the way to the use sparingly hundred-acre ranches where the mansions lorded a half mile back from the road. White columns. White shutters. Billowing fields for horse riders to bob their felt-helmeted heads. White fences keeping out the greater expanse of nature. Old money and breeding rights.

My hips ached. On a dirt road I set the cruise control and thrust my navel into a stretch like an ironing board packed into the passenger seat on moving day. The last sip of my coffee

---

30 [Sic]

was cold and gross and I thought about Mel. I checked my phone while minding the road in the peripherals of instinct. I had no texts.

Per Emma's glowing recommendation, I tuned the radio to Mark and Mantis. Mark had the helium voice I'd expect jockeys to have—horse jockeys, not radio jockeys—Mantis' voice was raspy and dry like a retired hair metal singer who chews cigarettes. A caller told the story of the time he took a piss while drunk and forgot the condom was still on. Sound effects. Pop. Splash. Mantis' dry, raspy laugh. I switched the radio off. In the quiet I realized the bottom of my car sounded like a power wash.

I pulled into the dirt lot of a country market at an intersection between more fenced pastures. The single gas pump and price gouge suggested a geographic monopoly. I did a 360 degree inspection of my wheels and stopped at the front bumper. I tucked my tie into my shirt and did a slow pushup to avoid the dirty ground. The bottom of my car hung like a launch ramp for daredevil pebbles.

A tin bell announced my entrance by clunking against the door rather than chiming the way it's supposed to. A trucker leaned his tanned elbow suave on the counter. He sized me up as a city boy and turned back to the attendant. I waited behind the trucker for several minutes as he spit tobacco juice game at the old woman. "Well, I best be moving on. Working next week?"

"Every day."

He tapped a chapped knuckle on the counter and turned to go. He gave a curt nod to the air past my face and left.

"Gas?" she said with a voice like Mantis.

"Hello. No. I'm having trouble with my car actually. Something's hanging down. I'm not particularly knowledgeable about cars."

"You really ain't buying anything?"

"Do you have an automotive section?" I surveyed the single aisle of snacks.

"Wait here." She went into the backroom and returned with a red toolbox and strutted outside.

I didn't know where to stand or put my hands. I settled on placing them on my hips in a sort of inquisitive half bend forward to bear some semblance of being useful. The power tool revved underneath my car where her work boots protruded.

She emerged. "Skid plate came loose. Sealed her up. Should be good." She cleared her phlegm like a camel.

"I appreciate it."

"Sure. Anything you need? Coffee? Chips? Smokes? We got a five-dollar minimum on cards."

"I don't smoke, but I'll stop by for gas on my way back. I'm full right now."

She nodded with all the enthusiasm of a mother listening to her child spout on about their favorite animal. "I'll be here." She picked the heavy toolbox up under her arm and the tin bell clunked as she went inside.

I had enough emasculation for one day so I filled up at a BP at the entrance to the highway. This station also failed all consumer expectations. Two of the six pumps were inoperable. Two-for-one jars of moonshine sat on the counter beside the tobacco and lighters. The attendant looked like he'd spent the morning tending to a farm. Apparently a BP in BF Egypt doesn't meet the revenue threshold for corporate to crack down on breaches of the franchise agreement.

I listened to a playlist of the one hundred or so songs I like and switched it off after skipping forty or so in a row. Cliffs rose up on both sides of the highway. A sign blurred past the passenger window bearing the image of falling rocks under the word ATTENTION. It begs the question whether begging ATTENTION actually earns the attention of the reader.[31] A spray-painted piece of plywood marked my exit: EXIT SIX

---

31 I think it does. *See* my preface.

- CRAWLERS 50 CENTS.

The next ten minutes took me through barren woods at a steady decline. Carrington lurked in a deep valley encased in crags and coal.[32] My car rattled the steel bridge marking the entrance to Carrington proper. A serpentine stream dyed black slithered beneath. A filthy double-wide with a suspect concrete porch attachment. A windowless, brick, box structure serving some electrical purpose. Grass stained the siding of every home as if from decades of sloppy mowing and yet none of the lawns were mowed.

No cross streets. The map announced my destination was a half mile on the left. The entire town seemed a single street. Black smoke billowed beside a rusty silo. I passed under a crooked pipe running above and across the road like a C-clamp. I passed the chain-link fences enclosing the mine. I reached solid woods again and realized my phone had a 1x signal. The map dropped service. There was zero traffic so I made a U-turn.

I slowed the car to a crawl as I scanned every storefront. Coffey Niehoff, LLP was indistinguishable from the other soot-caked houses other than a piece of neon green poster paper taped to the window bearing the firm's name in permanent marker. The sign beside it read: Sorry We're CLOSED. A window on the upper floor was foggy from a hot shower. It was 11:14 a.m.

I circled back to what seemed to be the heart of town. A pet store. A corner store. Gross houses. The awful Cliffside Motel. More gross houses. A church, and then the towering Roland. Roland's bar was a log cabin style hall tucked between the legs of a 30-foot-tall, red-nosed, wooden miner with a pint in one hand

---

32 The elevation of Carrington ground zero is approximately 750'-900' above sea level. Digital reconstruction by Unit B's topography sub-team estimates the valley was originally between 900'-1000'.

and a pickaxe in the other.[33] I parked and stretched my legs.

I went in. Two men in hardhats were two beers deep. They watched the bartender's ass as she leaned over the bar to get the TV in the corner to receive the remote's commands. Where do dive bars get those tin beer advertisement wall decals? Do they come free with shipments of product? Is there a catalog? Do bar owners actually buy that crap?

"Do you guys have WIFI?" I asked.

"Guys? It's just me, hon." The bartender chewed her tobacco or gum. Her skin was as tan as white can get with deep creases. She looked forty, fifty, or sixty. "Yeah we got some. Works best in the corner."

It was a good thing I charged my laptop the night before; the outlet in the booth had no ground. One of the miners feigned a day dream in my direction. The suit made me stand out. He whispered something to the other miner and they laughed and returned to their day drinking.

The bartender came over. "What'cha drink?"

"Water, thanks. Do you have a breakfast menu?"

"Water. Right. No. We don't. Could make eggs, I guess. Got those. Fries too if you want a kind of hashbrown."

"Scrambled is fine. No fries. Thanks."

"They're gonna be fried."

"That's fine."

The WIFI was so slow. I read Scott's novella of an email about deposition hacks and tactics. I wedged myself in the corner of the booth with the screen parallel to the wall and muted the speakers. I closed out the routine pornographic pop-up ads that heralded the cam site. GoddessMELgoddess had gone live from midnight to two—a much shorter show

---

33 Arguably the best piece of evidence supporting the sunken town to be Carrington. It was a much needed moment of lightheartedness after the weeks of excavating corpses for the crew to unearth the giant plaster head of the jolly miner.

than usual—no doubt she was upset about our fight. I skimmed the archived chat log, all those greasy requests from the horny slugs and Mel's vacuous, kittenish replies.

The undercooked fried egg jostled sad and translucent on the paper plate. The bartender said five bucks would cover it and I handed her my card as if it weighed thirty pounds. She had come from a door leading to a staircase where her apartment was now down an egg.

I went on a walk to pass the time. It was cold. A young pastor greeted what I could only assume were alcoholics at the door of a church seemingly built for burning witches. She smiled down at me from the stairs. Pretty sure AA support groups only incubate fond memories of drinking.

The landscape was a child's refrigerator painting. Splotchy brown mush across the bottom, thin brown stripes jutting out from the brown mush. One or two shapeless blotches of yellow. White space, black clouds.

I followed the black clouds up the loose gravel road to the bustle beyond the chain-link fence. Men hauled tools and rocks in callused hands. Echoes of iron on stone. Orange finger-painted incandescence illuminated the cave. I contemplated how wide the radius was from me to the next most intelligent man.

A man strode from the clamor toward me. "You Local 44?" He removed his canvas glove and put his hand through the fence to shake mine.

"I'm not with a union if that's what you're asking."

He retracted his hand. "Head back down the road then. It's dangerous and I got a rig coming through the gate in a minute. If you wanna know about mines, there's a museum down that way."

The "museum" was a cobwebbed shed like a 1600s frontier school. I kept walking. My phone got a signal and Scott's texts and missed calls came pouring in.

Change of plans. Call me.

Make it to Carrington? Call me.

EMERGENCY! CALL ME!

EXPEDITION NOTES

OCTOBER 6, 2022 | 10:18 P.M.

The steeple and cross protruding from the top layer of soil was what attracted the men who discovered Carrington in the first place. At the steeple's base was the first corpse—a child with a bloated stomach. The autopsy revealed two pounds of dirt in its digestive track. 570 grams had been partially digested into the lower intestine, indicating the dirt was consumed at least six to eight hours prior to death. Several dozen more corpses had consumed as much as six pounds of dirt pre-mortem. It's as if they were trying to eat their way out after the town sunk into the earth. Many of the corpses had bloody fingertips worn to the bone. It would seem they spent the final moments of life suffocating and digging. All corpses had leukocoria—white film over the pupils.

The bodycam footage of the officers who first arrived at ground zero has been analyzed extensively by Unit A. The snowfall had not stuck that December and so the officers walked across frost-kissed, loosely-compacted earth. They confirm the body of the child and request a coroner. The officers discuss between themselves that the child likely got lost and froze. They then discuss how the smell shouldn't be so bad.

One of the officers sees something on the ground a little ways away and when he approaches it turns out to be two fingernail-less hands protruding through the soil. They call in a bigger team.

There are too many oddities to recount from the full investigation. For example, one of the corpses had been shot in the stomach twelve times. Hopefully, the Committee will release the footage to the public in conjunction with my transcription and notes. Although, with atrocities of this caliber, it often takes years before the full record is produced, at which time the rest of the world has moved on. Perhaps a documentary series will one day be made. Sometimes I wonder if I'm the only person who truly cares at this point.

This morning I knocked on Sahar's door and she actually opened it.

"I'm sorry," I said. "It's nice out and I can't think to work today and apparently horse racing is a fall thing so put on your biggest hat you packed. We're going to Keeneland."

Sahar would rather carry a grudge to the grave if it meant she wouldn't have to apologize. Luckily, I never need an apology and the way she slapped my knee when the horses closed in on the finish line told me she'd moved on from our fight at least a little. It helped to have blue sky, even if we still had to grip our rum and ciders tight to keep our fingers warm. You could tell Borlú wanted to give chase every time the horses passed the bleachers.

"I re-read the Wade Transcription yesterday," she said.

I swear I felt butterflies. "Really?"

"It's not fair you've been doing all this yourself. I made a list of areas for follow-up. We should go to the courthouse and find the Rothacker v. Souers casefile."

"I can't believe that never occurred to me."

"I got you."

The horse that won the race was taking a victory lap in front of the pavilion. "Did you read Canvas Eighteen?" I asked.

"The really small one? Yeah," she said.

"I think Richie caused the cave-in."

"Did I miss a line about him packing a thousand pounds of dynamite?"

"He wished for the tunnels to collapse."

She poured some cider out onto the bleacher step below

us. "My thoughts go out to them. That shit's cold," she said.

"I think the Tint grants wishes."

Her eyes widened and locked that way. "Okay..."

I drank the last sip of my cider. "What would you wish for if you had that kind of power?"

"I wouldn't," she said.

"Come on. You wouldn't wish to know what horse to bet on?"

"I don't wanna be rich."

"So, if you had infinite wishes, you wouldn't use even one? Come on."

"Nope. Who knows the collateral damage from something like that. It's unnatural. I wouldn't want to hurt anything. The world's fucked up enough."

"So, wish to make the world better. Okay, here. There's a gun to your head. You have to wish. What do you wish for?"

"For you to shut up and watch the horses."

CANVAS TWENTY

The jar is half empty. Gotta write it all out. Scott's text read:

> Plaintiff's attorney called. Said she's too upset to leave
> her house. Something about vultures picking over a
> woman who lost her children blah blah blah. Below
> the belt crap to throw us off our game. Why we hit
> the road early for these things. Deposition's at her
> house now. 5 Eldridge Ln. Call me when you get this.

I texted back got it and it failed to send. I had five minutes.
I jogged to my car and counted my blessings the shithole was
so small.

Eldridge Lane was on the opposite side of town. I passed
more copy-pasted dirty double-wides distinguishable only by
the detritus under their crimped steel carports.

Ms. Rothacker's double-wide was the second property
in from where the lane dead-ended into cliffs. Her lawn was
well-groomed compared to the eye-sore manor looming beside
it. She had no driveway and a dying sedan hogged the street
space out front. The road was narrower than ordinance should
permit so I parked in the dead-end beneath the cliffs.

I leaned over the a/c and cooled my sweaty face. I
glossed over Scott's notes like cramming for a naked test in
a nightmare. I slung the tape recorder over my shoulder and
turned off the ignition.

Beneath the shadow of the manor, something tickled
my cheek then rasped my ear. I touched my thumb to my
earlobe. There was a drop of blood. Something black and small
swooped across my vision and I lost it in the tree line. It dived
again and flapped and pecked and scratched and I tasted its
feathers. I ripped it from my mouth where it burrowed and
threw it down hard into the gravel. My silhouette reflected
back in the clouded eye of a dead baby bird. Ants clamored
its feathered edges. Something tickled. I plucked a maggot off
my tongue and spat.

Holy shit it was the bird that fell in the well.

I knocked rapidly and the flimsy screen door clapped like a child's woodblock in music class. A man and a woman perked up at the kitchen table.

"Door's open," she called out as the man rose from his chair and waddled into the tiny living room. He tried to tuck in the sweat-damp lumps of dress shirt hanging over his straining leather belt.

"Barrett Niehoff…Nice to meet you…" He was out of breath from the ten-foot trek.

"Richie Maltessouri." The acidic taste of rotten milk had spread to every corner of my mouth.

"You don't like Richard? Richie sounds like you're a kid."

"Richard is fine. Where's the bathroom?"

"Come on, I'm only teasing. Scott said you were going stag. He called you the deposition magician."

"What can I say?" I scraped my tongue with my front teeth to trap the sour spit between my teeth and lips. The plastic sofa cover had a wide-bottom indent centered to the TV. The stuffy air hung beneath yellowed corners of wallpapered ceiling. Barrett unfolded a damp handkerchief from his pocket and dabbed his neck.

"You're a good kid, I can tell. But the gloves come off in there. It's nothing personal."

"It's our ethical duty. I need to use the bathroom before we get started."

"Tell him no." Ms. Rothacker smoked a cigarette at the kitchen table. She hadn't stood up. Her eyes and the words she spoke pinned me to the screen door like thumbtacks.

"Be nice, Molly. We're in for a long day as it is."

"Said no."

Barrett rolled his eyes so only I could see and tilted his head toward the bathroom door. His chins reverberated long after the tilt had stopped.

"Your client put her through a terrible week. You understand."

So I threw up in Ms. Rothacker's sink. I stumbled over a plastic stool decorated in rocket ships and it launched across the adhesive tile floor. I ran the tap at full blast to mask the sound of opening the medicine cabinet. I put her toothpaste on my finger and scrubbed the bird taste out as best I could. The bathtub held a cluster of toys and empty no tears shampoo bottles like a daycare after a flood. I touched the bristles of the children's toothbrushes in the plastic cup. Both were bone dry.

As soon as I opened the door, Barrett cornered me. He laid out certain "ground rules" about his client that had no basis in civil procedure. He asked me about my morning. He asked me what local spots I took in. He asked me how I liked Roland's. He was stalling.

"Nice of Lorraine to hook you up with some food, she doesn't normally serve food I don't think. Believe me I'd know." He laughed. "On your way outta town there's fast food."

Scott's deposition tips were softening in my memory. "I have a long drive back. I'd like if we got started on the sooner side of things."

"By all means. By all means. But..." He lowered his voice and leaned his B.O. in. "Go easy, kid. Her kids were kidnapped."

"I think we can both agree that's bullshit."

The kitchen was bottom-shelf sugar cereals and bags of frozen crinkle-cut fries. "Molly, this is Richie Maltessouri, Cyrus' attorney."

"Hello, Molly." I held out my hand.

"Ms. Rothacker." She put her cigarette in her lips and crossed her nightgown arms beneath her raw eyes. "So what? Cyrus can't pay alimony or afford a real lawyer? This an after-school program?"

I sat down across from her at the white, tile-top kitchen table. I laid out my notepad and tape recorder.

She took another drag of her cigarette, held in a belch and exhaled it all in my direction. "You're lucky you got into all this law business, you must be fuck all useless at any hard work. You're as tall as my kids."

"Now, Molly," Barrett said. "Once he presses record the judge hears everything."

"Getting it out of my system. Want a snack?" She motioned to the variety pack of chips on the edge of the counter. "Got fruit chews too. Everything kids like."

"Just water, thanks."

She turned in her chair and filled a Dixie cup from a watercooler beside the fridge. Dollar store alphabet magnets held photos of the twins. I tucked the corner of my notes beneath the recorder to keep the oscillating fan from blowing them across the room.

"Are we all ready?" I said.

"We're waiting on you," Ms. Rothacker said.

I pressed record and watched the timer increase to one second. "This is Richard Maltessouri, attorney for the defendant in the matter before the court of Rothacker v. Souers. Deposition number one of Plaintiff Molly Rothacker. Date October twenty-sixth, two-thousand-seventeen. The time is one thirty-three p.m. Ma'am, please state your full name."

"Molly Heather Rothacker."

"And this is Barrett. Barrett Niehoff. Counsel for the plaintiff."

Hours of useless information passed.

"How old are the children?" I continued.

"Both six. Both are twins." (No shit, you don't say?) "Olivia's a couple minutes older than Austin if it matters."

"It doesn't. When was the last time you saw Olivia and Austin?"

She packed the cigarette box against the edge of the table and reloaded another. "Five or six days ago."

"Can you be more precise?"

"Friday. She last saw them Friday," Barrett said.

"Ms. Rothacker, is that correct?"

"He's the lawyer."

"Ms. Rothacker, I'm going to ask you again, when exactly did you last see your kids?"

"Friday morning."

"What time exactly?"

"Don't know."

"Where did you see them?"

"Here."

"Here, as in your kitchen?"

"The house, yeah."

"What were they doing?"

"Leaving for school."

"At what time?"

"Jesus. When kids leave for school."

"Maybe we should take a break," Barrett said, eyeing the variety pack of chips.

"I wanna get this shit over with." She uncrossed her legs and crossed them the other way, pulling her nightgown down around her knees.

"The last time you saw them they were leaving for school, correct?"

"Yeah."

"And how do they get to school?"

"School bus."

"Where is the bus stop?"

"End of the road. That way."

"Did you see them get on the bus?"

"Yes. I always watch them from the window. I need a Coke." She rose and swayed.

"I got it." Barrett pulled her back down by the shoulder. He spent the entire deposition monitoring her movements. His legal pad was barren of all but doodles.

"Did you call the school when they didn't come home?"

"Of course. What mother wouldn't?" She began to cry.

"Let's take five," Barrett said.

She wiped her eyes. "No... I can keep going."

"What did the school say?"

"Said they had a policy where the drivers don't leave unless all the kids are on and... And they hung up and called the driver... And they called me back... And said he said he dropped them off at the corner like always."

"Did you talk to your neighbors?"

She erupted. "Cyrus has stalked me before. He parks around the corner over there. Sits there and watches the house. Did for years after the divorce. Years. Ask the police. They came every other week. I know he grabbed them. Parked right there. He sells cocaine, did he tell you that? Bet he told them they were going on another one of his fancy trips to turn them against me. Told them something. Or his new whore took them. They took my children." Her words sunk to spit bubble sobs and incomprehensible wails.

"I think that's enough for today," Barrett said.

"Agreed. This concludes deposition one of Plaintiff Molly Rothacker. The time is five forty-four p.m." I switched the tape recorder off.

I gathered my things as Barrett comforted his client. I crumpled my empty paper cup and went to step on the foot switch of the trashcan.

"I'll throw that away." Barrett rose and held out his hand for my crumpled cup. I lowered my foot. "No! Please. I'll take it." He held the trash lid down and ripped the cup from my hand. He then put his damp arm around my shoulders and escorted me to the door. "Tell Scott I said we should grab a beer sometime."

I crossed the lawn past the kiddie pool filled with floating toys and leaves. I peeked back. Molly and Barrett were nowhere to be seen. I raised the lid on the trashcan at the curb. Beer bottles from brim to bottom.

My phone gleaned a signal. I had two texts.

The first text was Scott:
How'd it go? Sometimes depositions are like trying
to find a needle in a haystack when you don't have
the address to the farm.

The second text was Mel:
I've been thinking and I completely understand why
you feel like you do. I'm not using you. I really do
wanna be with you. I've never been in a long distance
relationship. Please call me.

The phone rang twice. "Hi."
"Hi, Mel."
"Can you pick me up at Blue Grass Airport tomorrow at
one forty-five?"
"What?"
"I bought a one-way ticket. I don't know anyone in
Kentucky. Can I stay with you?"
"For real?"
"Yes."
"Yes. In a heartbeat."
"You're my hero. I'll ship my things later."
"I'm sorry for yesterday."
"I may love you."
"Me too. I'll see you tomorrow."
The smog from the mine turned the sunset into a symphony
of deep indigo, blood orange, and violet. I was standing in
the middle of the road gazing upward and revolving like a
stargazer.
The corner of my eye caught the tiny disturbance. The
curtain in the window swayed where it drew shut. Someone
in the manor was home. They'd been watching me. I sensed
it when I first arrived too. I turned toward the manor and
trudged through the knee-deep weeds. I figured a canvas of

the neighbors in advance of litigation might lead to a cherry on top. Instead, it led to an iceberg beneath the surface.

Aphid nests. Chipped paint. A hangnail downspout. I twisted my ankle on the edge of the grass-reclaimed walkway connecting the driveway to the veranda. My first set of knocks returned cavernous echoes and silence. The sidelites were opaque from the layers of dust inside. I knocked softer, like a pebble down a well, and closed my eyes to hear the splash. The pebble never hit the bottom. I sensed the artificiality of the silence. I sensed the tense apprehension beyond the threshold.

I knocked hard. "I saw you watching me through the window. Open up."

Something startled. The sound of shuffles and closing doors. A muffled voice. The jangle of locks. The front door opened two cautious inches and I lowered my gaze a foot from where I expected the face to be.

"Are you a policeman?"

"No. Sorry for disrupting your evening. I—"

"That's okay then."

"Okay. I'm an attorney on a matter involving your neighbor's kids. Olivia and Austin Souers. They're missing."

"What is going on with that?"

"That's what I'm getting to the bottom of, sir. My name is Richie Maltessouri."

"Are you..." The old man picked at the edge of the doorframe, scrunched his face, and quickly retracted his hand, shaking it as if he had been pinched. "...a detective?"

"No, sir, I'm a private attorney representing the kids' father."

He stared through me for an intolerable amount of time with unfocused eyes as if in a daydream. "I'm Sam," he said.

"Would it be alright if I asked you a few questions? Do you live by yourself?"

"Yes. I am alright with that."

"Does somebody help take care of you?"

"Not really," Sam said.

The way he acted I half considered him a drug addict. Forearms covered in cuts like a heroin user. His filthy home like a crackhouse. The way he took so long to put words together and even then spoke with such uncertainty. A door at the top of the stairs was boarded up. Amara's room. Saving on heat, I suspected at the time. How could he ever get upstairs? I followed him past the same heavy, whatever-wood-is-dark doors that now separate me from the marionettes outside. One of the intricate doors wobbled in its frame. "Kitchen's over here," he said.

A sink overflowing with dishes and tuna cans. Wilted window plants. A bouquet of unpleasant smells. Mold.

"Want water?"

"No. Thanks." I pulled a chair from under the kitchen table and a cobweb stretched and tore. I wiped the dust from the seat with my sleeve before sitting. My senses, invigorated by Mel's decision to move, were partly blind to the intolerable filth. Mel, sweet Mel.

"How is she feeling?" Sam said.

"What?"

"My neighbor."

"Of course. She's a mess, honestly. She thinks their dad kidnapped them. It's possible. Did you know the kids?"

His brow winced almost imperceptibly. He picked at his callused hands. "Maybe coming and going from cars. Used to play in the yard some. Been a month at least."

"Used to?"

"Umm. Before. Before when they went back to school." The dying sun bathed the room in a burning red and twisted shadows from the overgrown backyard. "Maybe they ran away," he said. "I ran away their age."

"Were your parents worried?"

His jaw clenched. His jaw stayed clenched. "No, they were not." He placed both hands on the seat of his wheelchair as if to lift himself slightly off the seat.

"Are you close with your neighbor?"

"Some."

"Can you tell me about her?"

"She's nice to me."

"I suspect she has a drinking problem. Does she? Do you understand what I'm asking?"

He smiled and took a breath. "Yes. She has that. A drinking problem. Amara told me that she was talking to her and she started yelling at her for no reason just because but that Amara was trying to ask her to not be so loud with her friends at night was all." He rubbed his eye and his wedding band reflected a ray of the fading sunlight.

"Is Amara your wife?"

"Amara is my wife."

"So she helps take care of you? Is she home?"

He shook his head. "No."

The sound of a lid falling from a shelf came from down the hall. It wobbled in faster and faster rotations until it came to rest flush with the floor. I turned. "Could that be her now?"

Sam stared wide-eyed toward the origin of noise. "It's the wind. I have a window open." He rubbed the back of his hair. "If it's okay with you, I got chores before Amara comes back since it's so dirty. Are you married? Does she like things clean?"

"I live with my girlfriend," I said. "She just moved in." I realized how little I knew about Mel. "I don't know how neat she is."

"Do you want to marry her?"

"Maybe. I don't know. Ah hell, sure. Why not?" Something clattered down the hall again. "Can I use your bathroom before I go? I've got a drive."

"It's so dirty, maybe wait and go at a gas station?"

"I'll only be a minute. Is that okay?"

He scratched his lip with his teeth. "It's the left door down the hall."

I lightened my footsteps and crept past the door on the left. One of the intricate doors shook against the door frame ahead of me. Something wanted out. I glanced back over my shoulder. No Sam in sight. I focused my ears. His wheelchair had caused the floorboards to creak earlier. I listened for creaking behind me. The door rattled.

The handle wobbled in my grip as I applied increasing degrees of force like a pot heating to boil. I cracked it from its frame and the black cat charged out between my ankles and scampered down the hall.

Inside were dozens of canvases stacked in lopsided towers. The stuffy scent of a year's shed skin flakes. Streaks of spilled paint crusted to the floor. Flecks and splatters of paint up the countless spines of the packed bookcases. A stack of odd still life paintings. All these details were in the periphery—my focus was on her portrait.

A six-foot tall canvas of a beautiful nurse seated beside an iron-lattice table in the dead of winter. The tint glittered in the light of the sunset burning through the windows. The nurse's face was an unfinished patch of canvas. Amara, I know now. It's here beside baby's crib. Sam eventually finished it.

My mind was swimming as the colors floated through me like a warm river. It twisted and turned and sped me away deeper into the loss of time.

"I brought you water, are you okay?" Sam's voice pulled me back to the present. "You been looking for a long time." Sam wheeled from the doorway into the study. "Don't judge me for it."

"Judge you? For this? This is beautiful."

"Thank you."

"I…" I felt hazy as my brain spun in my skull.

"I brought you water." He handed me the glass and the sensational cold revitalized the sponge of my throat. He draped a dishcloth over a half-empty jar of marvelous omni-hued paint.

"You're really talented," I said between gulps.

Sam rolled the stem of a paintbrush between his fingers and watched it twirl. He tossed the brush onto the palette.

"Who is she?"

"That is Amara."

"A gift for her? That's really thoughtful."

"I'm trying to bring her back."

I felt awkward for assuming they were still together. He even said she didn't take care of him. The sun had gone down long ago and my head began clearing of the effects of the tint. The cat weaved in and out and back again between my legs.

"He likes you a lot."

"I'm not sure why." The cat coiled his tail around my knee and arched into a satisfying push-up. "It was nice meeting you. Again, apologies for intruding."

"It's okay. I liked it."

"When you see Amara, could you have her give me a call? I'd like to ask her about your neighbor as well." I fished a business card from my jacket and handed it to him.

"Who is this?"

"I'm sorry?"

He turned the card to face me and Rowan's photo stared back at me.

"Your girlfriend?"

I laughed. "No, she's—"

He wasn't listening. "What's this word here?" He pointed.

"This one?" I read: "professor."

He laughed so loud. "Amara's a professor! They're a good wife to have." Images flashed of goddessMELgoddess and Hello Kitty dolls and the countless times I pumped my credit card number into a porn site. Only an idiot would have corrected his mistake and said—actually, my girlfriend works in porn and we've never met in person. "I know, right," I said. "I'd better marry her fast before I lose her, right?"

I fished in my jacket pocket again and handed him one of

my business cards. My stupid photo face smiled back at me with cake crumbs in its hair. "Have a nice night." I turned to leave.

He held the business cards side by side. "Y'all fit."

"You can have Amara call my cell. It's the one on the bottom."

"Okay, that says cell. Got it. It's a good feeling wanting to marry someone."

"Sure is." I stumbled over the infatuated cat as I made my way out onto the veranda. I buttoned my jacket against the freezing night. Sam sat in the doorframe.

"Are you afraid she might say no when you ask? I was afraid Amara would say no."

"Umm. Yeah, actually. Very scared. But I'm not sure I want to yet, either. Take care of yourself, Mr.?"

"Alley. I can help her to say yes, you know." He smiled. "I need about two days. I'll paint you something to make her say yes. Come back on Monday for it."

"Like a gift? Paint what?"

"It'll make you both really happy. Come back Monday?"

"Wow, thank you, I guess. Sure, I'll be here. You do make incredible art. Wait a sec! I saw your two self-portraits this morn—"

A dog bared its teeth and lunged at me from the lawn where it was held by a leash tied to a stake. The cat hissed at it. The dog barked. The cat jumped toward it from the porch and scratched its face and scampered off around the house. The dog whimpered. "Poor thing," I said. "What's your dog's name?"

"That is Samson. A stray I can't make stay away."

EXPEDITION NOTES

OCTOBER 7, 2022 | 9:22 P.M.

The Lexington Circuit Courthouse was an expectedly blocky and unremarkable building. They must have taken the spiky pigeon repellant strips off the windows since Richie's time.

All the floors hurt your knees so Sahar and I took the *Rothacker v. Souers* casefile out into the hall where there was a bench. It was Sahar's idea. We divided the file in half with Sahar working from the complaint forward and me working from the dismissal backward. I had been able to find Souers' answer online to use as an exhibit in Scott's deposition, but otherwise the pleadings were unfamiliar. The bulk of the dispute had been over custody after the kidnapping charges were dropped, so there were a lot of loose-leaf exhibits related to the parents' parenting history Sahar and I had to weed through.

"Have you seen this stuff before?" I said.

"Some of it," Sahar said. "Scott mostly took care of the matter. I drafted our discovery responses, if I remember."

"Gotcha." A clerk poked their head out the door to the judge's chambers and asked us what we were doing. I walked over to them to explain we were lawyers and had no intention to take anything out of the building. The clerk checked me up and down. "Next time stay in the library," she said. "We don't make copies of a lot of this stuff." This is why I always dress nice.

"What's your opinion of Sam? I don't think we've ever talked about him," I said to Sahar later on.

"Sam from the transcript? I think he's lonely. Sweet. Definitely has some form of ASD. He's the only sympathetic character in the whole thing."

"Character?"

"Yeah. Like a play. But no one would pay to see it. The plot's impossible to follow."

I picked up the order of judgement. "Maybe they really are all made-up."

I always read the last paragraph of judicial opinions first because they tend to give away the result and that way I know what the judge is building toward. "Have you seen the deposition transcripts?" I asked Sahar. "It says 'having found all kidnapping claims moot, and in consideration of the evidence and transcripts now before the Court, Plaintiff's motion to amend custody order is denied.' I'm not seeing any transcripts here."

Sahar flipped through her stack. "Nothing here either. The clerk did say they don't make copies."

Probably best I leave what Sahar did next out of the record.

CANVAS TWENTY-ONE

"Isn't that a low blow?" Sahar said.

"She filed kidnapping charges against her kids' dad."

"It feels like a smear campaign."

"Rich gave us ammo opening mom's trash, now we need to dump it across the bench. Custody disputes are always bare knuckle. We need to scour her social media. I wanna pull every photo of her with a cocktail. I wanna pull every status about day drinking with the girls. The judge sees everything."

"I see," Sahar said quietly.

"Earth to Rich. Come up for air there, boss." Scott flicked the back of my computer monitor. I looked up from my fruitless search of "Sam Alley artist."[34]

"Yeah, I heard. Play up the alcohol. Show she's poor. Drugs. Bad mom. Whatever. Pull no punches. I get it," I said.

"Do you feel alright?"

"I slept bad." It was true. The thought of sharing a bed with Mel in less than a day kept me caffeinated through the night while the blue screen of my phone pervaded my pupils with Wikipedia pages on painting techniques.

"Is something wrong?" Sahar said.

"No. Just thinking about the case."

"Well, don't make us look bad." Scott straightened my crooked diploma where it hung. "Make sure to get some sleep tonight. It's okay if you need to cut out early today. Burnout after an all-nighter is dangerous territory for your health and your career. There's no need to pretend to be busy if you're in here surfing the web."

I rubbed my temples. The headache started the night before. Sam must have started painting then. It hit like a blackjack. I prayed for two hours to the toilet where my head throbbed against the refreshing cold seat. I took a cold shower. My headache was like a laser pointer to the eye. I twisted the

---

34 Searches reveal several artists by the name. None of any noteworthy success. None are our Sam.

shower valve off and began my normal, unconscious towel routine: first dry my hair, then chest, then stomach, right shoulder, right arm, left shoulder, left arm, upper back, lower back, left leg, right leg—but I blacked out between lower back and left leg and came to with my finger tracing the w of the word *Row* in the mirror fog. The sun had rudely risen. I put on my socks and tied my dress shoes then untied my dress shoes and put on my pants. I briefly remembered the significance of it being Friday and seized the moment of clarity to fish a marker from the junk drawer in the kitchen. I scribbled *Pay Hundred Suns* on my palm as a reminder of my debt. I must have walked to work at some point since that's where I found myself when Scott flicked the back of my computer monitor.

The clock above Scott's head read 1:35. I was late to pick up Mel. "On second thought, is it alright if I went home now? I'll leave my phone on my pillow in case something urgent comes up." I was champing at the bit to see Mel in person.

"Nothing important will come up. Your health is what's important," Scott said.

Heading out of town on Versailles Road was a greenish gray drive along fields and rows of low-income apartments. The oil pan that lubricated the wagon wheel. I chugged a bottled of water to dilute my nausea.

A plane roared overhead as I strained to untangle Blue Grass Airport's knotted exit signs. SHORT-TERM PARKING. LONG-TERM PARKING. EMPLOYEE PARKING. SERVICE PARKING. TERMINAL. A handful of cars dotted the long-term parking. Imagine a man on a business trip trips over the railing of his hotel balcony to his explosive death below. How many 27 dollars-a-day parking fees would his car accrue? Is that a claim against his estate? They have a system for tracking curious vehicles like that at LAX and JFK, I bet, but probably not at Blue Grass. These racing thoughts only inflated my migraine.

I drove the ritualistic dance of airport irritation. Changed lanes. Got trapped behind a cab opening its trunk. Changed lanes again. Watched the cab drive off honking for god knows what reason. The radio filled the car like crinkling tissue paper. The signal wobbled on the knife's edge between NPR and a country station where the dick singer squawked like a cock.

I saw Mel's wig first and parked parallel to where it beamed like a lighthouse beckoning sailors. It was Pepto Bismol pink. Despite her head looking like a blown-up bubblegum bubble, she was relatively dressed down compared to her cam show outfits but still provocative enough to elicit double-takes from both male and female travelers alike. She had a lime green zebra suitcase with a long barcode tag and two bulging trash bags. She illuminated the blue LED of a vape pen beneath her bottlecap sunglasses. She stood with a foot on the luggage carousel like a lookout on a party boat. Around and around the carousel went.

That was the moment Sam took control of my body and mind.

The car stereo shifted with blaring static. My breathing quickened. The puppet strings unfurled. The fait accompli. I was smiling, smiling, smiling, tearing up, and smiling. The pink wig fell from focus. The fog cleared. The radio stabilized. My phone rang.

"Hello, Rowan."

"Hello, Richie."

"I never gave you my number."

"Pick me up after my shift for a date?"

"It's a date."

I drove off right as Mel's fake nails wrapped around the passenger door handle. Her bubblegum head deflated in my rearview mirror. My phone rang immediately.

"Richie, what the hell? That was me. Come back."

"Oops. Didn't recognize you. I'll come back."

I looped back around, popped the trunk, and loaded the trash bags and green zebra luggage.

"What's in the bags? They're so light."

"A surprise." Mel kissed me with my eyes open as I pictured Rowan. She pulled me hard by my tie. "Hey. Kiss me. Don't make me chase you."

"Sorry, it's just...we're blocking traffic."

Mel was like a video advertisement at a gas pump—she was always turned on and you couldn't shut her up. She told me about her blowout with her roommate. The creeps in business class. Some astrologist/fitness influencer she was certain I'd love. Ohmygod look at the cute lil' horse fountain. Blah, blah, blah. I was thinking about Rowan.

She stood in the center between the kitchen and the living room, her luggage heaped at her feet. "Your place is so empty." She tapped her index finger to her pursed lips like a realtor. "Perfect! So much easier for me to decorate this way. Ohmygod, there's two kitchen sinks! His and hers!"

"I'm out of food. I'll leave some money on the counter."

"Wait, where are you going?"

"It's Friday. I have work. I have a filing due at midnight."

"What's ten more minutes?" She pulled me between her hips by my belt loops and jumped onto the quartz countertop and kissed me. Her raspberry lip gloss gagged me. I bit down hard. "Ow!" She spat blood into the "hers" side of the kitchen sink and traced the inside of her lip with a fake fingernail. "Babe, that's gonna swell."

"Sorry. Got caught up in the moment."

"Now I know what I'm dealing with." She attacked me again. Her tongue tasted like raspberry and blood. I pulled her by the wig away from my face.

"I really gotta go."

Outside Coffeel, a frizzy-haired, sixty-years-late, bohemian kid was reading the second or third page of a frayed novel with no cover. He glanced at me and then back down in disappointment after seeing I was a dude. I palmed the sweat from my forehead in the glass, straightened my collar, and pulled open the door. It sucked hard against the frame in its usual way.

"Richie, right? She's washing dishes." Blondie Von TightPants had changed his name to BlueHair McBand-Shirt.[35] He poured beans from a plastic bin into the grinder then handed me the water I ordered. My headache blared. I chugged the water. Mr. McBandShirt's jaw dropped as the water streamed down my suit. "I'll just go get her," he said.

The tint-painted Sams were gone. All the walls were blank—waiting for something inevitable and terrible to fill the emptiness. The frigid air and the long wait gave my armpits time to dry after the half mile jog from my apartment.

Rowan snuck up on me. "Hey, Dick. Way to be late," she said.

"Is this a preview of the date?"

"I don't know. Are you taking me to a movie? Hey, let's sit next to each other in the awkward dark and not talk. You know, get to know each other. Who's idea was it that that's a good first date?"

"Hollywood's. Or nineteen-fifties consumerism. Wanna grab coffee somewhere instead?"

"Dick."

She drove us to the heart of campus in her coworker's pickup and then we strolled. Bugs musically whizzed past us. We walked and talked as we passed the library, the business school, the seminary. Someone called to us from a jeep while we waited to cross the street. "Y'all fit," they said.

"What'd they say?"

"Said you ain't shit," Rowan said.

"The mouth on you."

"Just you wait."

The date unfolded like cycles of rapid eye movement. Another cycle began again and suddenly we were in a New Age

---

35 I believe they were working when Sahar and I visited Coffeel, but their hair was pitch black with matching black shirt and black overalls (Gus Van Gothface?).

store. Hippie t-shirts and "tobacco" glassware. An employee pandered to us while we oogled the display case of crystals and stones. Jade, amber, lapis lazuli, citrine. Sunstone, larimar, kyanite, ametrine. Topaz, nephrite, aventurine, tourmaline.

"How about this one?" I said, picking up a stone.

"What's it do?" Rowan said.

I rolled the tag over in my hand. "Says it's good for psychic attunement. Looks cool."

"Looks ugly. You pick me one and I pick you one."

She bought me something pink and I bought her something black.

"This place is ridiculous," she said. "Only in a university town."

"Or L.A.," I said.

"True. Are you superstitious?"

"No."

"Obsessive?"

"Not in a flick the light switch three times before entering a room kind of way."

She snorted. "What kind of way then?"

"I count syllables sometimes."

"Syllables?"

"Sometimes. Not all syllables. Only people's names. I think certain numbers are good luck for certain careers. Some numbers are bad luck."

"What numbers are bad luck? Thirteen?"

"Exactly. Nothing good comes in thirteens."

"What about Wilt Chamberlain?"

"What's that?"

"Never mind. So you're into numerology basically?"

"No. My conclusions are just my own instinct. Row-an Rayne. Three. Three is good luck for anything I think. It just feels right. A perfect name, Rowan Rayne."

"Perfect pornstar name maybe." She tilted her head and closed one eye as her fingers counted off. "Rich-ie

Mal-te-sour-ri. Six. What's six mean?"

"Makes me think of something sharp. Something prickly."

"Prick's about right. It's gotta be bad luck. Hey, we're three and six. Together we make the devil's number."

"Thirty-six?"

"Three sixes, dick. The number of the beast."

"Sure. If you believe in that crap."

She turned to a plexiglass shelf of baubles. "I had a migraine before we met up. Thank god it's gone."

"Wait, me too—"

"You need this." She picked a tiny clay pot with a tinier clay lid off a shelf and handed it to me.

"What is it?"

"Come on."

I thought a moment. "I really don't know."

"I thought you're from New York?"

"I was only there for school and all I did was go from the dorms to class and back. That was my whole New York. I grew up everywhere. I got shuffled around in foster families. I sucked."

"Still do." She plugged her nostril with her finger and snorted.

"You okay there?"

"Cocaine, dumbass. It's a thing you keep cocaine in. I've tutored high schoolers who know that."

"Remind me to never let you teach our kids."

"Yeah. I'd make a seriously shit mom."

God, I hate Sam.

My phone buzzed nonstop in my pocket. After the fourth minute or so I checked it. No Caller I.D.

"You better answer that. It's probably SCOTUS," she said.

I took the call in a secluded book section between a tie-dye curtain and a shelf of Kama Sutras.

"Who is this? Just leave a mess—"

"Good evening, sir. Am I speaking with Richard

Maltesouri of two one two Rose Street, unit six three six, Lexington, Kentucky, four zero five zero seven?" It was a woman's voice. The voice was so devoid of emphasis it may have been automated.

"Sure. Who is this?"

"Good evening, Mr. Maltessouri. This is a courtesy call from Hundred Suns' collections department. A reminder that tonight, Friday, October twenty-seventh at eleven fifty-nine p.m. eastern is when the acceleration clause on page sixty-six of the Hundred Suns loan agreement increases the amount due from the three thousand dollars U.S. principal to principal plus one year of annual interest at the six-hundred and sixty-seven percent annual rate per page three of the Hundred Suns loan agreement. As a courtesy to you, I can take a credit card number over the phone for the three thousand principal now."

I couldn't keep up with the numbers. "Hold on," I said.

"Certainly, sir."

I logged into my checking account through the app. The balance was more dismal than the day before. I brought my phone back to my ear "My direct deposit hasn't come in yet." I looked down at the marker on my palm. *Pay Hundred Suns.* "I won't forget to pay."

"Splendid, sir. If the full principal is not repaid by eleven fifty-nine p.m. eastern time, tonight, the total due escalates to..." I heard calculator clatter. Rowan stuck her head through the curtain. She wore a fortune teller's bandana and bobbled her head like a genie. "...Twenty-three thousand and ten dollars U.S. Failure to pay by tonight's deadline will automatically forward your account to our field collection professionals."

"Field collection professionals?"

"Do enjoy your date, Mr. Maltessouri." The receiver clicked and a dial tone rang through my head like a car alarm. I blacked out the rest of the date.

EXPEDITION NOTES
OCTOBER 7, 2022 | 1:39 A.M.

On second thought, though I'm hesitant to write this because Sahar may one day read it, it's my duty to record our exhibition as fully as possible to aid the public in the search for Richie. It would make no sense for me to leave out one of the best pieces of evidence even if it reveals Sahar's deception and she ends up facing charges.

We went to the headshop Richie and Rowan visited. It was difficult to locate—tucked back above a record store. You had to take the back stairs and then go down a series of halls. There's no sign from the street.

The visit was pointless until we were about to leave. A little girl was by herself playing with a display of dreamcatchers. There's no way she wandered in given how hidden the place was. I suppose she might have been the cashier's kid. Regardless, the girl snatched Sahar's purse from the register and ran. Sahar's legs tangled in Borlú's leash so I took chase. I stumbled over myself hurrying down the steps and twisted my ankle but the girl wasn't very tall and so she wasn't very fast and so I caught up to her.

I ripped the purse from her hand and the contents spilled across the sidewalk. The wind blew most of the papers into the street but some stayed stapled at my feet. The girl got away.

It was the transcript from the deposition of Molly Rothacker. Here's page sixty-three:

A   Friday morning.

A   Don't Know.

A   Here.

A   The house, yeah.

A   Leaving for school.

A   Jesus. When kids leave for school.

The entire transcript is one-sided and double-spaced like that. No questions. Only answers. The opposite of this investigation.

Right before the theft, I bought Sahar a stone that was supposed to alleviate anger. It must have transferred her anger to me. I'm not actually sure what I'm feeling now. It isn't quite anger. I think it's closer to fear. She knows what happened to Richie.

CANVAS TWENTY-TWO

Rowan and I laid together in the darkness. My headache was gone but I laid sleepless. The LED clock cast a red 2:40 across the wall beside the nightstand. I rose and stumbled into my rumpled suit pants.

"You leaving?"

"Can't sleep. I've got work on the kidnapping case anyway."

"Aww. Lawyer steps into a phone booth and takes off his suit and tie to reveal the suit and tie beneath it and becomes Super Lawyer. When will I see you again?"

"Tomorrow night. Tonight, technically."

"I better."

"You will." I kissed her. Black marker streaked her body from the forgotten reminder to pay Hundred Suns.

EXPEDITION NOTES
OCTOBER 7, 2022 | 11:22 P.M.

I can't figure out how Rowan got Richie's phone number
before she called him at the airport. It's far-fetched, but
let's assume for now that Rowan knew Richie was a
lawyer and then searched online for Lexington lawyers
by his name. She then had his last name and subsequently
got his phone number from one of those questionable
websites with peoples' personal information. This leaves
an even more puzzling question: Why did Richie agree
to go on a date with her?

As Richie has made crystal clear, he despises Rowan
because of her weight and demeanor. He likely despises
her further for having put him in his place at Coffeel.
The explanation adopted by the Committee (at least until
Milsap's flash flood theory gave everyone an easy way
out while justifying the millions of tax dollars wasted)
is that Richie is going through a manic episode. The
head psychologist in Unit A proposed this explanation
on the basis that hypomania can sometimes accompany
headaches and bring about risk-taking behavior such
as increased sexual activity. You can understand my
skepticism.

Today, Sahar and I drove to the corner market where
Richie had his car repaired. We got in the car and she
asked if I wanted to listen to music and I said no and
that was the last words we spoke before our arrival. She
would occasionally dote Borlú as he sat with his tongue
lapping up the trees and buildings as they sped past his
window. Otherwise, the air was dead.

The market was about an hour south of Lexington
and the drive is exactly as Richie describes with the
fenced fields and imposing estates. The market is

now boarded up with the pump disconnected. Sahar suggested we head back. I ignored her and walked to the farmhouse about an acre back. I knocked and we waited and no one came. The second time I knocked, the door came loose in the frame.

"Don't you dare," Sahar said.

So I didn't, and for a moment I called out from the porch, but after my calls went unanswered, I did.

An old man on oxygen sat on the back porch. "Sir, your door was open."

"Did I forget? Are you with hospice?"

I told him we weren't and that we were lawyers and hoped he could tell us what he remembers about the market before it closed.

"You're here about the murder?"

"Murder?"

"My wife, Clarice."

"I'm so sorry."

"Beat to death in a robbery. I couldn't set foot in it again."

"Did they catch who did it?" I asked.

"No evidence they said. What about my wife's body I said. There isn't no body they said. Or maybe that's not what happened. Did Clarice die? No crime they said. No. I'm misremembering something…" He was clearly out of sorts and so we left.

Sahar drove on the way back. Neither of us spoke for a long time. My silence was intentional and I would have kept it that way the entire drive but she spoke up. "What would you wish for? Assuming you're right about everything. Right about the Tint granting wishes."

I was shocked. "I haven't given it any thought."

"Come on. You haven't had any breakthroughs on this wish theory? I'm your partner. Your constable. Your job is to stay up late chain-smoking, cracking the case.

Always with a bottle in your hand. And in the morning you tell me to go chase down some lead or rough up some drug dealers or something and it leads to some breakthrough and I go, 'wow, boss, you were right all along!'"

Borlú jumped the divider from the backseat and sat on my lap and licked my face. "In that case. My deductions lead me to believe that all clues point to Carrington. You said it's a vacation, right? Let's do some sightseeing. We're halfway there as it is."

"Joe, no. And quit calling it 'Carrington.' Call it ground zero. Have some respect for those people."

"If it's just a valley now, where's the harm in it?"

"I'm driving and I say no."

"We've found nothing the entire two weeks we've been here. Carrington is our best chance."

"We aren't permitted."

"Respect for those people. Why do I feel like I'm the only one who cares what happened to those people? Hundreds of people died and nobody knows why."

"Because you are the only one who cares at this point. It's sad to say but it's true. Those people didn't even have names. It's like that analogy about the cat in a box. You only care because you opened the box and saw it was dead. You're the only one who thinks the last few Canvases will somehow make things clearer. It's a terrible thing but terrible things go unresolved every day. Aren't you exhausted? Everyone else is exhausted. We've been chasing a ghost for three years. Given up our lives for three years. Those people were killed in a bad landslide. The Canvases are just some weird sparkly paint. Everything else is coincidence."

"How do you know?"

"Because of all the lies about me! You don't know how it feels to have your life ruined by some stalker. We aren't going to ground zero. All we'd be doing is wasting gas to see some trees."

This time the silence felt heavy. As if we drove the rest of the way with deployed airbags pressing in on us from all sides of the front seat. I waited until we reached the hotel. "I'd wish to learn the truth," I said. "No matter what that means for you."

CANVAS TWENTY-THREE

My headache blared all Saturday. I wasn't sleeping but I wasn't tired. I spent the day alone at the office. I blinked and it was Saturday night and I went back to Rowan. My headache went away whenever I was with her. Like we weren't allowed to be apart. Sunday was the same.

Baby's tucked in with elephant. I still can't bring myself to say her name. As if doing so would mean I wasn't dead after all. I must leave her here once I've drained all the tint. It makes me sick to my stomach thinking about her so I try to remember she isn't human. She came from... She came from wherever elephant came from.

I blinked and it was 3 a.m. on Monday. The fluorescent light of my office hummed. The light fixture littered with the bodies of dead insects. The words I wrote ached beneath the point of my pencil.

*I'm sorry for the inconvenience I...*I balled it into the trash.
*I'm sorry for the selfish thing I...*I tossed it and missed the trash.
I didn't mean to... I tore it in half.

I took a break to pace beside the venetian blinds. Two lights illuminated in a gunmetal sedan across the street. A white cellphone rectangle and an orange cigarette dot. Were they there the day before? Different sedan. Was it the same sedan? Was it the day before?

In the breakroom, the air pot wheezed and spattered. I emptied a fresh bag of flavorless grounds and waited for the machine to brew. The microwave read 3:30 a.m. I blinked and the microwave read 6:00 a.m.[36] The fresh coffee was already cold.

I penciled more drafts on my fake wood desk. A far cry from satisfied, I popped the cap off a pen to trace the pencil.

---

36 Losing your sense of time is not a symptom of mania.

Dear Mel,
I'm sorry. Moving here was a mistake. We aren't
in love. You know it too. Take as long as you need
to go. I'll be at a hotel. Please don't call. I'm sorry.
-Richie

I ruined several envelopes before I liked the way I'd written her name on the front.

The sunrise reflected off the gunmetal sedan back into my eyes. I lowered the blinds. I took a ton more aspirin. The hallway lights flicked on. Keys jangled along to footsteps.

"Hello? Who's here?" Sahar said.

"I am. I'm in here."

She stood in the doorway with her coffee thermos. "I didn't expect anyone else would be here yet. You look awful."

"Thanks. You too."

"Six fifteen is early even by my standards. I have to finish our answer to the kidnapping thing."

"I did it over the weekend."

"Did what?"

"The answer. I wrote it yesterday."

"What? I worked all Friday on it. Did you at least build off what I'd written?"

"Nope. Yours didn't make sense after the mom's deposition."

"What the hell? Caselaw didn't change."

"The strategy changed. I already sent my version to Scott."

"Well, I'm still sending mine. Scott said I write the brief. What the hell is wrong with you lately?"

"And I did a better job."

She stared at the water stain on my ceiling. "You're the biggest asshole I've ever met."

"And you went to a school ranked in the high seventies."

"You know I'd have no remorse killing you, right?"

"Cock-a-doodle-do-ooooo. Good morning to yoooou twoooo." The hanging buckles of Emma's leather jacket clinked as she came down the hall.

Litton Steenken had the most outdated cyber security package on the planet—not a single website blocked. Surely a violation of the ethics rule requiring adequate safeguards of client information. The global document-sharing system was worse than most free services. The firm adapted with all the momentum of a snail preserved in amber.

I muted the speakers and unplugged the speaker jack to be extra safe. I logged in. The familiar pop-up of a woman voraciously fingering herself assaulted the screen and I x'd it out. Account. Click. More pop-ups. Click, click. Billing information. More pop-ups. Click, click, click. Credit card information. Click. Delete, delete. I ctrl+f'd the words "deactivate" and "cancel." 0 of 0.

My checking account was a drained cadaver. Monthly $19.99 charges to ultraGLOBEbilling.[37] Countless $4.99 microtransaction spear wounds by the same biller. It had to be the site. I found the customer service number online and they told me the reason I couldn't find the account deactivation link was because there was none and that you had to call to cancel. Twenty minutes later, they told me my kittycamcentral[38] account would delete automatically at the end of the billing period per my request. "Thanks," I said, looking out the window. The sedan was gone.

"Ohmygod!" Emma's mouth was a frozen scream of lipstick stained teeth. Her eyes were glued to the blowjob on my computer screen.

---

37 The name of the entity has been changed to avoid any public harassment of—and subsequent lawsuits by—the otherwise inconsequential third-party company.

38 *See supra* note—with the caveat that the D.O.J. have already indicted the website's founders on a dozen sex trafficking charges.

"I clicked on spam." I clapped the monitor face-down onto the desk. My pencil cup spilled across the keyboard.

"Tsk tsk tsk."

"It was a virus or something."

She lowered her voice. "Sweetie, it's okay. I do it too. Mantis and I sext the entire day. Brought you a croissant and a cup of my famous instant coffee."

"Cool. Thanks." I popped the lid off the aspirin. It was empty.

The workday went on. I wiggled my teeth in my fingers. They seemed looser. I tongued them to sense whether or not I was paranoid. They felt coated in fur. Maybe that bird gave me a disease. I'd forgotten to brush them that weekend. I'd forgotten a lot that weekend. My eyes were dry. The contact solution dribbled above my tilted-back head and down my cheekbone. My inbox chimed.

> Come by my office.
> Thanks,
> Scott

He was leaning back in his chair against a shelf of desk pictures. A little league team. A wife way out of his league. A mounted behemoth of a snapper. The plastic-enclosed game ball from Super Bowl XX whatever. Sahar was already there.

"Shut the door, Rich." I did as he said and Sahar crossed her razor-burned legs away from me. Scott clicked his pen a few dozen times. "Rich, when I say you do X and Sahar does Y, I mean just that. You do X and Sahar does Y." I sensed Sahar's prickly satisfaction in the chair beside me. "We're a team. Respect your teammates. Don't hog the ball."

I had a foster sister at one of my foster homes that got rid of me by being a tattletale. Sahar and her would be best friends. "Two heads are better than one. Now, having said all that, I read both of your briefs. Sahar, your strategy is sounder, but Rich, your writing is better." Sahar gagged as though it were a greasy pick-up line.

"What do you mean hers is sounder?" I said.

"You're too hung up on the mom's alcoholism. It's legally irrelevant."

"Alcoholism is the linchpin," I said. "She was shit-faced for the goddamn deposition for Christ's sake." Sahar winced.

"I'm not arguing, it doesn't help us." Scott's eyes darted back and forth across his word processor like a ping pong match. "Take this sentence here. 'Sam Alley, the plaintiff's painter neighbor, confirms the plaintiff drinks heavily at all hours of the day, leaving the children to play unsupervised in dangerous conditions.' What are you talking about? Painter neighbor? What dangerous conditions? This is all hearsay, and arguably unethical."

"What? He's a goddamn Van Gogh and his yard is a goddamn jungle."

He pulled back from the smog of my breath. "Reel in the language, boss. I thought about the case over the weekend and Sahar is right. We shouldn't throw so much dirt on the mom. The judge is old-fashioned and manners go a long way with him. Her alcoholism might serve as a change in circumstances to justify a change in custody, but our focus now is the kidnapping charge. Custody doesn't matter if there aren't any kids."

"Her trash could still be at the curb. I could go now and get photos," I said. "No hearsay there."

"Richie. Drop the alcohol angle. I won't say it again."

"I'm going back today to see Sam anyway."

"To see who?"

"To see Sam. The neighbor."

"Right. The painter neighbor." Scott and Sahar exchanged glances.

I stood up and paced. "I could question plaintiff some more while I'm there and get more out of her. That's a hearsay exception. Catch her off her guard too. Maybe she'll be passed out. That'd be perfect. I could swing by before I pick up my painting from Sam."

"Did they not make you take legal ethics at Columbia?" Scott said.

Sahar chimed in. "A lawyer can't talk to a represented party about the represented matter without their lawyer present as well.[39] We need to get Barrett Niehoff's permission before we can talk to Ms. Rothacker. Your plan is malpractice. It's also insane."

"I'll just ask Sam about her then. He's got everything we need. There must be a dozen exceptions to the rule. I'll leave now."

"Richie, sit down. Under no circumstances are you going back to Carrington. Sahar and I will handle the in-person interactions. You've got me worried."

"Fuck that." I struck my fist against the wall and a chunk of plaster broke off.

Sahar jumped out of her chair and backed into the corner. Scott rose to my level. "Sahar, go to your office. I'll come by later. Close the door on your way out." She did.

The two of us stood awhile listening to the muffled office noises through the thin walls. Scott searched the floor for words. "I stayed in Lexington over the weekend to play golf on Saturday with a couple buddies," he said. I was already irritated running late to pick up my painting, but now I was getting furious. "I lost four hundred bucks on a stupid bet. It was real bad. I keep a stash for guilty pleasure in the office. A 'what wife doesn't know won't kill her' account."

"Can I go?"

"No, you can't. So anyway, Saturday I swung by the office to make a withdrawal and I saw you were here."

"I was working on the brief."

"Do you remember talking to me?"

---

39 Ky. R. Sup. Ct. 3.130(4.2). Every state has adopted some form of the rule.

"What? No."

"I didn't think so. You seemed like you were sleepwalking. I thought you were drunk so I asked if you drove and you said you hadn't so I left and let you be. I stopped by that night to check on you and you were still here."

"Yeah, lawyers work long hours."

"I drove by on my way to church. Still here. I stopped by Sunday after dinner, same story. Last night I was so concerned I couldn't sleep. Do you remember talking to me in the breakroom at four a.m.?"

"What?"

"I talked and you sleepwalked. Look, it's obvious you haven't slept or eaten in days. Emma said she brought you something to eat this morning and you threw it in the trash, coffee and all. This isn't normal behavior, Rich." Scott watched his thumb pick at the edge of the desk. "My brother was a lawyer too. I don't tell many people that. I wanted to be him my whole life. Straight As, star athlete, class president. He was unstoppable. But you can't compete at that level forever."

Scott heaved a choppy breath. "Bipolar, mania, no one ever talked about that stuff back in the nineties. He died driving the wrong way onto an off ramp. Collision with an oncoming car. They told me he fell asleep at the wheel but I had seen the weeks leading up and I know he was wide awake and saw the headlights before he died. I know he was manic and must have felt invincible."

"I'm fine and I feel fine."

"That's the problem. You feel invincible. I see the same signs." He spoke each word slowly as if to a child. "Today you're going home and you aren't going to leave until you sleep. Understand? If you still can't, please call me so I can take you to the hospital. Do you understand? Sahar and I will cover the cases you're on. Right now, your only job is to get better."

"I need to go. Sam has my painting."

"Right...the painter neighbor. I'm driving you home."

Scott dropped me off at the community mailbox wall of my apartment building. I shived the slot with my mail key and it spilled its guts of pizza coupons and plastic-paneled envelopes like used car salesman smiles addressed to "our neighbor at..." I read a final warning from my bank and threw it all in the trash.

The property manager snuck up behind me. "Mr. Maltessouri, is your bike okay?" The property manager had the demeanor of a meter stick.

"What?"

"I texted all the residents." I hadn't charged my phone in four days.

"Okay."

"Well, yesterday, my day-off mind you, one of the residents pulled into the lot and a white pickup was parked in the garage gate keeping it from closing. The resident called out his window, that's Mr. Hartford who called out his window, in 12b. I shouldn't have said that. Anyway, a resident shouts for the truck to move and two men come out running with two bikes each. They jump into the truck bed and it speeds off. Practically picked the bike racks clean. Please check if yours was taken so I can update the police report."

"Yeah, I don't have a bike."

"Really? Shame. Who doesn't have a bike? It's great exercise, you know. The funny part is one of the thieves came in to use the lobby bathroom and hit on one of the residents right in front of the security camera. I hope it makes *Cops*."

"Neat."

"I'm surprised your girlfriend didn't tell you about it. She's the one they hit on. While we're on the subject, is she a permanent resident now? Your lease requires that you update us about additional residents. Page two, I think. Liability and things like that. You're a lawyer, you understand."

"Yeah, she didn't mention it."

"That sort of thing can be hard to tell your man.

Mentioning when other men flirt with you. Gosh, you men get so jealous." The rusty squeal of my mail key made better conversation.

"I'm in a hurry," I said.

"One last thing." She checked both ends of the lobby and lowered her voice to a whisper the volume of her regular voice. "You smell, how should I say, bad, Mr. Maltessouri. We try to keep a certain atmosphere of luxury at Rosearms."

The elevator carried me up. I crossed the hall like a cat burglar and held my breath with my ear to my apartment door. There was total silence inside. Sleeping until two in the afternoon was par for the course with Mel but if I opened the door, the latch would echo through my unfurnished apartment. I knelt and the welcome mat dirtied my knee. The envelope bent from the first unsuccessful attempt to jam it under the door. The gap was wider near the hinge and I slid the letter to Mel across the threshold.

I took the freight elevator lined with cloth move-in pads like an asylum isolation chamber. The inspection plate was up to code. A fisheye camera stared. A friend in retail told me every other security camera is an empty plastic bubble. A cost-saving cut corner. A retail panopticon. I hoped that was the case with the elevator. The property manager annoyed the hell out of me.

The note caused me to freeze after I put my key in the ignition. The note had the stereotypic magazine clippings glued to paper. It laid flat against my windshield beneath the wiper.

Pay by EOD.

I turned the key and the wipers and fluid obliterated the note. All I cared about was my painting.

EXPEDITION NOTES

OCTOBER 8, 2022 | 8:05 P.M.

The Rosearms property manager pulled records confirming a massive bike theft had occurred in October 2017. She informed us that the condo association had a strict rule about not sharing tenants' names and personal information but that she assumed we were part of the "crazy, weird F.B.I investigation that keeps coming back. I told ya'll already you need a warrant for that." Still, she confirmed what we already knew: no Richard Maltessouri had ever lived there.

I spotted a maintenance man power washing the parking lot as we were walking back to the car. I asked him if he had worked at the Rosearms Apartments in 2017.

"Since 2005."

"Any break-ins?"

"No. Are you reporters?"

"Yes."

Sahar stepped in. "Joe, stop, we should go."

"What about the bike theft in fall 2017?" I said.

"Oh yeah, there was that. I thought you meant were there any break-ins in the units."

"Were there?"

"Not a single one since I've been here."

"Have you ever had to fix a pressurized door closer?"

"Joe, let's go."

"Oh sure. Those jam, sure."

"Did you ever clean or throw away a hallway rug covered in blood?"

Sahar was mad. "Joe, what the hell? That's enough. Thank you so much for your time, sir. Sorry to bother you..."

"Yeah, I had to fix a snapped door arm once. You don't forget that. Takes forever to find a replacement."

My heart skipped a beat. "When was that?"

"Few years ago. Rug on floor six had blood all over it too. It was a whole thing because the unit's door had been kicked in. Man that really was a whole thing. The association voted to up security over it."

"Do you remember the tenant?"

"What's there to remember?"

"Do you remember his name?

"Well, no. I mean, no one was living there. Might seem weird someone broke into a vacant unit but probably drunk college students throwing a party and one of them kicked the door and cut himself."

Sahar had already gone back to the car.

CANVAS TWENTY-FOUR

The steering wheel was slick with sweat. Daydreams drifted in the center of the road like drive-in movies. I was on cloud nine drifting toward my own sparkling Sam Alley painting. The corner market appeared in an instant and it occurred to me that Scott was right about one thing—I hadn't eaten in days. The shelves were crowded with local preserves and honeys but little by way of protein. I bought a bag of peanuts and a soda from a rattling vending machine. The cooling fan whined like a mayday propeller. It sounded as exhausted as my reflection looked in the machine's glass.

The white fences and porches of wicker and birch gave way to prairie then highway then cliffs then woods then a bridge above a black industrial stream and then Carrington.

I parked beside Ms. Rothacker's trash can where it laid on its side at the curb like shed snake skin. I crouched down and peeked into its stinking mouth. Empty. Regardless, the best evidence would come from the drunkard's mouth.

The pulsing static of ten thousand cicadas stuffed the evening air.[40] The low sun cast fingerling shadows across the toy-cluttered lawn and my stretched silhouette joined them. The living room curtains were drawn. I knocked and waited and listened to a distant laboring lawn mower.

The door opened and my heart tore through my chest as though tied to the doorknob with wire.

"Olivia?"

The little girl's jeans were torn around swollen black ankles. Her shirt was caked in mud. Her nose was broken. Her two black eyes stared through a rip in the screen door mesh. An ant skittered across the screen.

"My god. What happened?"

She said nothing. She swayed gently like a bloated corpse on the edge of tide and beach.

---

40 The sound couldn't possibly be attributed to cicadas, let alone thousands of them. Cicada season in Kentucky is May and June—not the end of October.

"Who did this?"

"Olivia, get back. Who are you?" Ms. Rothacker came around the kitchen corner, makeup streaked. "You. What the hell do you want, you dickless little vulture?"

"Olivia. She's..." The amber light from the open door ripped across the curtained darkness and up the laminate couch to illuminate a grass-stained tennis shoe and a boy's scabbed, purple leg, "...and Austin."

"Is this all part of that sick bastard's plan? Send you to make it look like I did it. Like Cyrus didn't beat them? You rapists. You sick bastard's lap dog."

"What happened?"

"Was it you or his skank who dropped them off in the yard?"

"What?"

"I'm calling my lawyer." Her shaking hand knocked the ashtray beside the phone. Ashes snowed onto the dirty carpet.

I turned to Olivia. "It's okay." She stared through me with no expression or pain.

"Don't! You! Talk! To! Her!" Ms. Rothacker beat the handset against the receiver, punctuating each shrill word with a ringing bang. "Get out!" The headset missed the receiver and walloped the corner of the end table and plywood exploded like a gunshot. She sunk to her knees and heaved breaths like a paper bag. She sobbed. I backed out of the room slowly. The children watched through the torn screen door as I crossed the lawns.

The sprinkler arc swayed back and forth across the verdant green of Sam's lawn. It drenched the bags of grass clippings set out to the curb. A smell of worms and fresh paint filled the air. I followed the woven hose to where it coiled like a snake beside the veranda. The faucet drip pooled a bath of red in the fresh mulch. A push mower rumbled and decayed in oscillations behind Sam's house.

My thumb peeled sticky off the veranda railing—fingerprint stained white. The siding, the trim, the stairs, the railing—all were painted white. Sharp white. White like swimming dots of TV static. The lucid veil of trepidation. A white dog house.

I spat in my palm and swirled the white paint. I bent down and wiped my hand in the wet grass. I tested the first stair with my toe. The paint had already dried so I climbed. I sniffed the bright white door. It was dry so I knocked. I heard a loud bang from within and to my right as if a bird careened into break-neck death against a pane of glass. I heard footsteps like a soldier's march down the hall. The front door swung out to the full limit of its hinges.

"Who are you? What do you want?"

His eyes were six inches above mine. "Mr. Alley, it's me. Richard Maltessouri. Remember? The lawyer from Friday." His brow tightened more at my every word. "You said you'd paint me a painting."

His brow relaxed. "I did? Sure. I guess I did. Of course. How are you?" He crossed his arms over his white undershirt and tucked his hands into the armpit pockets of sweat.

"I'm doing well. You look great."

"Why's that?"

"I mean…you're out of your chair. I guess, I'm embarrassed for assuming it was permanent."

He kicked each of his shins in turn. "Sprained ankle was all. Was using the chair while I healed. Old bones take a while to mend. You'll learn one day. So what do you want?"

My mind drew a blank as white as the house. "The twins showed up."

He had a sudden tone of anger in his voice. "There are no twins here. Just me."

"Your neighbors next door. Olivia and Austin. The twins. They're back home. Someone hurt them, but they're back home. Just in case you were worried."

"Don't know them."

"Okay," I shifted my weight between my legs and the porch boards creaked, "Friday you mentioned their mother drinks."

"Sure." His hands stretched to the high corners of the door frame like the Vitruvian man.

"Could you give me more specifics about that? It would help my case."

"Beers outside with her friends. That sort of thing. Normal stuff." He was nothing like the real Sam. The simulacrum the tint had created was not only physically inaccurate, but it was articulate in a way Sam never was. He stood as a purposeful barrier. The hall behind him was spotless. Mirror lacquer floor, banister cleared of cobwebs. Far back in the kitchen was an opulent spotless sink beneath a glimmering tile backsplash. A padlocked chain coiled around the knobs of the great study doors.

I pointed to the chain. "Is that because of me?"

"What?" He turned. "No. Just wanted extra security is all." He stepped out onto the veranda and closed the front door. "I'm still not sure what it is I can do for you now, Mr... What was it?"

"Maltessouri... Richie."

"Well, Mr. Richie, it was awful thoughtful of you stopping by to tell me those kids are good."

"No problem. I also came by to pick up my painting."

"Oh, right. I changed my mind actually. No painting. Sorry about that. Would have called if I had your number."

"I gave you my card."

"Must have lost it."

The push mower rattled the manor windows. It turned away and the sound ebbed back down.

"Is Amara out back? Can I talk to her?"

"No. She'd hate to be interrupted. We've been choring all day and there's a lot more to do." He rubbed his palms together like using a bow drill. "Thanks again for stopping and telling us about the kids, Mr. Richie. Half this clean-up is about making the yard safer. Such a mess before. A kid could've really hurt himself. You have a word for that I think."

"I have a word for that?"

"Legalese, I mean. A legal doctrine. You know, for when kids drown in pools and fall down holes on peoples' property and what not."

"Attractive nuisance."

He snapped his fingers. "That's it. Kids tangled in barbed wire fences. That sort of thing. Breaks your heart."

"Okay." I walked backward down the veranda steps. "I'll get out of your hair."

I turned around and the yellowed fangs snapped. The golden hound stressed the chain to its limit. The stake in the ground bent. The beast drooled and chomped and barked at the inches of air between us. I froze.

"He's leaving. The man is leaving. The unsafe man is leaving." The false Sam hopped down the steps and knelt beside the beast. He wrapped his arms around the hound's dirty coat and whispered into its shorn ear. "He wasn't here to steal Sam. The man is leaving."

The beast's glaucoma eyes softened at once and it sat back on its hind legs. Its tendons held tense like a folded spring.

The false Sam stood up. "Drive safe, Mr. Richie." He climbed the steps and went back inside the painted white manor. The door latched in several places. Rabid drool dripped from the dog's jaws as I stepped off the grass onto the driveway. My palm print was white from grabbing the railing in fear. I breathed through the lightheaded adrenaline hangover.

Olivia and Austin stood at the edge of their yard holding their mother's hands, watching me. Olivia's leg bowed out at a disturbing angle. Austin's head hung like a ragdoll's.

"Get the hell off my property!" I turned around. The second false Sam wheeled a push mower onto the driveway from behind the manor.

"Mr. Alley? I—"

"You've got ten seconds." Sam abandoned the mower and bulled toward me in long strides. "Ten! Nine! Eight! Seven! Six..."

I dove into the driver's seat, baffled by the exchange. The skin of my finger pinched between the key's jagged edge and the steering column. I gaped over my shoulder as I left Eldridge Lane behind. The second false Sam stood in his driveway beside Samson. Olivia and Austin pulled their mother by her hands toward Sam's back yard.

The light in my apartment building's elevator flickered and I counted the corpses of a dozen dead insects in the frosted plexiglass. Starved for warmth, they wriggled into a cage they could not escape. The elevator opened to my floor. The stench of the garbage chute hit me at once. Cat litter and rot. I kicked the jammed chute door. It wouldn't close. I held my breath. The hallway bulb went out. There was no moonlight. My eyes adjusted to the traces of dim light and the pitch black walls slowly populated with rectangles of slightly lighter darkness. The furthest rectangle was my apartment door.

The rug fibers crunched beneath my feet like crushed velvet. My door was open a sliver from the frame. A distant, silver light cast across the floorboards inside. "Mel?" My whisper was too soft to reach the bedroom but loud enough to defeat the purpose of whispering. "Mel," I said louder. I waited on the doormat for the arrival of courage or foolishness. One or the other came and I slowly opened the door. Something about the weight and resistance felt off. I flipped the light switch but the lights wouldn't turn on. The light along the floorboards was the light from the open door of the empty fridge. In the bedroom, the light of my phone illuminated the gawking eyes of the insufferable stuffed animal gang like horrific animatronics. Glossy eyes and grinning teeth. I opened the ajar closet door wider. I thought it was strange she left her clothes, but it was stranger she left her jewelry.

A soundbite door slammed shut behind me. I spun around toward the sound. A light shined up the wall from the crack beside the bed. I laid on my stomach across the tangled knot of sheets. I reached my hands down into the space against the wall and fished up Mel's open laptop. She was logged into the cam site. She was still live. My pale face shined back at me from the screen. She had been live for six hours. I read the slugs' comments in the chat:

> two on one that's hot
> love that bondage
> you kicked the camera
> can't see anything
> what's with the screaming? is the show still going?

My stomach dropped with the laptop to the floor. I tripped over a stuffed animal as I scrambled out of the room. As I ran down the hall of my apartment, I saw why the front door felt wrong—the pressurized arm at the top was bent back and snapped in half. A muddy boot print was beside the doorknob. My dress shoe lost traction and slid out from under me. I caught myself with the door and picked the slippery surface off the bottom of my shoe. It was a crumpled envelope addressed to Mel in my handwriting. It was unopened. It was spotted with blood. The trail of blood led across the hallway rug to the elevator.

EXPEDITION NOTES

OCTOBER 9, 2022 | 5:59 P.M.

I just think it's messed up Sahar is barely talking to me. The questions I'm asking her are valid. She should feel glad I don't report her for obstruction of justice.

Today we took the remote deposition of Melanie Cybulski. Ms. Cybulski was in Orange County, California. Sahar led the questioning; I was second chair.

BY MS. AYUBBI:

Q Have you ever heard of a Richard Maltessouri?

A Only when you people keep asking me the same bullshit.

Q Is your answer no? You've never met him or otherwise heard of him?

A Nope. Never.

Q Let's move on. Can you please tell me about your educa--

Mr. Blackhurst: Why did you come to Lexington?

Ms. Ayubbi: Joe, I'm lead.

Mr. Blackhurst: Sorry.

Ms. Ayubbi: Ms. Cybulski, do you have an answer to his question?

The Witness: Can you say it again?

Q Have you ever been to Kentucky?

A Why do you people keep asking me that? The kidnappers took me to Richmond.

Q So you have no reason to believe you've ever been to Kentucky?

A Never been. No way. I'll tell you what

I told the detective DEA people. I was doing bad at UCLA. My parents wanted me to take a year off until I could take stuff seriously. I remember that. My dad wanted me to go to aesthetician school or something I'd like more or find a job or whatever. He called it makeup school. Asshole probably thought I should cut hair 'cause all women wanna do that too he thinks. I probably ran away. But there's like zero reason I'd ever in a million jillion years come to Kentucky. Like think about it. I don't know anyone there. I don't know anyone in the South.

Q I agree. It makes no sense for you to have ever stepped foot in Kentucky.

A Right. I swear it's like I went to bed in my dorm and the next thing I know I'm in a police station in Virginia. Still not Kentucky so why do people keep asking about Kentucky? Look--My roommate and I were taking like twenty kinds of pills that semester and got trashed literally every night. I'm sure those sex traffickers roofied me.

Mr. Blackhurst: The sex traffickers being Hundred Suns?

Ms. Ayubbi: I think we can wrap this up. I don't have any more questions.

Mr. Blackhurst: Do you remember them abducting you in L.A.?

The Witness: Not really. Sure. I guess.

Mr. Blackhurst: You have to answer yes or no, truthfully.

Ms. Ayubbi: Joe, you can't hijack--

The Witness: I don't think so. Maybe if I think hard enough.

Mr. Blackhurst: Tell me about the abduction.

A If this is about the criminal case, my lawyer said I don't have to talk about this anymore. I'm still anonymous in that case, right?

Ms. Ayubbi: We're not at all connected to the Hundred Suns trial. I apologize for my colleague, we shouldn't be asking you about that. It's beyond the scope of the interview.

Mr. Blackhurst: It isn't beyond scope. Mel, if you said you remember being abducted in L.A., give us the details. The proof.

The Witness: Fuck you, dude. Look--I'm done. I've got class.

Ms. Ayubbi: That's okay. Thank you for taking the time to speak with us, Ms. Cybulski. I apologize for my colleague. You won't hear from us again.

Mr. Blackhurst: Did you keep a list of your camshow customers?

[Ms. Cybulski leaves the call]

I need to get rid of Sahar.

CANVAS TWENTY-FIVE

Rowan filled the top of her automatic coffeemaker. She put the lid on the tin of cheap grounds and put it back in the cheap cabinet. She switched the water filter on the tap for a faster stream to rinse the coffeepot. She whipped the pot in circles like a glass of wine. She dumped the brown water in the sink and it sloshed up the stainless steel side and stained the front of her wedding dress.

"God dammit," she said, dabbing the stains with a ratty dishcloth. "Happy Halloween, by the way. Way to not dress up."

I mumbled to myself, "...five days."

"I can't hear you over the water."

"We haven't slept in five days."

"Six."

"Six?"

"Pretty sure. I used to pull all-weekers in grad school."

"All-weekers?"

"Yep. Weird I don't feel like total shit though. Normally, you feel like total shit." She set the pot to brew.

"I should see a doctor. I need drugs or something."

"Your problem is this ass is bomb."

"I'm serious. Something's wrong with me."

"We all got problems. Research sabbatical would be great if the University actually paid." The percolator started to drip.

"As a kid, what helped me sleep was to think of dreams as a sort of communal thing," I said. "I'd imagine a cloud of grape jelly. The super sweet sort that sits in the little bowls at restaurants with the butter and the cream. I'd pretend me and all the other kids in the orphanage each had a straw we'd poke up into the cloud and drink the jelly with. Straws that look like barber poles."

"Sounds like you're already on drugs." Rowan spanked the percolator. "Hurry up, son. I gotta run." She turned to me. "I was two minutes late opening one time. I mean seriously six-o-two tops, and this bitch regular ratted me out. Total boomer. Friends with the owner, I think." Rowan's voice intoned to high society snoot. "Fancies her cappuccino precisely twenty-two degrees chiller than one doth normally heat the milk, my dear. Foam? Heavens no! Crema, darling. Crema." Her white-gloved hand glided like a swan as she spoke beneath her veil. "Whoever invented 'the customer is always right' was a boomer I bet."

"Would you marry me if I were broke?" I said.

"Hell no. I require a big ass ring." She had bought the most expensive wedding dress the Halloween shop sold.[41] She pulled off the veil and beat it like a foyer rug and stuffed it back over her greasy hair. "I gotta head out."

"I'll leave too. I should get to the firm early. I need that money to afford a big ass ring. I also need to change."

"Why don't you go home and change? At the apartment I'm not allowed to see."

"There is no apartment. I'm a homeless mooch."

"I figured." She poured a cup of coffee and mimed tossing it in my face. "That'll be two-fifty." She held out her open palm. I put my hand in hers and we stayed that way for awhile, sipping.

"And here come the coffee poops," she said.

"Gross."

She skipped across the studio and closed the flimsy bathroom door. A switch flicked and the bathroom fan groaned. I tip-toed to the coat rack and unbuckled her purse. Lip gloss, tampon, tubes, other baubles my touch couldn't readily identify.

Her voice was faint through the door. "I'm working a double. I get off at five. Come get me off after that."

"Sounds good." I tilted the purse into the light and saw neither wallet nor pocketbook.

"I haven't worked on my book since last week."

I heard toilet paper tear. I fisted the pockets of her coats

41 Halloween Planet USA let me dig through their transaction records (a shoebox stuffed with receipts). A rented costume wedding gown from October 2017 had never been returned. It has accrued a late fee of $2,200.

and felt something in a jean jacket. The toilet flushed.

"Guess I'm outta soap," she said.

I pulled out two twenty-dollar bills rolled over each other like a joint. The bathroom doorknob rattled. The money slipped from my fingers. The bathroom door opened. I bent down and crammed the bills into my shoe.

"What are you doing?"

I flattened onto my stomach and peeked under the fridge. "I saw a roach run under and I wanted to be your hero."

"Tight."

"Must be way back there. I can't see it." Rowan straddled my back. The linoleum was cold against my racing heart.

"Wanna nail me quick?"

Students in costumes hauled heavy backpacks to class. We passed ghosts and witches and characters from popular TV shows. We kissed at the corner and she crossed the street and I continued on toward downtown. The sky hued pink above the streetlight-speckled sidewalk. The pink rose into tangerine and then violet and then into the deep blue. The icy October morning stung my nostrils as I breathed out life in little clouds.

Three men in costumes smoked cigarettes beyond the two rung fence of the Copper Roof. A cowboy, a sailor, and a biker. The cowboy sat on the picnic table like it were a shoeshine stand. He tilted the rim of his hat. The sailor spat. I crossed under the buzzing neon sign of a closed tattoo parlor—the quarter mile marker to Litton Steenken. Behind me, a voice like broken teeth called out.

"Yo, debtor."

I stopped and turned. The sun tore through the envelope of concrete street behind the cowboy. "Reach for the sky." He reached into the toy holster and pulled out a real nine millimeter. His arm extended up, perpendicular to the sidewalk. The gun snapped three times and bullets ripped into the atmosphere above. The biker and sailor were already over the fence and chasing after me.

I lunged forward—my first two strides long and stumbling.

I caught my weight above my pounding knees. The sailor was closing in fast. My hand gripped a brick building as I whipped around the corner. My knee collided hard into the wing of a decorative concrete angel. "Fuck you," I said to the angel as it toppled over and shattered against the pavement. I ran on with a limp.

Rough fingers caught and tore my shirt collar. Whiplash. The sailor swung my face into his fist. Torn lip. Canine tooth down a sewer grate. The sailor reeled his fist back behind his ear. The tendon in his forearm exploded open. A geyser of blood and bone broke skin. He fell to the ground clutching his mangled arm, whining like a kicked dog. The bullet was one of the cowboy's warning shots—what goes up must come down. I doubled over into a run like a frightened four-legged animal. I ran by a dead-end alley and the sailor's screams reverberated off the surfaces of dumpsters. I looked behind me, backpedaling. The biker knelt beside his wounded comrade; the cowboy was gaining on me.

The gunmetal gray sedan cut me off in the crosswalk. My knee crashed into the corner of its bumper and dented the hood. "Fuck you," I said again. I pulled myself up by the side mirror and scrambled in the direction of the trunk and away. I heard the driver's door open behind me. The cowboy yelled for him to get back in. The driver closed the door and struggled a three point turn.

I ripped open the door of a liquor store. The clerk glanced up. The glass door clapped against a display and shattered along with a dozen cascading liquor bottles. A bottle of whiskey skid across the linoleum and broke against the wall. A cardboard chip display soaked in the flood of alcohol. The clerk ducked under the counter. I jumped over the counter. My leg knocked the cash register to the floor with the ring of a forcefully hung-up telephone. My head struck the plexiglass overhead display and showered the clerk and I in cigarette cartons. "Take what you want, don't hurt me," she said. I rose and a bag of tobacco popped under my dress shoe. The cowboy stepped through the broken glass door. I scrambled through the back hall of back-stocked boxes of bourbon and candy bars. I shouldered through the backdoor. Kratchkabub-chink. Sirens closing in. I ran down the alley. My aching knee pierced through the mire of sloshing adrenaline.

A police car screeched to a halt in the maw of the alley, cutting off my escape. I dove behind a stinking green dumpster. I chased my breath.

Red and blue light pulsed along the white brick walls. The siren switched off. An amplified voice bellowed. "Boyo behind the dumpster, come out with your hands above your head and lay on your stomach where I can see you." I did as he said. In a funny way, I felt saved.

The officer was short with the stereotypic mirrored aviators, purposeful five o'clock shadow, and a sinewy body. He cuffed me without reading my Miranda rights. At least I knew anything I told him would be inadmissible. He opened the backseat and tossed me in beside a gorilla-sized Native American man wearing a headdress. We sat with our hands cuffed behind our backs.

"What is it about Halloween that makes college boys think with their testes? You boys play nice."

Baby dropped stuffed elephant out of her cradle and wouldn't stop crying for a half hour. She just needed to be held. The cop car made a left then another left then a right. The man beside me stared sullenly out his window, his feet rested on a bag of fertilizer.

"APB possible 10-62 in progress at MLK and High. Available units please respond." The officer twisted the dial on the transceiver and it clicked and the interface dimmed. We passed the razor wire of the courthouse jail and continued on through residential neighborhoods.

The officer spoke between handfuls of sunflower seeds. "Dardanelle, meet Mr. Maltessouri. Mr. Maltessouri, meet

Dardanelle. You can call him D. D, make him comfortable." A
sudden burst of speed pulled me back against the leather seat.
Dardanelle took his hands out from behind his back where no
handcuffs restrained them and he pounced on me. My head
bent at a 90 degree angle against the hard plastic door frame
as his massive body straddled me. He dug his D battery fingers
below my ribs. His fingers pressed hard between the tendons.
The tendons separated like strands of raw ground beef. Agony.
His fingernails cut skin. The worst pain I've felt. My empty
lungs gasped but drew no air. "D's a pro," the officer said
before cracking his window to spit sunflower shells. Dardanelle
pressed the same spot repeatedly until I cried and begged and
then he pressed harder.

"D, that's good. His whining's giving me a headache."
The cruiser slowed back to normal speed. Dardanelle pulled
his fingers out. He kept me pinned to the seat. "How's life
treating you, boyo?" The officer nonchalantly checked his
mirror, switched on the turning signal, and changed lanes.

My words felt like popped hernias. "Who are you?"

"Not one for foreplay? Wanna get right down to the
pussy-pumping business?" The officer smiled and winked back
at D in the rearview mirror. "We're accountants. You owe our
employer twenty-three thousand and change." He tossed more
sunflower seeds in his mouth.

"You're Hundred Suns."

"Uh-huh."

The cruiser hit a pothole and Dardanelle's belt buckle dug
into my hipbone. The officer coughed hard. He took a drink
from a bottle of water. "Down the wrong pipe." He pulled
off his sunglasses. He dabbed a tear from his bloodshot eye.
He only had the one.

He put the aviators back on and his tongue traced the space
behind his bottom lip for seeds. My reflection in his aviators
reflected back at me through the rearview mirror. "Think of
us like client services," he said. "D and I are assigned to wine

and dine you, make you comfortable. Keep you happy until you pay your bill. How may I be of service to you today?" He nodded at Dardanelle through the mirror. The behemoth man pulled me down off the cruiser seat to sit on the floor between his boots. My cuffed hands caught momentarily on the seatbelt and the motion pulled something in my collar. Dardanelle straddled my shoulders beneath his knees like a rollercoaster harness. His arm coiled my neck in a chokehold.

"I can pay." I forced the words through clenched teeth and closed throat.

"Melanie will be jazzed to hear that, lemme tell ya." We hit another bump and my Adam's apple pressed into my throat like a stone and I wheezed tickled, cut-off coughs. "For her sake I hope you got it on you. D, gimme the rundown."

Dardanelle molested my pockets. He pulled out my empty wallet, phone, and the rolled-up twenty-dollar bills. "Dude's broke, Apollo." He tore off my watch. "Watch is nice."

"Keep it. Toss the phone." A back window rolled down and Dardanelle threw my phone out over a pasture. He put my watch on an inch in front of my eyes without releasing the tension around my throat. His hairy wrist bubbled around the stressed leather band. He pocketed the forty dollars and returned to an even stronger chokehold. I turned blue.

"I got..." I struggled to supply air to my words.

"What's that?" Apollo said.

"I got...paid...on...Friday."

"Speak up so the fans in the back can hear." D jabbed me in the side with his boot heel. "Shit, he pissed." Dardanelle spread his legs wide to avoid the puddle of urine.

"I can...withdraw everything I have now. I got paid...on Friday."

"You said that already and we did that already."

"...What?"

"Your account is already zeroed. Our finder's fee. Still need the twenty-three thousand you owe us."

I coughed between words. "What...are you talking...about?"

"Our higher risk clients, like yourself, are put on a payment plan. Principal plus interest will auto transfer to us every time that fat lawyer paycheck of yours comes in. Think of it like a mortgage on Melanie's life."

"I didn't...set that up."

"We did. We're client services. Remember? Our job is to make your life easier."

Dardanelle wiped his piss-stained boot on the plastic divider between the leg spaces.

"We really can't make it any easier on you. All you gotta do is keep making a paycheck. I guess you gotta figure out how to eat and whatnot, but you're a smart guy. It'll give you a taste of life on the Rez." D smiled. "And if you stop paying. Well. We bought Melanie the best life insurance policy. Real gold standard. Why we don't cash it in now, don't ask me. The boss is religious or something. Believes in karma, I guess. But I don't, so don't push me. See, I find the worse I treat people, the faster I get what I want."

"That's for real," Dardanelle said.

"Welcome to your new life, Mr. Maltessouri," Apollo said. "Can I call you Dick?" Dardanelle tightened his chokehold.

Apollo pinched sunflower seeds into his mouth with his fist. "I'm sick of this asshole, D."

Dardanelle pulled my head back by the hair. His knees held my skull like a vise. His fingernails cut my lip as he pried open my mouth. He pinched my cheeks with a hand like calipers while his other hand reached into the white plastic bag and brought out a fistful of wormy manure. He fisted it into my mouth. I gagged and puked. He slapped me and the puke burned my eyes. He fisted another handful of manure into my mouth and then chewed my mouth like a nutcracker. It was coarse and sour as it moistened and caked in my throat. A taste like vermouth and propane. I swallowed a fat, runny glob and blacked out.

EXPEDITION NOTES

OCTOBER 10, 2022 | 3:44 A.M.

Canvas Twenty-Five is where the Wade Transcription ended—fell into incomprehensible madness is a better way to put it. The entire Hundred Suns chase is news to me.

In the Wade Transcription, after the line: "[w]e passed ghosts and witches and characters from popular TV shows," Klay Wade tells an entirely different story about trick-or-treating: "I watched her go door to door collecting her little candy gonna get fat like her mommy." Unit A took this to mean Richie and Rowan actually went trick-or-treating and Richie was disparaging her as usual. The transcription then devolved entirely to expressing hatred for "her mom." It of course seemed odd that Richie would know Rowan's mom, or have an opinion about her at all. Events from Klay's own life had taken over the transcription. He murdered his wife and daughter shortly after Halloween.

Sahar tore into me after the deposition. Said I was harassing and scaring a rape victim. What is she even talking about? There's no indication Mel was raped by anyone. She said I should sleep more but who can sleep when they're this close to cracking a mystery they've devoted four years of their life to solving. Richie's door was kicked in and the Rosearms maintenance man's testimony proves it. Why would she want me to sleep? There must be another agenda to this trip I'm not privy to. The Committee allocates assignments on a need-to-know basis where you're told only what you need to perform your part without an eye for the big picture. What is it they sent Sahar to do? She made me promise never to investigate at night without her. Says she hates going out at night ever since the Canvases were discovered. Says it's panic attacks and fear of "her stalker." His name is Richie. Call him by his name. But he isn't a stalker. Oh so I can't go out at night, can I?

Just got back. The officer I spoke with at the police station found nothing about the foot chase. The liquor store owner remembers nothing. She said break-ins happen a lot. Both said I should really come in during regular hours with all these questions. I knocked hard on Sahar's door and she didn't answer. Borlú didn't bark.

She's going out at night.

CANVAS TWENTY- SIX

"Mister, wake up."

I was numb. My eyes opened inches from the face of an intricate iron horse. It grinned and spewed water with its head tucked low as if to run me down. The taste of manure returned to the foreground of my senses and I threw up. The sick bobbed on the water like oil.

"Mister, get out or you'll freeze." The woman's scabby fingertips under fingerless gloves lifted me beneath my arms. I couldn't feel below my waist. "One, two, three." Purple skin exposed to freezing fire. The edge of the fountain darkened beneath the deluge of ice water streaming from my pants.

"Stay here, mister. Stay right here." I couldn't wiggle a toe to save my life. The homeless woman limped away from the fountain of stampeding horses into the light snowfall. She stopped on the sidewalk and dug through the refuse of her loaded shopping cart. The clatter of pawed empty cans and the song of distressed birds caught in the year's first snowfall. The snowflakes landed and melted at once in the grass. A thin film of ice encased my lower half. The homeless woman hurried back across the frosted park to where I sat on the edge of the fountain. She draped a black trash bag over my shoulders. She knelt and wrapped my legs in more trash bags. She slapped the sides of my thighs down to the ankles and back up again. "Are you drunk? You could have drowned."

My answer was chattering teeth.

"You did me a kindness once," she said. "I never forget. Did that sister of yours leave you here?" The muscles in my neck locked solid in a spasm. No words came.

"I know what it's like," she said, "being on your own and so low." She sat beside me on the fountain's edge. "Those people, they stare, but we can't go on blaming them. We all don't know ourselves enough to be judging anyone else. Easy to stare at you freezing there and think how he put himself there in that awful way. Like it's your fault. You might have played a part but they don't wonder who else mighta put you down that path in the first place." She picked at the green patina of an iron horse's hoof. "My brother is who put me here. Out in the cold. I was a baby. Had no one else. I hated him. I hated him with a hate that spread to the face of every man I saw. Sixty years hating him and seeing his face in every other man and hating them all too. Good strangers don't deserve us treating them that way. Don't do it."

A sunbeam broke the cloud wall and warmed my legs.

"Forgive your sister for leaving you. Not tomorrow, not later. You forgive her right this moment. Or hate'll become you. Took me sixty years to see my brother had probably been hurting so badly to abandon me there like that. Took me sixty years to forgive him. And you know what? I love him. Don't remember him, but I love him."

Violet stood up and buttoned her frayed wool coat. She stared into the falling snow. "Leave her here," she said. And like that, she was gone.

EXPEDITION NOTES
OCTOBER 10, 2022 | 2:55 P.M.

Sahar was silent the entire walk to the fountain. The fountain had coins in it but little else. We sat on its edge just as Richie had.

"See—we're just sightseeing now," she said.

"How do you not understand?"

"Excuse me?"

"How do you not get how important this is? We've never read this far into the record. Every new lead, no matter how silly or small, is still brand new."

"And we've still found neither hide nor hair of the made-up man. How much more proof do you need?"

"Which is why we keep going."

"We had all the proof Maltessouri wasn't real the first time they deposed me and I said 'I don't know anyone by that name.' But no, you all had to go and ruin my life more. Never take a woman's word at face value. There's no way she's right. Let's send teams and teams of men to figure this thing out. This woman must be lying."

"Did you murder Richie?"

"What did you say?"

"Did you kill Richie and bury him?"

"What did you say?"

"It's a lead. Are you moving the body at night? I'm exaggerating. That's silly. You're only covering your tracks at night. Not actually moving his body. Perhaps parts of his body? Did you chop him up and put him in trash bags? Did he have any Tint when you killed him? What are you using it to wish for? Did you feed him to Borlú?"

She slapped me so hard my vision flashed white. My eardrum still rings.

I could hear in her voice she was crying behind the shouting. "You want wishes? You want magic?" She threw her legs over the edge of the fountain and waded in. She fell to her knees and plunged her arms into the freezing water. "Here's a wish." She threw a coin from the bottom of the fountain at me and it sped past my head. "Have another one." She pelted me with a quarter hard enough to sting my forearm as I protected my face. Borlú was barking and pressing his front paws against the lip of the fountain. "Here's another. I wish for infinite fucking money to throw at you!" The coin ricocheted off my shin.

"Stop!"

Her arm went limp mid-throw and the quarter skimmed the surface of the water. It left expanding ripples which broke against Sahar's soaked coat where she sat in the water sobbing. "I wish for you to be my friend again," she said.

"Are you okay, ma'am? Mister? I don't want you to hurt each other." The homeless woman ran to stand between us.

"Get the hell away," Sahar said.

"I remember you."

"I've never seen you before."

"You have, you have. You were the girl who threw the fork at the window at Angelo's. You completely shattered it."

Sahar stopped crying as the blood left her face.

"I remember I came in to see what was the matter and you were so mad at me. You don't remember? Well I remember. It's easy remembering someone who threw a fork through a window. Especially easy to remember because you ordered two meals for yourself. Hard not to remember."

"Get away from me."

"You don't remember? It was just a couple years

ago. I know it was you."

"Get the fuck away from me."

Sahar climbed out of the fountain. The water streamed down from her clothes. She took Borlú's leash and got up. "I'm leaving this fucking city." She reached into her pocket and pulled out her key to the Canvases' case. She threw it into the center of the fountain. "I'm going home."

Violet was already gone. I turned back and Sahar was already so far away it was as if she were running. I should have removed my shoes and socks first but I jumped in after the key without thinking.

CANVAS TWENTY-SEVEN

Manure stained button-down and pants like sheets of ice. A pair of sorority girls crossed the street to avoid me. I staked out the firm's front door. The lunch group came out on cue. Emma and the other administrative assistants lit up cigarettes. A group of old attorneys walked out. I turned my face to the brick wall as they passed me breathing through their mouths. I pulled open the frosted glass door of Litton, Steenken, & Mendez for the second to last time.

The elevator dinged and the down arrow illuminated and I darted into the stairwell. I peeked up the center space of the stairs and focused my ears. Only the sight of pipes and the stomach growl sounds they make. I took the stairs two at a time, looking down at my soaked pant legs.

I crashed into Sahar and she fell back onto the cold metal of the stairwell landing. "Are you okay?"

She sat up wincing and rubbing her lower back. "What the hell?" She opened her eyes, "Jesus, are you okay?"

"I got mugged."

She covered her mouth and pinched her nose with the same hand. "That's horrible. Are you okay? Where did it happen?"

"Near my apartment. I've been at the police station filing a report all morning."

"Why are you all wet?"

"The shower at the police station."

A slow smile crept across her face. "Do you want me to tell Scott?"

"No. I just need to get changed."

"I should tell Scott."

"No."

"You have shit smeared on your chin."

"Don't."

"I'm telling Scott." She smiled. "For your own good."[42]

She turned and ran and was already two steps ahead of me. I lunged forward and my hand caught the tail of her blazer. She stumbled and the fabric tore in my hand. She could run, but I could only limp.

When I made it through the stairwell door she was halfway down the hall. I dove into my office. The sleeves of my filthy, soaked dress shirt fought for their lives to stay on my wrists. I balled it into the trashcan like a soaked rag. The act of fighting off my shirt left me light-headed and I stood a moment shirtless leaning over the desk. I might have cried if I had the energy. I peeled off the freezing suit pants. My leg hair had matted to my skin like balls of hair on a shower wall. I pulled off my underwear and threw them in the trashcan with the stinking shirt and stuffed it all beneath the desk. I tiptoed to the spare suit hanging on the back of the door. My soaked socks squelched beneath my feet. I steadied myself with the doorknob as I stood like a flamingo and pinched the first sock off. The door swung open and I crashed against the wooden armrest of the chair and down onto the floor.

"Are you alright?" Scott said standing over my naked body.

"I'm changing," I said.

He averted his eyes and closed the door. He pulled me to my feet and turned his back. I put on the dry suit pants. He turned back around. "Those are fist bruises." He pointed up and down the swollen black rot creeping from my navel to my neck. "They had a ring on, too."

"I got mugged."

"Sahar told me you'd say that. I've been trying to reach you all morning."

"They took my phone."

---

42 She wants to get rid of me. It was never about the expedition for her. It was always about deception. But now she's the one on the run. Something must have motivated her to kill Richie. I know she killed Richie.

Scott collapsed into the chair. "Get your shirt on. Do you need to go to the hospital?"

"They checked me over at the police station. It's just scrapes and bruises."

"I'm not talking about the bruises...wherever they came from." He cracked nine of his knuckles in slow succession. He wrenched the tenth back and forth but it made no sound. "You need help."

"I need money."

His cheeks billowed and expelled a puff of air. "Barrett Niehoff called me last night. Late last night." My heart sank. "He said you went to Ms. Rothacker's home uninvited. She said you harassed her and her kids."

"I discovered she was lying about the kidnapping and had the kids the entire time. She beat the shit out of them."

"We don't know that. Barrett's revising the kidnapping allegations to attempt. I haven't talked to the prosecutor yet to hear what they're doing but they arrested Cyrus this morning."

"If Cyrus was the one who beat them then he should be in prison. I don't care. I need money."

Scott stood up. The muffled chatter of the admin assistants coming back from lunch could be heard through the door. "Barrett's also filing an ethics complaint against you with the bar association.[43] You spoke with a represented party without their lawyer present. Dammit Richie, you spoke to an opposing party, who you knew was represented, at her house at night. She said you went through her trash, too."

"It was at the curb so I peeked in is all."

"You could lose your license. I'll ask you one more time."

---

43 I just made a call; the Office of Bar Counsel of the Kentucky Bar Association has no record of such a complaint ever being filed. The Association did have an attorney bar number that would have been issued in 2017 that had been inexplicably skipped over. The Association assured me its system is not foolproof and the occasional clerical error is made and that no harm would ever come of it. Sahar and the Committee must be behind it.

He took a deep, wavering breath. "Do you need to go to the hospital?"

"No."

"Then I have to let you go. The firm can't afford a malpractice suit and I can't help you if you won't let me."

"Please help me. I need money, Scott. I owe bad men a lot of money. Scott, I desperately need money."

He took my diploma off the wall and handed it to me. "You have a bright career ahead of you once you learn to prioritize your health before it. I hope you find someone who can teach you to appreciate that. I'll always regret I couldn't." He came around the desk and put his hands on my shoulders. "Please, Richie. Get yourself the help you need. Gamblers' group. Therapist. Whatever help you need. I can give you the number of a psychiatrist who specializes in bipolar."

I shook myself loose. "These men might kill me." And so Scott left me.

Emma had been listening in and invited herself in. "I'm so sorry, Richie." She hugged me and whispered in my ear. "Was it the porn? I think they have software watching our screens. Did Scott say anything? You'd tell me if Scott said something, right?"

I limped down the hall holding my diploma with both hands. The words were pointed outward like some plaque beneath a melting wax sculpture. Sahar leaned against the wall beside the stairwell door. She watched me limp toward her down the length of the hallway. "Let me get that for you," she said as she held open the stairwell door without breaking eye contact, smiling. I threw my diploma down the stairs and the glass broke against the steps. She shrieked.

"I'll take the elevator."

EXPEDITION NOTES
OCTOBER 10, 2022 | 11:58 P.M.

Sahar got Richie fired. She stabbed him in the back. I can feel it in my gut she killed him. Or knows who did. The Committee must be behind her actions. Who else has the resources to cover up murder of this magnitude? I need to move quickly. She checked out of the hotel. Hopefully she meant it when she said she was going home. Home for her is Cincinnati. That's where she grew up. She'd drive if that's the case. Which would mean she's on her way to the airport to get a rental car. Or already got a rental car and is making the drive now. I need to call them. But there might be other rental car places. I'll call them all. This is assuming she meant it when she said she's going home. I shouldn't believe anything she says. She could also have meant home as in Chicago where the Committee is located. She'd fly. I need to check flights.

The next flight is tomorrow morning. She's probably staying the night at another hotel. I'll call around. I should buy a ticket to catch her at the terminal. Or I could leave now and drive to Chicago and gather the Committee before she can and explain how she's obstructed the expedition from the start. But that's a six-hour drive. I could call but I know Milsap would get ahold of the truth and twist it to buy Sahar time. It's in his interest our expedition fails. He wants to publish. Publish his stupid goddamn stupid flash flood theory. He doesn't care about the truth. He cares about being a guest on talk shows. He'll get the Committee to vote on having me removed. I need to beat Sahar to Chicago. But what if the entire Committee is behind her? I need more evidence. I'm on my own now. I need to find Violet again. I need to take her deposition. But

I'd need a stenographer and tomorrow is Saturday and they would need 24 hours' notice. And I don't know where to find Violet. No, I must transcribe to inform my next move and go from there. Sahar may well be going to Cincinnati. I've never seen her so shook up. I need to get out of my head. Whatever I do, I need to wait for my clothes to dry over the shower. I must look ridiculous typing naked like this.

CANVAS TWENTY–EIGHT

Banks were once the most opulent buildings, second only to theaters. Nuanced stone between marble floors and breathtaking painted ceilings. Now they're all carpet mats, brown counters, and promotional materials shouting *FICO*.

"I can help who's next."

I lurched forward. "I need a loan immediately."

"Please take a seat over there and I'll let our bankers know." I waited in line for a line.

My fingernails wore the armrests of the fake leather chair. I thought about the pain of Dardanelle's fingertips digging under my ribs and how I already missed Rowan. Fibers of the pleather chair flaked off and stuck to my sweaty palms.

"Mr. Maltessouri." The banker looked about eighteen. "Come on in."

Her office was as plain as the rest of the bank—brown furniture and promotional materials. The void of personal decorations suggested the office was shared.

"How about that game? Didn't think U.K. was gonna pull it off in overtime."

"I hate football. I need a loan immediately."

She shot me with finger guns over the laminated placemat of credit card comparisons. "Let's hook you up."

She clicked a few boxes in her monitor.

"A loan, right? Not a mortgage?"

"Right. I didn't say mortgage."

"Right. Let's see. They keep changing the software on me. It's slow today. Starting a business, are we?"

"Sure."

"Very nice. Very awesome. I've got the entrepreneur bug, too. Got an idea for an app that lets landlords pool and invest their tenant's security deposits. Think about it. Time value of money. You might not know about it but that's just money being wasted that could be earning interest. The app would take a cut. What's your idea?"

"I'm opening a restaurant. That would never work."

"Your restaurant would never work?"

"No. Your app. By law, you have to keep security deposits in separate accounts. Assuming you got a surety bond on each account, it'd only work if the interest you're earning is in excess of those costs. Plus the fees associated with investment. Plus tenants move out before any interest could significantly compound. Plus landlords could do it themselves and cut you out as a useless middle man. And even if it worked you'd be predatorily gambling with low income people's money to benefit yourself. It's gross and stupid. But mostly just stupid. I need about thirty grand."

"Like I said, it's just an idea. I'd need a coder to build it anyway."

"How much can you lend me?"

She turned back to the monitor and clicked aimlessly. "I can give you the pre-approval paperwork to do over the weekend. How's next Tuesday sound?"

"For what?"

"For our next meeting when you bring back the pre-approval paperwork." She opened a filing cabinet and pulled out a single piece of paper and slid it across the placemat.

"This is asking for basic contact information and income. I'll fill it out now."

"That won't work. We have a policy."

"Tell me the policy."

She leaned in. "Look, I'm new. My manager isn't here and I haven't been trained on business loans yet."

"When is he back?"

"Tuesday. She's on vacation."

"Is there another banker who can do it?"

Her eyes darted to another place in the monitor and she clicked the mouse. "Nope. They're booked up until about next Tuesday too so I'm still your gal."

"What about tomorrow? I can come back tomorrow."

"I'm off tomorrow."

"What about another branch?"

"Sir, I have to ask you to lower your voice. We require pre-qualification to be done at your home branch, which is us. The earliest I can do is 9:00 a.m. next Tuesday."

"Okay, then I'm closing my account. I'm taking my business to a bank that helps."

"By the looks of your balance we literally wouldn't be losing anything."

I ripped the placemat off the table and whipped it at her. She shrieked and cowered. "Security!"

A heavy hand fell on my shoulder and gripped hard. "Time to go." His NFL sportscaster lookalike suit was straining to burst.

"I'm closing my account."

"Not today."

The man scooped me up under the arms and locked his fingers behind my neck. My feet dragged across the carpet past the silver vault.

"Let go of me."

"Shut up."

A queue of patrons watched me. A Felicity filmed me with her phone.

"I'm calm. I'm calm," I said. The pressure behind my neck was red and white. He turned me around to face the gawking audience as he pushed his back against the steel bar of the exit door.

He hurled me down hard onto the alley pavement and left me with the puddles and the trash. I needed money. I walked several blocks and saw my reflection in a jewelry store display window. Rows of diamond rings winked up at me. Prosaic price tags. Diamonds—tiny misers of nature's beauty. The teensiest of symbols compacted under the pressure of desire. How could one of billions of anything be so coveted? The old jeweler scrutinized me through the window. I headed back to the firm.

[Sketch of a diamond ring]

I staked out the door for two and a half hours crouched behind a dumpster. A muscle in my hip spasmed like a taut rubber band being flicked. Scott was always the last man out.

He didn't see me. My hand caught the germy door handle before the latch could catch and lock. I took the stairs two at a time, being mindful to step over the shattered glass of my broken diploma. I pressed my cheeks to the cold door to check the hallway through its skinny window. Both ends of the office were dark and still. I passed my office. It looked the same as my first day—empty walls, drawn shades, cheap desk, old computer.

I noticed the shoebox digital safe under Scott's desk immediately but still trashed the room. Books splayed across the carpet where I'd pulled down his bookshelf. The shelf leaned at a 45 degree angle against the desk. I opened every desk drawer and threw the contents in the air like I'd won the lottery. I smashed the photos of his wife and the little league team and I threw the behemoth snapper down the hall. I checked the bottom of the safe for a post-it note with the combination. There wasn't one. Scott wasn't a complete idiot. His computer was password protected so I threw that down the hall too. The safe containing his what-wife-doesn't-know-won't-kill-her stash was small but too heavy.

A door opened. Kratchkabub-chink.

Rap from a radio down the hall. The janitor went to the break room first. I was out of time; I smashed the glass display case and tucked the Super Bowl XX whatever ball under my arm and rushed out of the building.

Beneath the saloon lettering "Antiques," blinked pink neon in an interstitial rattling buzz that read "Pawn Services." Inside, it was less an antique shop than a warehouse. Tin knick-knacks and milk crates of waterlogged records. A maze of stalls organized by forgotten categories. Books, glassware, toys, electronics. The stalls' identities worn away by decades of lazy shoppers leaving their change-of-heart purchases on the nearest shelf. The ancient woman behind the register had no fight left in her to keep the place organized.

"I'm closing up, dear." Her eyes peered over her glasses lodged in the wrinkles of old age. The register space was a raised platform where she sat pricing tattered fifty cent books.

"I have something you'd be interested in," I said.

"I'm interested in closing up." She shifted her hips in her ergonomic chair.

"It's worth thousands and will sell itself."

She rolled her eyes. "It isn't the ball, is it?"

"It is the ball."

She held the ball and stared at me. "Young man, I'm closing up."

"It's a Super Bowl game ball." She glanced at the ball for the first time, albeit unamused.

"Which one?"

"I'm drawing a blank. The pirate one."

"The pirate one?"

"Florida was in it, I think."

"Florida was in it, you think. This ain't your ball, is it?"

"It's my dad's. It was my dad's. I inherited it recently."

Her cheek wrinkles ironed out. "Poor thing. I'm sorry for your loss. I really wouldn't be comfortable estimating a price on it though. To be honest, pawning was never me. My husband ran that. He died recently too. If six years is still recently. That ugly sign out front is on the grid with the floor lights. Six years it still ain't burned out."

"I imagine it's worth thirty grand at least."

She laughed. "Vivid imagination."

"Do you have a computer? Could you check what others sold for?"

"Yeah. In the back. Only way I sell anything anymore."

"Can you check for me? I'm just trying to get rid of it. The memories are just too painful. I'll give you a deal. I need to get rid of it."

She clutched the dusty brass railing and stepped off the register platform onto an arthritic knee. "Alright. The pirate one you said?"

I nodded. She wrote the word "pirate" in a small spiral notebook and ambled across the concrete showroom. She went in a backroom and out of sight.

I hopped onto the platform. The antique cash register was quaint and ineffective. I tugged the worn lever and the drawer popped open. To my surprise, it burst with cash. I began filling my pockets when a sparkle caught my eye in the glass display in the counter beneath the register. A diamond engagement ring. I pocketed the ring and ran, leaving the money where it laid overflowing from the register onto the floor. Something in the window display caught my eye—an antique shawl-collar tuxedo was in the window. I was so madly in love with Rowan. I didn't do these things. Sam made these things happen to me.

I took a shower at Rowan's while I waited for her. Her shower was like a dude's—a bottle of combination shampoo/body wash, tub blackened with footprints. I put the tuxedo on. It was precisely my size. My headache pulsed so I made a cocktail of aspirin and melatonin—the only drugs Rowan had, surprisingly. I was lying on the couch when the spotlight shined.

The brightness penetrated the cracks of the venetian blinds and refracted off the hung glass frames of Rowan's concert bill collection. I laid paralyzed in fear by the sheer overload of light. I breathed slowly with perked ears to hear even the smallest stirring. The light blinked on and off to the rhythm of a muffled metal song. I sat up and squinted through the blinds. It was a police cruiser spotlight. My heart skipped a beat but then I recognized Dardanelle by his massive frame and my heart skipped a lesser beat. The twerp next to him was Apollo.

Rage insulated me from the frigid night air. I pushed open the steel exit door so hard it swung open and snapped back against the limit of its hinges. Apollo pointed the spotlight at me and I stormed forward blind.

"What'd you do with Rowan?" I said.

"Cool it, boyo. We came to ask you what she's doing."

"I'll kill you both if you hurt her."

"Lower your voice. D and I have been driving all over hell and back cuz of her and we're not in the mood for confrontations."

"What?"

"After we tossed you in the fountain—wasn't that a nice touch? I surprise myself sometimes with my machinations and what have ya's. After we dropped you off at the horse pool, we went to scoop up your fat little girlfriend." Apollo palmed his nightstick as he spoke. "She borrowed someone's truck or something, at least the plates didn't come up as hers. We tailed her all the way to this BFE little mining town. To this huge ass house. So she gets there and just stands there on the porch with a bouquet of flowers for hours. Hours and hours just freezing. Tons of people there. Party I think. Too many people around to scoop her up. Called in reinforcements to keep an eye on her. D and I got better things to do. They said she's still there ten minutes ago. She gangbanging those twins? Spit roast? The wedding dress is some real kinky shit, boyo."

Dardanelle's laugh loosened up a loogie and he hocked it.

"What twins?" I said.

"Two old dudes whose porch she's hanging out on. She a hooker or just a whore?"

I hit him hard in the jaw. Apollo spun and caught himself with the cruiser mirror. I was impressed with myself. He spat teeth. Blood coursed down his chin. He stood up straight. "Bit my fuckin' tongue."

Dardanelle twisted my arm and pushed me to my knees. Something in my collar popped. Apollo stood over me. "I'm starting to warm up to you." His nightstick clapped against my ear and my skull bounced off the cruiser door. Dardanelle put me in a chokehold. I clawed at his arms. My ears rang. Dark pink flooded my vision and then black.

EXPEDITION NOTES

OCTOBER 11, 2022 | 1:14 P.M.

I stayed up all night. I can feel Sahar's still here. She's following me. Watching me, I'm sure. Waiting for me to slip up. I think maybe that little girl is working with her. I saw the girl in the bank. The bank was useless and treated me similarly to how they treated Richie. Acted like I was a nuisance or a danger, said I was acting crazy or something I don't know. Asked me to leave. The point is the little girl was there.

Went to the antique store. I didn't bother questioning the owner. She wouldn't remember anything. But I saw the little girl spying on me from an aisle of antique toys. When I chased after her she dropped a porcelain doll and it shattered. The owner came over and the girl escaped. I paid fifty bucks for a stupid old doll.

Sahar knows where I'm headed next. She's scared of me. Scared of the evidence. She can't stop me. Wish I had a gun. The next Canvas is short. I'm going to Carrington tonight. Should get a gun.

CANVAS TWENTY-NINE

The day or days faded in and out. I still have no clue what day it is. They tied me to a chair toward the back of a greenhouse between rows of dead beans shaded by brown mesh hanging plants. The whole structure was made of flimsy plywood, PVC piping, and plastic sheeting. The zip tie cut off circulation to my hands where the feeling of polka dot static crawled. The tendon over my elbow pinched against the folding chair. I faded out again.

I came to at sunrise or sunset. I heard shouting and a distorted speakerphone voice. My hunger felt like a broken rib. I faded out again.

"Wake up. I wanna torture you." Apollo pressurized the hose with his thumb and the freezing water stung my naked body. The moonlight cast a sapphire gray over the room through the layers of snow on the roof.

"Apparently D's your buddy, boyo." Apollo switched on a box fan. The agonizing cold air gusted over my drenched body. "He spent the whole night keeping me from torturing you. Made a few good points too. Boss wants this. Boss said that. Orders were to tail you and intimidate you and collect off you and kinda just be scary dicks in general. I think we can both agree we did a decent job at that. But then you went and gave me a lisp." It was true. His words were punctuated by whistles. "See, D's what ya call a pacifist. Hates unnecessary violence. I think it's cuz of the business with his mom on the Rez. He was just a tot then. Bangers broke in and, well, banged her while he was in the room. He slept through the whole thing. Next day, Rez police pulled him out of school to tell him the bangers came back and killed her that afternoon during round two. Sad, I know." He lit a cigarette and savored a puff as he watched the box fan drain my body to icy blue. "Two lessons from that story, boyo. One, D hates violence. Two, D's a heavy sleeper." He put the cigarette out on my kneecap. The skin melted and smoked. I tried to scream but I was gagged. Apollo smiled pink swollen gums.

He took a pair of rose trimmers from a nearby pallet. "You look like you saw a ghost. Relax. You ain't gonna die. You're just gonna get you dick snipped off." He kicked a milk crate in front of my knees and sat down. "Sorry if my hands are cold."

I had no strength to stop him from spreading my naked knees. "Oops. Left the safety on." He clicked the orange switch on the side, unhooking the jaws. The rose shears squealed as he clicked the handles together.

He pulled it taut from my body. He bit his lip and squinted. He puzzled as he flourished the blades at different cutting angles. "Figure I'll cut like this. That work for you? Blink once for yes. Blink twice for yes yes." He laughed, took a deep breath, and exhaled. "Wow, I've got butterflies. This job always finds a way to stay fresh. This is probably gonna be gross. I've never cut a cock off before so bear with me. Not that I'd call this a cock." He turned and blocked the box fan and blood and feeling returned to my body. "On three." I tried to clasp my knees, his knees held them open. "Got that out of you system? Trust me, a clean cut is in your best interest. I couldn't care less."

He clicked the rose trimmers. "One…"

He placed the blades at the base of skin. "Two…"

He stared into my eyes.

"Three."

Blood spurt across my face and stomach. The rose trimmers fell to the dirt.

The long blades of garden shears stabbed out of Apollo's collarbone. His jugular sprayed onto me in heartbeats. Apollo's hands rose and he grabbed the blades. He looked down at his impalement. He screamed until his lungs filled with blood and then he burbled. He slumped forward between my naked knees and died with his head resting on my thigh. The garden shear handles stuck out from his back like a tuning fork. Wide-eyed I spurned my lungs to draw breath. I was unharmed. Warm blood pooled under the soles of my feet.

Dardanelle's eyes were rolled back in his head. He leaned down and tore the garden shears out with a disgusting sound. A sticky strand of blood connected the blade to the hole in Apollo's back like an umbilical cord before snapping like drool. Man, I thought that was so gross when I saw it. Half the marionettes' have wounds at least that gross. I'm used to it now. He opened the gruesome blades and stepped behind my chair.

Snip.

My arms fell limp to my sides and sobering blood returned to my corpse-blue hands. Dardanelle dropped the shears in the dirt and crossed the greenhouse in heavy steps. He pulled back the plastic sheeting door and sleepwalked into the night.

I moved with adrenaline and instinct. I pulled the rose trimmers off the ground and cut the zip ties around my ankles. I used the garden hose to wash the blood off my body and I dried myself with a burlap sack. The tuxedo was piled in a corner; I pulled it on. I felt the engagement ring in the breast pocket. Apollo's shoe size was only a little smaller than mine. I crammed my toes in. Apollo's single eye stared up at me. A cluster of ants had congregated around his blood. I read the text messages on his burner phone. Dozens of missed calls and angry texts from who must have been his boss. Request for a backup crew. Rowan's address. My address. The gun in Apollo's holster was a realistic looking toy. The tag of his shirt read HALLOWEEN PLANET USA RENTALS - YMCA COP.[44] I took the toy gun and his keys.

A cloud blotted out the moon. I unlocked the cruiser and stabbed the ignition. It rumbled to life beneath my frozen fingers.

The warmth of the cruiser headlights bathed the figure of a perfect warrior born unlucky to the 21st century. The warrior

---

44 I need to go back and dig through their receipts again, but there's no time. I gotta get going.

shambled aimlessly into the distance. I turned the cruiser and the headlights collapsed the snowy grasses of the field in shrinking acute vision against the axis of the dirt road shoulder until the light was parallel and the snowy grasses vanished from relevant existence. That mind-hijacked warrior—named Dardanelle by his mother—marched deeper into the snowy Kentucky wilderness following the purposeless reckoning of Sam's collateral influence. Sam, the destroyer of countless lives.

I'm sure they've both frozen to death by now. I'm running out of tint. I owe it to Sam to keep going.

EXPEDITION NOTES
OCTOBER 11, 12?, 2022? | VERY LATE (OR VERY EARLY)

I made it to Carrington after dark. I wouldn't have known I was there if it weren't for the latitude and longitude. I called out for anyone to hear but no one was there. I walked the rows of saplings cascading deeper and deeper into the valley. A shape took form ahead of me in the darkness, tall and narrow. A tower. When I reached its base and touched its stone I realized what it was.

[Here I'd sketch a towering well]

The well rose about twelve feet from the soil that had drowned the town around it. The birch tree leaned against the well, dead, creating a sort of ladder up over the lip. I would have climbed the tree had something else not caught my eye.

What did I find? Joe, what did you find? It's so bright. Focus on the words. Wake up. Focus. On the words. Its light twinkled between the bottom-most stones of the well. A sparkling scrap of denim flapping in the freezing breeze. I pulled it free from the stones. The words are finger-painted in Tint. Focus on the words. They read:

DEAR GOD, DON'T WORRY ABOUT ME. I PRAY THE PEOPLE OF CARRINGTON TAKE CARE OF SAM.

Sahar lied that she doesn't go out at night. I heard the footsteps crunching the leaves in the distance. I stuffed the note in my pocket and hid behind the well. Sahar held a flashlight in one hand and pulled Borlú by his leash in the other. His legs were locked but he couldn't find traction so he slid helplessly across the dead leaves. She was crying.

Suddenly, the sound of screaming cicadas erupted from the trees. The pain in my ears caused me to scream as well and I stumbled from behind the well. Sahar screamed from me startling her. Borlú was barking. He wouldn't stop barking.

I caught very little of what she said through my hands clasping my ears.

"I'm afraid," I think she said.

"The cicadas!" I shouted. I couldn't hear my voice. I only felt the words resonate in my skull. "The sound is peeling back my skin."

"What?" She remained composed through the screeching. "Give me your hand. You're scaring me." She said something like that.

"Why?" I shouted louder. "You've come to slit my wrists? Like you did to Richie? Where's your knife?" I circled around her. "Or should I turn my back so you can use your gun?"

I shoved her away and she stumbled over the fallen birch. Borlú attacked me at once and bit his teeth into the sleeve of my windbreaker. The pain was a fraction of the pain in my ears. I shook my arm and tried to pull it away but his jaws were locked. I kicked him hard and he let go. He limped away, whining, before collapsing beneath his weight. Sahar ran over to him. "You broke his leg," she must have cried. She cradled him in her lap.

I had to escape the sound. I walked backward through the saplings to keep my eyes on her. To see her pull her gun. She stayed still. She held Borlú as he licked his leg.

I see the colors.

CANVAS THIRTY

The rising sun shed bloodied golden light across rows of low crops beating in and out of the narrow field of view beside the driver's side window. The tinny jingle of keys against the steering column. The fog of my breath clouded sight of the yellow painted lines forming an almost constant median. The cruiser maxed out around 120.

I reached a crossroads and crushed the brakes. No landmark on either horizon. A speckle of trees behind fields of further farmland. I turned onto a one lane dirt road. The cruiser lurched along gravel divots and frozen mud. I steadied the wheel to trace the crimped tracks that lay ahead of me. Pothole after pothole, the chassis scraped and stones rocketed into the fenders. Sunlight winked through the prison of skinny trees and sleeping branches and the dead leaves fed the muck beneath the tires and it was still so dark. I switched on the cruiser's CB radio and scanned a dozen varieties of crunchy static distortions. I clicked it off and from the silence grew a different distortion. A low buzz grew to a grinding roar. Thick black exhaust. The road turned a bend through the ribcage belly of trees and I saw the thresher.

The machine crept and blocked the entire width of road. The massive arm of blades raised above the plexiglass cab. The blades rotated. Around and around. Five mph. I brought the cruiser within a foot of its bumper. My knuckles turned white depressing the horn—barely an audible tone in the symphony of diesel bellowing from the thresher.

"Move!" I saw visions of Rowan frozen on the veranda. "Move!"

A buck sprinted out of the barren tree line and launched headlong into the spinning blades. A cluster of bright sparks as the antlers sheared and snapped. Crunching, yowling. Fur and blood across the plexiglass cab. The driver veered and the thresher careened into the ditch, pinning the carcass to the snowy bank. The blades buried the cab in dirt. Rocks kicked back and chipped the cruiser windshield as I drove by the wreck and regained speed. The buck must have been Sam's influence. His wish had to come true somehow. I had to make it to Rowan. The fuel light lit up.

The corner market materialized a mile further like a mirage. I parked the cruiser beside the single pump. A closed sign greeted me in front of the darkened lights within. The dashboard clock read 6:45 a.m. A woman in overalls and a checkered coat hiked on bad hips from an inland farmhouse toward the pump. She drew up beside the passenger door and motioned to roll down the window.

"Morning, Officer." She chewed her last bite of breakfast or tobacco.

"I need gas."

"Not open just yet. Gimme ten minutes or so."

"There's an emergency."

"Out here? It's too cold for that."

"Some farm equipment went off the road."

"That I believe. I'll get the pump warmin'."

"Thanks. I'll wait."

"Out here? It's too cold for that. Come inside. You can get the first cup from the pot."

I twisted the ignition and stepped into the frigid air. The cruiser popped in places beneath the hood. The attendant frowned at my tuxedo.

"Undercover?"

"Off-duty."

"We met?"

"No."

"Well, come on in anyway."

She selected a key from a bulging keyring and unlocked the market door. She flipped switches on a wall pane and delayed light hummed and then burst like popcorn. "Pump switch is in the office. Cream and sugar?"

"Black. Thanks."

She walked behind the counter and into the backroom.

The door closed behind her to rest an inch ajar.

Too many minutes passed. "Are we good outside?" I said. No response. "Is the pump on?" No response. The click of a telephone set back in the cradle.

I checked both ends of the road through the glass door. The sun had cleared the horizon now. I pulled the toy gun from my pocket. I stood at the register with my hand concealed between bags of chips.

"Is everything going okay?"

"Just waiting for her to drip," she said.

Thin maple floorboards creaked as I crossed the invisible barrier between the shop floor and the space behind the counter. The toy gun pointed forward from my hip as I approached the backroom. "Am I good to use the pump? It's an emergency." Pensive silence of duelists waiting for the others' wrist to twitch.

"How's the skid plate been holdin' up?" she asked.

I opened the door and glimpsed her sitting in a chair beneath shelves of supplies before the shotgun muzzle flashed. I ducked behind the wall as the door exploded sawdust.

"Did I get you?" she asked.

I tenderly pressed the tattered tuxedo and the skin beneath. The buck shot had only singed the sleeve. "No," I said.

"Well, I got another barrel and I ain't coming out so this is how this plays out…" She cleared her throat of phlegm as if a Mexican standoff were a usual step to her opening routine. "…either you toss that gun in to me and wait for the sheriff. He's on his way. Or you get back in that stolen cop car and drive as far as you can until you run out of gas and see how far you can outrun a K9. Those your options."

"How many shells do you have?"

"One, probably more."

I leaned my back against the wall beside the smoking door. I listened to her chew.

"Didn't hear you leave and I don't have that pistol yet.

Ain't no third option."

"She's in trouble."

"I'm just fine."

"Not you. I need to get to Rowan. My head hurts so badly."

"Are you cryin'? Toss that pistol in."

I swallowed. "It's fake."

"You kidding me?"

I tossed the toy gun through the door and it hit the floor with a plastic sound.

"Son of a bitc—" She was interrupted by a loud crack of wood and a heavy cascade of rattles and thuds and snaps and the shotgun fired again. I sat wide-eyed with ringing ears. A stream of blue paint and blood crept past the door frame. The purple mixture ran into a floor drain. I peeked out from behind the wall into the room. Her caved-in head hung low between her knees. Her foot was blown apart. The shotgun barrel smoked in her lap. The shelf above her hung split in two. Beside the body a blue paint can teetered back and forth on its side next to a red toolbox with a corner of blood and hair. The penciled labels had faded away on the electrical box beside her so I flipped every switch until a little green bulb lit.

The bell clunked against the door as I went outside into the cold. The pump display illuminated 0.00. I lifted the nozzle. I heard the siren. I dove into the driver's seat and slammed the door. The sheriff's car peeled into the parking lot and crunched to a halt in a wave of gravel. The sheriff threw open his door and took a knee. He pointed his revolver through the space above the mirror.

"What's the situation? You state patrol?" he called out.

I took a breath. "It's a mess inside. Perp shot the cashier and then himself. The bodies are in the backroom. I need a moment to collect myself."

He pulled himself up by both arms. He craned his neck to peer past his belly and holstered his weapon. "Sad to say I'm a little relieved. But, poor Clarice."

"Dispatch said to hold everything down for reinforcements."

"Dispatch said what?"

"I guess the FBI have jurisdiction."

"Better listen then, I guess. I'm gonna take a look. Look bad if I didn't see the biggest shit storm to hit my town.

"It's not for the faint of heart," I said.

"Poor Clarice."

The gravel crunched beneath his shoes as he crossed the parking lot. The siren lights painted red and blue over the market windows. The bell clunked behind him. He had left his cruiser door open with the keys in the ignition. I was off again.

I drove through a vast expanse of snow cleaved by black highway's speckled asphalt like a drying photo negative. Slush arcing behind the wheels. To the side of the highway stood a lone fir tree coated in snow. Lace patterns and needles. Visions of Rowan in a wedding dress frozen on the veranda. I had already forgotten the corner market.

The new cruiser maxed out at 140. Cliffs rose along the highway like mountains of shoveled snow. A great gust of wind howled as it cut itself on the bladed edge of rock. The wind blew ferociously and lifted the cruiser an inch off its wheels. God and nature tried to stop me.

A clutter of pebbles like hail. A chink in the windshield. A loud thud on the cruiser roof. A rock the size of a human skull dented the hood and then another and then another. I steered the cruiser out of the path of a rolling boulder and another pummeled the cruiser. The windshield spiderwebbed and the brakes rattled beneath my foot. The car spun out on both axes. My neck whipped at cross purposes with the gyroscopic somersaulting earth. My head and hair swayed as if underwater as the world outside the shattered windshield flipped along a horizon of white sky and black pavement over and over again like a kaleidoscope.

The machine came to rest, rocking gently. My arms hung down past my head. The engine hissed. I unbuckled the seatbelt and fell down onto the roof. I crawled across the shards of broken glass onto the cold pavement. The cruiser sizzled where it lay upside down in the center of a boulder garden strewn across smoking asphalt. I was a miracle of scrapes and bruises.

I walked along the snow on the road shoulder. No other cars passed by that entire day. My calves burned from the incline of the road and the cold. Rowan frozen on the veranda. I walked for miles. The cliffs shallowed and wire fence crowned the tops of them like thorns. I made for the fence. I climbed the grim cliff face. I gripped handfuls of loose black gravel and protruding roots. Fingers purple with cold. The tuxedo ripped in the arm. The lip of the cliff jutted out above me at an acute angle spilling fronds of long yellow grass over its teeth. I wrapped the grass around my freezing hand like a rope and swung a leg up and over.

I got to my feet. The muscles in my legs had the sturdiness of a stack of couch cushions. The fence was rain-rusted chicken wire the height of me. I put my hands in my sleeves and pressed my full weight down onto the wire and it crumpled enough to straddle and I fell down hard on the other side. I laid watching the white snowflakes fall past a background of whiter sky and melt in my eyelashes. My body was content to die right there but my mind panicked from wasted time. My broken collar and death could wait. Rowan frozen on the veranda. Carrington wasn't far.

I stood in the blank pasture painted-over in infant snow. Pure white earth melted with pure white sky without division. Encased in the womb of a lightbulb. Ahead of me, the filament—a plain horse. The merry-go-round went around and around the day my mother abandoned me. No scrollwork in gold. A plain horse. She and I were bugs trapped in a white lightbulb.

My tracks disturbed the still field. The horse nuzzled the snow to graze. She blinked at me through her black marble eyes. Not yet a marionette. I touched her neck. The merry-go-round pierced the implanted thoughts of Rowan. I shivered.

I couldn't climb on for the longest time. My dress shirt came untucked as I slid down the horse's side. I beared through the pain in my shoulder and her shoulder blades dug into my aching thighs. I shifted to keep the contact off my bruises. I tucked my frostbitten fingers into her mane. Her warmth spread to me. We trotted along the wire fence above the road. We reached an unlatched gate and I kicked it open and we rode down the path to the highway.

EXHIBITION NOTES

Sahar came to climb the fallen birch tree and feed me to the well i know it

CANVAS THIRTY-ONE

Filled the fountain pen with the last of the tint. Be concise but preserve what matters. All of Carrington was in a fervor. Townsfolk went in and out of houses carrying shovels and buckets. They trudged through the inches of snow on the sidewalks and driveways. The buildings all had filthy windows that diffused the light within. Truck after truck layered in heavy soot as if from a forest fire. A pair of men shambled from a cellar and their eyes followed the hooves beneath me. They wore t-shirts in the freezing cold.

I buried my mouth and nose in my elbow as I passed the boarded-up pet store. Rancid air. No movement. Barrett emerged from the garage beside Coffey Niehoff in his dress shirt and suspenders. He dumped a pail of dirt onto a bigger pile in the driveway. His shirt rode up, exposing his purple gut.

Sam's house had become one with the sky and snow. The bristling white of shed snake skin. That's it. Of course of course of course. A line of townsfolk stretched from the backyard to the door of the Call-A-Ride parked at the edge of the driveway. A man in a neon yellow parka crowd surfed. The crowd cheered as they passed him above their heads like ants. The man in the yellow parka disappeared behind the house. I know now the man was screaming beneath their cheering.

Rowan's coworker's pickup was parked behind the Call-A-Ride. I slid off the horse and at once my thighs erupted with the pain of raw blisters. The horse took to a patch of grass poking through the snow. The pickup was the only car not coated in dust. I cupped my hands over the driver's window and saw a mess of wrappers and plastic fast-food cups. The bed was full of blackened snow. All the snow in Carrington was black except the snow around the manor.

The line of townsfolk had broken apart and returned to their chores around the manor. A woman chopped firewood. A group whitewashed the garage. Some went in and out of the side entrance, piling the furniture at the curb.

Samson bared his teeth from the porch as I approached.

A man placed a hand on its crown and calmed Samson before turning back to slap the white paintbrush on the shutter he was staining. His movements seemed so heavy and slow. The veranda steps felt sturdier, as if they'd been rebuilt. The front door was open and I walked in. The smell of wet paint, bleach, and hot cheese. The walls and doors were painted white. Even the floor was white.

"Excuse me, but I don't go walking into your home," a woman called down from the staircase. Behind her, a teenager slopped the uppermost stair with a mop dipped in white paint. The door at the top of the stairs was no longer boarded up.

"I'm looking for someone I was told was here."

"Perhaps I can help." The woman came down the stairs unbalanced like a toddler. "Who are you?"

"Richie. I'm looking for a girl named Rowan. I want to marry her. I'm ready right now even. See." My words came out franticly as I brushed the snow off my tuxedo. I took out the antique engagement ring and held it inches from her face.

"Gorgeous. I could help y'all with that. I'm Kellan. I'm the pastor at the church."

"I could tell from your clothes. Where's Rowan?"

"What's she look like? I can't read minds."

"She's in a wedding dress."

She put her hand on my broken shoulder and squeezed. I winced and pulled away. "She was here and now she's gone," Kellan said. "She'll be back soon though."

"Where'd she go?"

"She went with the hearse to the morgue in the next town over. She was the one who found Sam and you can't just find a dead body and not expect to answer a couple questions."

"Sam?"

"Did you know him? I've been crying all day. They think a heart attack. He was painting. Awful kind man."

"When did he die?"

"A few days ago they think. He was already gone when

the girl found him. He left the house to the church. He had no one else. We're fixing it up to sell it and start a fund for the youth group. Poor saint."

"When will Rowan be back?"

"An hour. Maybe a day."

I heard a sound behind the white study doors. The padlock was gone. My eyes hurt from all the white.

"It's tough on all of us. Is there anything else you need? I'm really very busy today, hon. Should get back to overseeing things."

"I'm sorry."

"Don't be sorry." She locked her arm in mine and escorted me onto the veranda. "You'll get to have your little wedding soon. Perhaps I call you when she's returned?"

"I lost my phone. And my wallet."

She pulled a small notepad from her pocket and a pen from her hair and used the white veranda railing as a surface to write.[45]

"You need sleep. My brother runs the Cliffside. It's a motel in town. I'll give him a call and let him know you're coming and he'll put you up, free of charge. I'll come and get you there. Call you there."

"Thank you." I surveyed the two-street map drawn on the paper.

"Get some rest, hon. We're all grieving is all. Take a deep breath with me." Together, we inhaled and exhaled. My breath was a heavy white cloud. You couldn't see her breath. "Now

---

45 DEAR GOD, DON'T WORRY ABOUT ME. I PRAY THE PEOPLE OF CARRINGTON TAKE CARE OF SAM.

I've read the denim note a thousand times. The truth is clearer to me each time like a brightening lightbulb. The fire as I ascend from the cave. Mustn't sleep until every inch of truth reveals itself. Couldn't sleep in all this fire.

The truth begins on Canvas Three. Amara says to Sam let's paint the house white, the whole house. It'd be cleaner, I think. Wouldn't that be lovely, Sam? We'd even paint the floors." And now here what do we have here what does Richie see when he returns he sees the house painted floor to ceiling white. So beautiful.

get going," she said.

Cavities of dirt speckled Ms. Rothacker's yard between children's plastic sandbox shovels. Olivia and Austin stroked the horse with heavy hands like clubs where it grazed at the edge of the yard. Dead leaves littered the driveway like soiled parchment. At once, the commotion at the manor ended and all the townsfolk went inside. Stillness and evening pressed inward through the woods of fir trees smothered in coal-black snow. Someone whistled from the street.

The gunmetal sedan creeped past. The window rolled down. It was the Hundred Suns cowboy. He pointed his index finger toward me and snapped his thumb down like the hammer of a gun. The manor door opened and Kellan came out and watched the sedan. The cowboy blew me a kiss and the sedan picked up speed and turned the corner and headed toward the town. I brushed an ant off the nape of my neck. The horse was gone.

I kept to the ditch as I followed Kellan's map. The black blizzard came and curtailed vision to faint scraps of distant glimpses. The black snow blew upward in clouds like murmuring locusts; on my lips it tasted of sulfur. The sun lost its grip and fell beneath the horizon. Wherever Hundred Suns was hiding, they had no way of seeing me. I followed the pastor's map. Faint silhouettes shambled between buildings in the dark.

A blinking street light through the black ash marked the turn I needed to take. Dark blood snow. Dark green snow. Dark blood snow. Dark green snow. I turned the corner, and stood beneath the towering Roland, across from the giant miner was the motel. The Cliffside was a single-story, U-shaped turquoise relic from the 1970s. The shades were drawn in every window. Cable TV and vacancy buzzed.

It took both hands to tug open the office door through the inches of snow. I slipped through the narrow gap. I stood awhile between the wood-paneled walls as the blood returned to my nose and ears. I rang the call bell reflecting static from the transistor TV. I rested my legs in the cleaner of the two chairs and considered how I'd propose to Rowan. I wouldn't need to propose. Once she's back we could ask the pastor to marry us on the spot. Excitement welled in my neck above my broken collarbone.

I rang the bell again. The take-a-penny, leave-a-penny had a couple quarters I used to buy a bag of stale pretzels from the wood-paneled vending machine. They tasted like mossy cigarette air.

My eyes adjusted to see the silhouette figure in the backroom staring out at me from the dark.

"You startled me," I said. "I need a room."

The figure didn't reply.

"The pastor said she'd call ahead and set me up with a room. Pastor Kellan? She said you were her brother."

The figure didn't move.

"I lost my wallet. If I could just wait in here a few hours that's fine too. It's freezing out. I just need a place warm to wait."

He stepped out of the shadows. "Of course! My sister called! My sister called! I know what it's like to be down on your luck!" The TV static illuminated the dirt on his face. A V-stain of sweat dampened his flannel shirt.

"Why is every one gardening? It's freezing."

"No gardening for me! Changing sheets!" The man had no sense of calibrating the volume of his voice to the size of the room. He lifted a key from a hook behind the counter and handed it to me with a mud-caked hand. "Room six! Three doors down on the left!"

"My name's Richie Maltessouri, if you need it."

"Slipped my mind! Can't have you destroying the place and getting away with it!" He lifted a pen between his thumb and ring finger and dragged it across the ledger.

"I don't have any I.D. Like I said, I lost my wallet."

The pen drew a meaningless line and tore through the paper. "Sleep well, sir!" He coughed a pneumatic cough.

I turned to leave and then turned back. "Are you here all night?"

"Yes!"

"I'm expecting someone to call for me. Your sister or a girl. Please call my room as soon as they call. I don't care if it's the middle of the night just call me. Same if any men come asking for me. But don't let them see you call. I don't want to see them."

"Yes! Rowan will be back soon! Now get some sleep, sir!"

There was no sign of life at either end of the parking lot. The buildings across the street were erased by the black blizzard. I walked past the motel room windows and reached a chipped red door with a crooked metal six. I turned the key and something rattled and fell inside the lock.

The dismal bed struck a fear of bed bugs. Sodden red curtains like a beaten rug. I drew down the canvas curtain by the dangling string. The bolt was busted, so I latched the security chain and pushed the waist-high dresser against the door to keep a vigilant barricade. I stacked the potted plastic plant on top as though it helps. I checked the connecting doors to the adjacent room—both were heavy and locked. The bathroom sink groaned before deciding to flow. I waited for the copper water to cycle out and scrubbed my face and filthy forearms. Bruises speckled my arms like leeches. Cuts like fire ants. My teeth chattered from the room's freezing draft. It felt as though the door was wide open. I cranked the heater and hung the tuxedo over it and stood naked watching the fibers thaw and then I put it all back on.

It happened after midnight.

Physical exhaustion total, my wired mind flashed a wedding with Rowan. I laid on the disgusting quilt in apprehension of the sheets. The bed sagged beneath me with an iron bar bowed across the middle of my back. Consciousness would begin to slip and then a crack in the wall would jolt my fried nerves awake again. False premonitions braced my heart for the telephone to ring with Rowan's safety. Any second now...Any second now. The bedside LED clock bled red light across the stucco ceiling. An ant bobbed and weaved the stucco bumps. Stupid ant would starve to death. The potted plant was plastic and the meat lying on the quilt was somehow still breathing. What a mess you got yourself into, ant.

I heard a sudden pop different from the rest. Instinct opened my eyes. I saw the coat hanger through the cracked motel room door. I laid still. Millimeter by millimeter the hook worked at unlatching the security chain. The chain swung loose and smacked against the door. Outside, a man whispered "shit," and another whispered "shhh."

It was quiet for a short while—all parties listening. The bedside lamp was my only weapon. I primed my muscles for the series of quick movements they'd have to make. Spring to action, smash the lamp over their head, lose them in the black blizzard. The door creaked opened and hit the edge of the dresser in front of the door. I feigned sleep through slit eyes. A familiar man shouldered his weight quietly into the door. His face strained. The dresser wouldn't budge. Whispers and another familiar man took his place. Again, the dresser held. More whispers. The figures passed across the amber light of the shaded window and went away.

I shot to my feet and peeked through the gap between the window frame and curtain. Through the falling black flakes, I saw a glimmer of the gunmetal sedan parked on the street. The YMCA cowboy and the YMCA biker rummaged through the trunk. My mind raced. No back window—my only escape was into the adjoining room. I cranked the air conditioning unit beneath the window to full blast and prayed its rattle would mask the noise I was about to make.

I opened my connecting door. The knob on the other side was locked. I stepped back to the foot of the bed and braced my good shoulder. I ran hard into the door. The crash was louder than I thought it would be. I backed up again and rammed the door a second time. I heard someone shout from across the parking lot. The pain in my broken collar pulsed like a taser. I charged again and again and again and then the space around the doorknob splintered. The dresser barricade jolted as the cowboy and the biker battered the front door. The potted plastic plant toppled to the floor, spilling dirt. I kicked and kicked and in the offbeat of kicks I heard a second series of crashes coming from the adjoining room; I heard its front door bust open and clap against the wall. The violent twang of the reverberating doorstop. "I got it," one of the men called out. They had surrounded me. I slammed my side of the connecting door shut and locked the bolt. I heard the splintered door on the other side open with a squeal of hinges. Both doors to my room reverberated from heavy kicks.

"Give up," the cowboy shouted through the crack in the front door. I lowered to a squat and pressed my back into the heavy TV stand. It slid an inch as the carpet burned the palms of my hands. The edge of the TV stand dug into my shoulder blades and moved another inch. The connecting room door splintered open with a crack and clapped against the inch of TV stand in front of it.

"In here," the biker called out. The assault on the front door ceased. I pushed the TV stand further and laminate wood shaved off against the door's edge. It came to a stop and would no longer budge. A crack tore like a wedge through the TV stand from the force of kicks. My mind raced. Wrap yourself in the blanket, dive through the window, lose them in the black blizzard. Wrap yourself in the fucking blanket, dive through the window, lose them in the black blizzard. Go. Now. "Behind you," one of the men shouted in the other room. There was an awful, sticky sound and the biker's body fell forward against the inches of open connecting door. He was seizing. A machine gun erupted and bullet holes hopscotched and tore through the wallpaper of my room. I rolled onto my stomach at the foot of the bed and covered my head with my arms. The bullets burst through the TV, showering my forearms in glass. I heard the cowboy scream before having the wind knocked out of him. The bullet holes arced up to where the wall met the ceiling and then the gun stopped firing. I heard a struggle and the loud snap of a bone. I listened to the cowboy gag on his own blood until there was too much to swallow and then the choking stopped.

I laid gasping the sixty years of cigarette smoke in the carpet. Flecks of singed wallpaper floated down around me like feathers. Warmth soaked my elbow as the blood creeped under the cracked connecting door. The biker's head, with a sliver of exposed skull, leaned against it. I gagged and listened as sullen footsteps crossed the adjoining room, dragging some object against carpet. The heavy footsteps went out into the parking lot and the dragging became scraping of metal on concrete. The shadow of a figure limped across the drawn canvas curtain of my room. The figure stopped in the center of my window. It lifted a shovel with both hands and I saw the blood dripping from its blade. The figure reeled back, gripping it like a bat. I froze and heard a clacking sound and then the figure's arms went limp again and the shovel dropped to the concrete. The figure turned and limped away from the window. I listened to the scraping of the shovel slowly die out as the figure crossed the parking lot and disappeared into the black blizzard.

I heard the steady drips of blood in the other room—the blood pooling around my stomach. It was already getting cold. I felt the coarse carpet imprinting in my cheek as I stared at the bedside clock counting the seconds in red.

I screamed as the hands grabbed my ankles and pulled me beneath the bed. My jacket gathered up around my neck and the carpet burned my stomach. Down past my feet I saw her grinning face poking up from the tunnel beneath the bed. No wonder the room was freezing. My legs dropped out into the cold earthen air. My head struck the bed leg as she pulled me under and then my head struck earth and I was out.

KILL HER FIRST

DEAR GOD, DON'T WORRY ABOUT ME. I PRAY THE PEOPLE OF CARRINGTON TAKE CARE OF SAM. My cave was this life and the fire was down below. No one expects. The denim note *is* the fire. The birthplace of it all. "Dear God, don't worry about me. I pray the people of Carrington take care of Sam." Amara wrote the note. She was the only other person who knew about the well. Perhaps she fell into it in her dementia. Suicide attempt or maybe an accident. The denim is a scrap of overalls or jeans. Canvas Three reads: "[Amara] wore denim overalls. She loved to wear denim overalls." Amara wrote the note. Amara wrote the note. "I pray" must carry the same command over the Tint as "I wish." Imagine the power. What would I do with it. Money likely. Fame definitely. Imagine the power of wishes at your fingertips. My fingernails can't scrape the Tint off the Canvas or the denim. All I need is a little bit.

The migraine feels amazing. All the evidence Sahar tried to bury but she couldn't put out the fire. My fire. She would have killed me to extinguish it. Should go back and kill her first. Her and that little child spy.

I turned my hotel room inside out looking for listening devices. Looking for bugs. Next I need to stand on the dresser and check each dimple in the ceiling for cameras. I already confirmed no flies or ladybugs on the window sill. No ants across the ceiling. I heard they have cameras disguised as flies. I heard that from my mind. I'll check the carpet too. I'll stop talking out loud just to be safe. Transcribe under a blanket under the desk away from the cameras. The Committee want my fire. They've known all along what the Tint is worth. A chemical weapon. I see that now. I've outsmarted them now.

CANVAS THIRTY-TWO

Consciousness flitted in squints of dim torch light like orbs of floating dandelion. Tuxedo jacket up around my ears, arms splayed out behind me, the bare skin of my back scraped the ground with her every step. One hand dragged me by the ankle, her other hand held the torch. She ducked beneath a cluster of roots hanging from the tunnel's low earthen ceiling. Swollen tongue. The smell of worms in the rain. I kicked. "Hush, hon," Pastor Kellan tightened her grip. "Hush, hunny, hush." A mine cart rail bowed my lower back and knocked the back of my skull. Black purple stars. Splinters dug in from the jagged wooden railroad ties. Scratches from the interstices of gravel between. I kicked her elbow with my free leg and the force snapped her elbow.[46] She dragged me by her broken arm deeper into the network of tunnels. I kicked and flailed. "Maybe I should put you to sleep." She threw my leg down onto the mine cart rail and I cried out from the pain of my already present bruises. She straddled me between her boots and torch light licked her vacant visage. "My brother hit those men back there a little too hard. We wanted them too, but a man can take a shovel to the head only so hard and my brother's still learning the sweet spot." She brought the toe of her boot to rest on my lips. "These are steel toe, you know." Wrinkles smiled beside her glaucoma eyes. She didn't breathe. None of the townsfolk breathed. "You wanna see how much steel toe a skull can take?" A line of ants skittered across her smiling face and down her clerical collar. I stopped kicking.

Deeper in, the walls populated with sporadic torches and battery-powered lamps. The arrhythmic clunks of pickaxes grew closer. My sleeve caught and tore on a crossbeam as we rounded the corner into the great hub. Dozens of townsfolk dug in the dark. They shambled with limp limbs bent at obtuse angles at the joints like marionettes. "Brothers and sisters,"

---

46 The corpse had an antemortem fracture of the elbow!

Kellan said. One in three had a shovel or tool—the others pawed at the earth with bleeding hands of sheared fingernails. Marionette children bit the walls and swallowed mouthfuls of dirt. A dozen rough tunnels converged at the hub. Down one, I saw marionettes pushing wheelbarrows full of dirt and stone up plywood floorboards to the surface. A marionette hammered nails in sheet metal to build another structure in a row of rusty sheds and lean-tos. The shell of a man turned from his work to look down at me. His right eye—clouded and oozing yellow. His left eye—a frenzied mass of ants devouring flesh. He turned back and drove in another nail. The subterranean sheds had ratty blanket doors. In one, three marionettes sat at a spool table holding air like cards, clacking their tongues. A queue of marionettes passed buckets of earth in unison as though ordered by a broadcast I couldn't hear. They clacked tongues in a sort of call and response. "Congregation," Kellan said. She dragged me down a zig-zagging tunnel. The clamor of workers dimmed to faint echoes behind us. I spotted the faintest movement. Sam's cat stalked us from a distance with its eyes locked on Kellan. The tunnel came to a T and Kellan stopped to turn. The creature pounced onto Kellan's shoulder. She dropped my leg and the torch and fought the cat with both hands. She wrenched hard as its claws tore across her eyeballs and cheeks, sinking its fangs again and again. I scrambled to my feet and grabbed the torch and limped away as best I could. Kellan screamed and clacked her tongue behind me as I hurried into the dark unknown. I turned a corner. Kellan screamed and clacked. I turned another corner. Kellan screamed and clacked and then I heard dull steel-toe stomps and the cat's dying whimper. I limped through pain without stopping. A pair of marionettes shambled across the intersection of tunnels ahead without seeing me. One carried a lantern, the other held a shovel like a halberd. They were hunting. The caves echoed with clacking tongues. I curtained the torch with the corner of my tuxedo jacket to reduce peripheral light. I wish Sam's cat goes to heaven.

Left turn. Right turn. Dead end and a ladder.

Mud-caked rungs rose fifteen feet to a trapdoor. I laid the torch on the ground and it cast prison bars of shadow through the ladder rungs. I pulled myself up with my left arm and draped my broken collar right arm over each rung for stability. Halfway up, I caught my breath and cricked my aching neck to look back at the darkness behind me. The torch was beginning to fade. The Committee will poison me.

The doorknob weighed a thousand pounds in my hand. I twisted the brass and bowed my neck forward beneath the weight of the wood and pressed up with my legs. Pain blazed in my collar and I climbed the top rungs. A rancid smell invaded. A pitch black room with the cold air of cement walls. Flies escaped toward the dying torch below. I breathed through my mouth and barricaded the trapdoor with a laundry machine. The Committee will use poison. I wasted a moment spitting a fly from my mouth. My eyes adjusted to silhouettes in the dark. An unfinished basement. I stepped forward with my arms out in front of me toward the jagged silhouette of stairs. The light switch would be there. Baby steps. I wonder when baby will start to walk. I'm already so proud of her. The sour smell grew stronger. My shoe stubbed a brick and I stumbled forward. I caught myself against the grout of the cinder block wall. I spread both arms and waved them like a drowning snow angel. The edge of my hand hit a small metal junction box. It was an outlet. I turned to climb the stairs when something tickled my ear. It was a string. I tugged the string. The metal beads rasped the metal socket above and the light came on. The brick I'd tripped over was Sam's rotten head. A seeping fresh dent from my dress shoe. The back of his head caved from blunt trauma. The eyes beside the shattered bone stared into my own from their sunken place. The skin of his neck and forearms tinged pale green. His body splayed at the foot of the stairs. A bloody shovel beside it. So many flies. I looked away and the assault on my senses spread to infect reason as well.

Halfway up the cedar steps, there lay a second corpse that was also Sam. Both looked to have been thrown from the top of the stairs. The second Sam's neck twisted to gaze past me at an angle that it shouldn't. I'll be dead soon too. For getting too close to the truth the Committee wants for itself. Or for getting too close to the truth they already know. Well it's my truth and I will share it. For Richie's sake. "Here you are." Pastor Kellan climbed out of the trapdoor onto the cold concrete floor like a tarantula. Her cheeks flayed to ribbons draping down her neck. Tears of blood coursed from the eggy pulp in her eye sockets. "Sam needs his servants," she said. She flung her arm with the broken elbow in a wide arc and a pickaxe clapped to rest on her shoulder. She stepped forward. I pulled myself up the stairs by the rail. I scrambled over the groin of the second Sam. I clambered on my hands and knees, face to face with the second Sam's rotten eyes. Bones cracked behind me. Over my shoulder I saw blood up to the ankle of Kellan's boot where it stood inside the first Sam's broken chest cavity. She lifted the boot with a strand of red. She shook it and viscera flecked the cement wall. I heaved the second Sam down the stairs like a sand bag. The corpse caught Kellan in the knees and she fell back onto the seat of her pastor gown. I reached the door. She swung the pickaxe point down through the first cedar step and pulled herself to her feet. She set to levering the pickaxe back and forth in the splintering wood, trying to pull it out. I burst through the door into the manor's entrance hall and knocked a frostbitten man onto the painted white floor.

"The deposition magician." Marionette Barrett Niehoff stared up at me through clouded fish-like eyes. He wobbled onto his side and pushed himself to his feet. Marionette Olivia and Austin watched through the lattice work glass of the front door sidelites. I turned toward the kitchen where more marionettes stood holding hand scythes and other instruments.

Torture. If they don't already know the truth that means torture. They might trust the transcription but they'll need the details of the denim note. I gotta hide it. Marionettes came through the front door, a half-dozen more tottered down the staircase. They crowded both ends of the hall.

Kellan emerged from below and spoke. "Saved me the trouble of pulling you up the ladder." She swung the pickaxe with the full span of her broken arm and it buried in the plaster wall. She ripped it back and wood boards splayed out like broken ribs. She swung it into the opposite wall, stabbing a tint painting of a revolver. Marionette Barrett tackled my shins and I fell over him. More marionettes turned me over and pinned my wrists. I struggled but my muscles burned white hot and every push had less strength than the one before like losing at arm wrestling. "You will be our brother, too," Kellan said, resting the cold pickaxe blade on my throat. Her tongue clacked and the marionettes followed her orders. My shoulder banged against the edge of the doorframe as they carried me onto the back veranda—two to a leg, two to an arm. My only fight left was to scream. I swayed low like a hammock full of stones and the snow licked my belt. The falling black snow soothed the cuts on my face. They'll waterboard me. Is Sahar CIA? Can't find her online. I swear she had a presence before. Marionettes came from all sides to follow. They carried torches and shovels like revolutionaries. Dozens of marionettes caked in black frost. Dark blood clung to the flannel fibers of the motel owner's shirt. The light of torches behind him winked through the bullet holes in his torso. The black snow fell on Kellan's flayed face to form a scabby sheen of ice the color of wine.

The marionettes carried me to the opening of the path through the woods. She used to have a footprint. She scrubbed it all. Sahar's a ghost. My voice was hoarse. The gunshot rang out across the yard and ping-ponged in the trees and cliffs before coming to rest in snow. The gun snapped again and I saw the muzzle flash on the veranda. Kellan and Barrett and the rest turned their blank gaze toward the voice. Above the crowd, Sam's arm shook. His spotted hand pointed the revolver to the sky and brought the barrel down to press against his temple. The townsfolk trembled. "Leave him alone," Sam cocked the hammer, "or I will kill me." In unison they dropped my arms and legs and the wind knocked out of me. Sam kept the muzzle flush to his head. "Come here, Richie." The horde parted and formed a path to the veranda. I limped. Pale moon behind passing clouds. The sea of marionettes. Their fingers twitched to grasp me as I passed, but they wouldn't disobey Sam.

I PRAY THE PEOPLE OF CARRINGTON TAKE CARE OF SAM.

Torches popped sparks. Shovels and axe blades glimmered moonlight. Dozens of townsfolk spilled out onto the street. Sam watched from the veranda unshaven, meek from weeks of little food. I steadied myself by the ramp rail. The torn tuxedo exposed my torn skin to the freezing cold. My shattered collarbone spread purple along my shoulder blade. The splinters in my back needled at every contraction of muscle. Sam lowered his elbow to rest on the arm of his chair. He tilted his head to keep it flush with the revolver. "Come and get warm." I didn't know, god. I didn't know what Sam had been through. The good man he was. He didn't deserve it. He didn't deserve to have so much taken from him. Marionettes lined the sides of the hallway like sullen mourners at a wake. Sam rolled his chair faster than I could limp. He turned into the study. The front door was open and a queue of marionettes traced the sidewalk and crossed the street and disappeared behind the tree line. The sound of moaning and chains. Samson bared his jaws from the porch.

In the study, Sam draped a sheet over a canvas leaning against a bookshelf. "You look a lot hurt," he said. "Very," I said. "Me too." The study looked like a bomb shelter. Littered canned food refuse and a bedpan. A military cot in the corner by the bookshelves. A sleeping bag had slid onto the floor at the feet of the finished painting of Amara—a beautiful young nurse with eyes sparkling in a snowy, still courtyard. The day they watched a finch. There was a cradle in the corner of the room. Milsap has the Tint. They found the well and drained it and murdered Richie and I'm next. No prison for me. Only death. I'm next. Sam sat at the desk beside the easel under the domed conservatory windows. He scraped the inside of a glass jar with a paintbrush and turned it upside down. The last drips of gold light pooled onto the palette. He still held his head at gunpoint. "Those dead take care of me," he said shaking the jar up and down—it was empty. "What?" I said. He scratched his hair slowly. "They bring me food and pillows and tell me they will take care of me."

I PRAY THE PEOPLE OF CARRINGTON TAKE CARE OF SAM.

Outside the windows, a sea of rotting eyes stared in at us. The same sea of eyes watch me as I write this sentence. They never leave. So many days writing and they never leave. They wait to take me. But I am their master now. I began to pace. "Is Rowan here? I need to find her. I need to find Rowan." A spark of a smile crept across Sam's face. "I meant to do good." His voice was barely above an exhale, as though praying. "I didn't mean for none of this. Wanted something good to come of this." "Where's Rowan?" "Come here and look." I crossed the room and stood beside the easel. He drew a thin paintbrush from the bundle in a mug. He dipped the bristles in the golden droplets of tint. He painted on the surface of the desk—a simple line and, at its end, a simple dot. Endless colors and deafening orchestral music seemed to charge the simple shapes and grapple one another for precedence over my senses. It feels so good. The denim note feels so good.

The line and dot glowed all colors at once but my mind held to the conviction that the dot was red and the line was wood and it was. The simple line and simple dot took form from the chaos like a trick image and there, on the desk, laid a matchstick. "It's a tint," Sam said. "It makes wishes come true." My God. "Where's Rowan?" "I can paint things with it and then they're there. I can paint people and they do what I painted. I painted me to walk and talk but it made two of me instead." "Where's Rowan?" "I painted Amara, but she..." He turned away. "I said where's Rowan?!" I threw the mug of brush water and it shattered against the spines of textbooks. I pulled Sam's head back by the hair to stare up at me. His Adam's apple rose and fell with the swallow of a man before a scalping. At the time, I didn't hear baby start to cry. "Tell me where Rowan is now." "Look." His free hand shook and pointed to the covered canvas leaning against a bookshelf. "I will tear your head off if you don't tell me where Rowan is." Baby cried louder. "Your painting I made you. Look." I let go of his hair and walked over to the canvas and lifted the sheet. A painting in tint of a marriage on Sam's veranda under a black snowfall. Rowan in her wedding gown, me in my tuxedo. Our business cards pinned to the corners of the canvas with thumbtacks. Sam spoke in wavering words. "It was coming true..." I took the match and struck it on the edge of the desk. I lit the corner of the painting. It caught fire and burned rainbow with sweet tasting smoke. The painting seemed to scream. Colorful sparks flittered and died until all that was left was ash and my headache finally lifted. I felt myself return. I was free.

I gagged and spat from the lingering taste of Rowan in my mouth. The gravity of the things I'd done hit me at once. The crimes Sam forced me to commit to make the wedding come true. Dardanelle's murder of Apollo to make the wedding come true. The tint forced the wedding to come true. Until the marionettes stopped it. The horde of dead eyes watched me pace. The byproduct. The cost. Sam had moved to protect the cradle in the corner. Baby continued to cry out. "I'm sorry," he said. I couldn't breathe. "I don't understand," I said. "I'm sorry," Sam said as he lowered the gun from his temple to comfort baby and, in an instant, the front row of the marionettes outside began bashing their fists against the windows. He raised the gun back to his head and the commotion stopped as fast as it started. "I have to get out of here," I said. "The blizzard," he said. "I can paint a car with a snow scoop on the front. We need more of the tint though." "Where do we get it?" "A well out there." He looked up at the tinted Amara. "The well makes the tint after it eats." "Eats?" Sam seemed to be speaking to the baby. "Animals first." Lips pulled taught around a tearful grin. "I told them it was a funny game. That the bottom was like a mattress. I told them to hold hands and close their eyes." The wind outside howled over the cliffs. Baby finally stopped crying. "The boy landed on his head but Olivia landed on her leg. I just wanted Amara back." He scratched the back of his hair. Pastor Kellan's shredded face smiled up at me from the yard. Sam sniffed and streaked tears with the edge of his hand. "They took a horse." Sam wiped his eyes with the edge of his hand. "It hasn't had horse yet. There'll be tint. It won't stay long. We need to go get it."

I pulled a sweater over Sam and the gun and wrapped his emaciated legs in a wool blanket. The marionettes cleared from the study doorway like cattle. I pushed Sam down the hall past their motionless limbs and into the kitchen. Ice-burned bellies torn open to form icicles like jaws of blood. The veranda ramp groaned beneath us as I pushed Sam off onto the snow. My sleeves brushed against the mob with their shovels and knives. Sporadic torches lashed light across the moldy gray film borne across their vacant eyes. "In there." Sam flicked the revolver toward the trail through the woods. Two lines of marionettes stood motionless sentry down the dark trail, still as statues. Sam's hand was blue as it shook holding up the gun. I took a torch from one of the marionettes and pushed it into a fold of leather in the back of the wheelchair. Light illuminated the corridor of horrid faces. Blood returned to Sam's frozen hand.

He began to speak. "Shut up. If you drop the gun, I'm dead," I said. I didn't know who you were, Sam. I didn't know.

We reached the clearing and I caught my breath and rested my arms. The marionettes marched out from behind us on both sides. They marched along the forest and cliffs to form a great circle around the edge of the clearing. They lined the outer perimeter and then the queue coiled into itself and formed a second and third circle like a python. Countless torches purged the darkness and through the light I saw the well. It screeched.

The thrum sang to me. I hear it too. I'm fading. Sahar must have already poisoned me. I'm dying. Can barely keep my eyes open. This is death. Snow crunched beneath Sam's wheels. A stone's throw to the well, I froze. The moon cast off its clouds. Silver moonlight reflected off the lips of the well and then its foul tongue lashed out. Black ants swarmed out from below. Waves of skittering ants crisscrossed over each other as they surged from the well. They dribbled onto the snow and scrabbled into queues. The oily columns spiraled like brushstroke night skies. Enough legs skittering at once to hurt your ears. The black spiral coiled into itself the way the marionettes had. More and more filled in until the circle became an impenetrable inky black and then the mass of ants piled over itself and rose and took shape into a teetering sculpture that swayed and dribbled ants like slaver. It rose taller and taller. They ceased coming from the well. The black sculpture loomed still before our eyes. And then the ants melted. Burning legs and antennas. Tiny appendages smoking and knitting together like the wax of candles. I covered my ears from the shrill scream of a million things dying at once. The odor of incinerating steel wool. The waxy sludge contorted as if on bones and the high pitch of the screaming ants sunk to silence and from this silence a single human scream came and I saw a mouth form in the wax and then eyes and then the black glowed to the color of her skin and hair and wedding dress.

"Richie," marionette Rowan said. "Gimme the friggen

gun." "Don't listen," Sam said. Rowan clasped her hands. "Pretty please, Richie. Gimme the gun. Pretty please." Sam thumbed the revolver hammer back. "I will shoot me." Rowan fluttered her eyelashes over clouded irises. She tottered across the clearing and joined the ranks of her mindless kin. They clacked their tongues. The frill of her dress left faint patterns that the falling black snow buried without trace. Rowan Rayne was the sole identifiable body of the hundreds unearthed in the excavation.

"Take me up to the well," Sam said. He brushed the snow from the stone with his hand. He hooked his arm over the stone basin and lifted himself from his chair to see down. The torch began to fade. "Only a little bit of tint. The bucket won't work." He sat back in his chair. He slowly scratched his hair and I could tell it calmed him. "You're too heavy for me. Pick me up." He held his eyes shut and hugged my neck. I hoisted him onto the edge of the stone. My broken collar screamed pain and the last of my adrenaline silenced it. I wrapped the rope around his waist. He tucked the bucket through the coils and down between his knees and tightened it all. I gripped the metal crank and braced my exhausted muscles and broken bones. Sam stared past his broke legs into the light at the bottom of the fall. His right hand gripped the rope and his left hand steadied the revolver to his head. The rope was the most terrible texture he'd ever felt but he would not let go. "Okay," he said. "I am ready."

There was never flash flooding, I know it and I can finally prove it. Amara's wish is the puppeteer. Amara wrote the denim note. "Dear god, don't worry about me" (she fell in the well and was trapped and starving and found the Tint), "I pray the people of Carrington take care of Sam" (they are marionette servants; literal puppets). Sam said it himself: "[t] hey bring [Sam] food and pillows and tell [Sam] they will take care of [Sam]." They won't let him die. The marionettes are the byproduct of the denim wish. "Sam needs his servants,"

Kellan said. It's the will of Amara's wish, strong as the will of God. But Sam played a second God and twisted Amara's will. Sam painted himself so he could walk and write (to save Tint. He was illiterate... [stop using gossipy little parentheticals, Richie said cut it out] (make me) [I already have] (oh yeah well you still have to end this argument in a close parentheses) [no I don't]]. It created two Sams and they had no will to protect him. They caged him and I don't know why. Never paint yourself. The marionettes freed him by killing the false Sams. Sam played God. No, Sam sold his soul to Satan. Or Amara sold her soul to Satan and Sam played God. Or both to Satan. Or Sam killed the false Sams. No God or Satan there is a rational explanation. There must be, right? Suicide. Amara lost hope in her dementia and threw herself down the well after first writing the note. But why wouldn't there be a returned marionette Amara? What the hell is the Tint? Where did it come from? Why is it here? Baby is friendly. Baby must be a creation of Sam's painting. Not the ants. Not the evil. But good. Like Sam's painted cat! She isn't evil. Sam's portrait of Richie caused him to fall in love with Rowan and vice versa. Where do the ants come from? They can't be ants. Where did the Tint come from? Someone knows. I must comb back through the record. I'm fading fast. Aliens? Bioweapon? Did the Tint perpetuate itself? Wishing for more wishes? What if you wish for Tint? It's awesome (in the true meaning of the word). Sahar and Milsap and Satan. They're in cahoots and they're at the top. One to lead as the false prophet/false expert, one to discredit and destroy the doubter/truthseeker. Milsap put Sahar on special assignments left and right, I know it. Secret assignments. When did they poison me? Three days without sleep or food. There's no way. The little girl! When I caught up to the girl in the pawn shop she must have needled me. Hair thin needle with arsenic. No, some slower poison. It doesn't matter. My death is inconsequential. All that matters is finding Richie. Richie holds the truth of the Tint. He saw it create the marionette Rowan. Why was the identity of every corpse of Carrington ground zero unknown but for Rowan? The proof must be ahead. I must preserve the record. I must distribute the transcription online before the Committee has time to edit/alter/bury/twist these words of the truthseeker. The public will follow in my footsteps and fill in the blanks where I can't. I must read on. Paint the house white Amara always said and the marionettes did just that. Richie wrote on Canvas Eight: "I wish that, as soon as I leave, the tunnels collapse and all the marionettes get crushed to death." There was never flash flooding, only a wish. Consciousness is fading. Dry mouth. Coughing. Poison with symptoms like a disease. The Committee will win the battle but lose the war. Must upload the transcription. Symptoms like a disease. My mind is racing. The Tint can save me. Wish for the antidote. Scrape it off with my thumbnail and use it. Use it and save my life. The Tint is God/Satan. Klay Wade was murdered and I was murdered. Use it to stop the poison seeping into my brain. Fingernails shorn off and bleeding on the Canvas. Scratch with both hands. They're all gone my fire extinguished by fire they're all gone all ruined I fell asleep transcribing under the desk I woke up from the smoke the entire bed on fire roaring it was all the Canvases but the final one sprinkler system tore through the charred remains rainbow smoke tastes so sweet the firsthand record is lost my record is all that remains Sahar and Milsap wanted the Canvases destroyed they sent their child spy I saw the little girl run out and I chased after her down the hotel hall and she dropped her stuffed elephant and the elevator doors closed between us but I saw it I saw the little girl floating in the air as if being cradled she buried her face in the air she was being carried she was crying and the elevator doors closed something invisible carried her someone invisible it really happened and I saw it I can prove it happened I have the elephant in the raincoat the police are here I've barricaded the door to my room so I can finish in all this ash and lingering rainbow smoke black ash like the black blizzard I have to finish the ax blade smashing in and out of the door to my room the firefighters will break through soon they think I have a weapon like I might hurt myself I've shouted again and again I'm unarmed and that it was the little girl with the elephant and that she's with someone who's invisible but they won't listen but why else would I have a stuffed elephant if it didn't really happen they're almost inside wrap yourself in the blanket dive through the window lose them in the black blizzard wrap yourself in the blanket dive through the window lose them in the black blizzard.

THE LAST CANVAS

I wish to understand how Sam felt.

He was a boy. A woman washed his mother's blood from his sister in a basin and afterward they let Sam hold her beside a candle as they wrapped his mother's body in blankets and took it all away. His sister opened her eyes to meet Sam between fits of sleep and he named her Violet. It was his mother's favorite flower. He laid her in the cradle and ran away. He never told anyone. Not even Amara. He could never put the words together.

I'm so sorry, Sam. You handed me the jar and I let the rope go. I didn't know you. I didn't know any of this. And I made it back from the well so you must have kept the gun to your head down there. Despite the broken bones. Why'd you do that, Sam? Keep me in your dying thoughts. Why'd you have to fucking do that for me?

Now, the sun peeks over the cliffs. The sunlight shines past the black icicles. It passes through the conservatory windows and sets these awful words ablaze. The tinted words are thin stains now. Shaking the pen does nothing and I wouldn't dare touch it to my tongue. Forgive me, Sam. Forgive me. Please, Sam. You didn't know what you were doing. How could you know. How could anyone know. God, tell him I'm sorry. I didn't know who he was or what he'd been through.

I feel how much you missed her. I feel how much it hurt. But, you did it buddy. You brought her back. Please God, tell him I'll take care of her. I'll raise her. I promise. I'll be the best parent the world's ever seen. I promise I'll raise Amara, Sam. She's crying again. My crying woke her up. I need to get her out of here.

I wish for a car with a snow plow outside. I wish for the keys to be in the ignition. The tint is almost gone.

I see the horde of marionettes watching from the yard. I see Rowan. I hear the floorboards creaking beneath their weight.

They will take me. I wish to be invisible to everyone[47] of them.

I wish this place and these things I did be forgotten.

And God, if there is no heaven, I wish for

I wish for

for

remember

I wish for heaven for

I wish for heaven for

Sam.

---

47 [sic]

AFTERWORD

I transcribed the last canvas only because I owe it to Joe. He sustained severe injuries as a consequence of jumping from his hotel room window on the third floor. He'll live, but he's being kept in intensive care while he heals, after which he'll be moved to a psychiatric ward until his mania subsides. Then he'll face criminal charges for arson and resisting arrest. Conflicts permitting, I'd like to be his defense attorney. Again, I feel I owe it to him.

Joe has battled bipolar disorder for most of his life. He told me this to comfort me during a breakdown of my own. He sat with me on the floor of the ladies' room for what felt like hours as I cried. He never left me and I won't leave him.

His disorder led to this most severe manic episode. Lack of sleep, irritability, pressured speech—I saw his symptoms intensify as our trip went on. I should have said something to someone. I'll always regret that. Mr. Wade, the original copyist, struggled with mental illness as well. The idea that the paint on the canvases caused these breakdowns is a manic delusion.

The experts agree that the mass grave was the result of flash flooding. It took the lives of hundreds and a deranged individual later hid their twisted manifesto among the bodies. Who this individual was and how they knew me, I don't know. I don't care. I'm able to sleep at night not knowing and so should everyone else.

It breaks my heart this obsession with a tragedy bred more tragedy. The Wade family lost their lives,

Joe nearly lost his, and I lost my sweet dog. But, I will never blame him for that. No one is to blame for their mental health. I wish Joe a speedy recovery.

And I wish everyone would just leave me alone.

/s/ Sahar J. Ayubbi
Attorney
October 14, 2022

Please sign up to submit evidence and
receive notifications regarding the
Carrington Investigation at

JOSEPHBLACKHURST.COM

Please consider leaving
a review on Amazon.